Compulsion

KATE SCOTT

HAMISH HAMILTON
an imprint of
PENGUIN BOOKS

HAMISH HAMILTON

UK | USA | Canada | Ireland | Australia
India | New Zealand | South Africa | China

Hamish Hamilton is part of the Penguin Random House group of companies
whose addresses can be found at global.penguinrandomhouse.com

Penguin
Random House
Australia

First published by Hamish Hamilton in 2023

Cover image by akinbostanci/Getty Images
Cover design by Alex Ross Creative
Typeset in 12/17 pt Adobe Caslon Pro by Midland Typesetters, Australia

Printed and bound in Australia by Griffin Press, an accredited
ISO AS/NZS 14001 Environmental Management Systems printer

A catalogue record for this
book is available from the
National Library of Australia

NATIONAL
LIBRARY
OF AUSTRALIA

ISBN 978 1 76104 655 1

penguin.com.au

We at Penguin Random House Australia acknowledge that Aboriginal and Torres Strait Islander
peoples are the Traditional Custodians and the first storytellers of the lands on which we live
and work. We honour Aboriginal and Torres Strait Islander peoples' continuous connection to
Country, waters, skies and communities. We celebrate Aboriginal and Torres Strait Islander stories,
traditions and living cultures; and we pay our respects to Elders past and present.

For Maura, Siobhan, Jonathan,
and all the other good eggs

CONTENTS

'There is no theory. You merely have to listen. Pleasure is the law.'
Claude Debussy

'If I could do anything, I would go with you to the middle of
our planet, Earth, and seek uranium, rubies, and gold. I'd look
for Unspoiled Monsters. Then I'd move to the country.'
Truman Capote, Answered Prayers

'Make a sudden, destructive unpredictable action; incorporate.'
Brian Eno and Peter Schmidt, 'Oblique Strategies'

NO YELLOW LINES

December 2003

The coke's white-magic alchemy made me bulletproof – a temporary state, but a useful one. Anika raked out another four lines with her deft surgical precision, and we gobbled them up. Then we lay back into the floor and waited for something to happen.

We'd been waiting all day for one thing or another. Drugs to arrive, water to crystallise into cubes, the right feelings and chemicals to accrete in our receptors. Above all, we'd been waiting for the night, and like everything, it was taking forever. The last five days had been hot – a fatal, combustible, organ-swelling heat that compels trees to abandon their fruit. The sun's last cherry streaks tore the sky with agonising slowness and the same Lee Hazelwood album played all afternoon, both of us too heat drunk to choose another. Yet part of me was coiled in readiness because part of me always was.

'So,' said Anika, lighting a cigarette. 'What should we do tonight?'

'Well, there's the Pink Fist show. We could cool down by taking an illicit swim, or soaking our feet in the fishpond of the botanic gardens, or riding the silk-lined elevator of The Elysium. Or maybe we could find The Unspoiled Monster.' I lit a cigarette too, as if smoke might diffuse the terrible want of this last impulse.

'Surely not.'

'Perhaps not,' I said. 'We could just stay here, put on Fleetwood Mac and finish the coke.'

'That is not the purpose of my coke. We need to hitch this buzz into the evening, or nobody will be finding anyone.' And then, with the right degree of censure, she said, 'We'll discuss The Unspoiled in the cab.'

Everyone knew The Unspoiled Monster. I suppose everyone knew me too, from the magazine, but The Unspoiled was a proper flaneur, going out most nights, to most shows, for at least a decade by then. He was famous in that highly localised way passionate spectators are famous just for showing up to things. He had impeccable taste, excellent bones. And the height of his particular beauty coalesced perfectly with the times.

It was a strange, tense, electric epoch. Sixty thousand body bags had been acquired by the city in case our machines failed on New Year's Eve. A redundant precaution, it transpired, but a contingent of us – young, hungry, predisposed to ecstatic nihilism – found the symbolism irresistible and decided to go out swinging. We cultivated our hysteria with terror and delight, proud of this

Baudelairian homage. We obliterated ourselves in each other and whatever else was nearby. We found a soundtrack in the dark drama of high-camp electro, music that equated glamour with self-immolation. Every week, new 12-inches materialised from an imagined 1983: minor-key hymns to pleasure and leisure, polaroids and sleek androids, caviar and crashing cars, strict machines and deep ravines. Hymns of neon-drenched, aspic-slick ennui, pinioned to the propulsive throb of Roland 808. We bricolaged old stuff in with the new, believing ourselves the first to really *feel* Suicide's 'Diamonds, Fur Coat, Champagne' or Gina X's 'No GDM' or Yoko Ono's 'Walking on Thin Ice'.

Shows ended, inevitably, with everyone on stage. Parties ended, inevitably, with everyone undressed. If The Unspoiled – sleek, pathologically promiscuous, the most ecstatic of nihilists – was engineered for anything, it was this. He only had to stand still. He only had to wait.

We met officially when I interviewed him for the magazine, when the job was still fresh and good. Then, I'd spend whole days on the telephone with musicians. They'd talk of their compulsions, their idols, their addictions, their loneliness, their fraught childhoods, their fractious relationships with bandmates, their sudden renouncement of guitars for keyboards, and their sudden renouncement of keyboards for guitars. They'd say, 'I've never told anyone this before,' while I twirled the telephone cord around my fingers, and they'd say, 'This record is best enjoyed with Courvoisier,' and they'd say, 'Come backstage after the show.' These conversations seldom went beyond 20 minutes, but intimacy was swift and palpable. Sometimes I'd get an earnest one who wanted to discuss Salinger or Sartre, and being earnest myself, this filled me with pink-cloud happiness. The Unspoiled

3

was newly evangelical about Věra Chytilová, as was I, and this seemed close enough. We compared proclivities, graphed shared obsessions, and started meeting in ferocious assignations. I'd found a perfect, alabastrine surface on which to smash myself.

The air outside crackled and rasped. Our cab pulled away from the curb, and Anika opened the windows to drink in the dissolving afternoon. It carried the perfume of jasmine, frangipanis on the edge of rot, and trace elements of promise. The sunset gathered like a flock of flamingos and broke apart with fanfare. We stalked overpasses and underpasses, speeding towards Pink Fist. Anika had decided this, but Pink Fist were my band, my discovery, and invisibly yoked to The Unspoiled, so only a six-car pile-up could keep me away.

'So,' she said. She shook out two pills, relined her eyes in a pocket mirror, and fixed me with her ersatz violet gaze. 'The Unspoiled. Is that a good idea?'

'Probably not,' I said, chewing my capsule, meditating on this. 'I haven't had a good idea in ages.'

It was true. Entropy had cut a broad swathe through my life. I'd acquired a stalker, an ex-husband, and industrial bronchitis with no serious effort on my part. The magazine, sick for 10 years, rose-cheeked for the last two as it fed directly from my veins, had lurched into terminal decline, its death rattle spooking the whole industry. I was 24, living deadline to deadline, barely half a person, and if anyone asked, having a very good time.

So while The Unspoiled radiated his obsessions outward, I conserved energy by honing mine to a radiant point: him. I loved the Cheshire Cat superiority with which he carried himself.

I loved how much he loved fucking, and how much he wanted everyone to know it. I loved that he was the poison and the cure in equal measure. I loved the chime of the words *idée fixe*. Below this, I envied him, with a fever-sick fury that could be mistaken for an urge to push him down the stairs.

The day was finally licked. The drive achieved the pace of inevitability, stars magnifying the twinkle of skyscrapers and skyscrapers imitating the twinkle of stars. The cab edged around a rattling bus, and the city pulled into focus: fire-bright, twitchy, leaking rum and sulphur. People leered from balconies, danced in traffic, and every bar played 'Africa' or 'Maniac'. Usually, I'd have paid the driver double to take me home then, but the pill had done its work early, hastened by heat, and I felt expansive, magnanimous, powerful. I braided Anika's hand into mine, and we dashed to the club, where I checked our names at the door.

The cavernous room oozed bordello light; sticky and sold to twice its capacity. I clocked the first wave of Pink Fisters – the ripped-stocking sybarites, the electroclash grads in lace fingerless gloves, the goth kids, the performance-art kids, the kids who knew their Bauhaus – pinned at the edges, but the black-denimed masses had well and truly come up from behind. My incantation of pinkfistpinkfistpinkfist, a secret held under my tongue, belonged to everyone now; passed from cell to cell, tissue to tissue.

'It's over,' I told Anika.

'Don't be greedy,' she said. 'There's more than enough to go around.'

*

We lost each other immediately, so I shoved my way to the bar. Someone yelled, 'Did you listen to my CD yet?', and someone grabbed at my skirt, but I angled my shoulder to a weaponised 'V' and kept moving. The abiding fact of The Unspoiled was his eel-slipperiness; never being where you wanted or expected. He didn't own a phone, so finding him required going into the night, ostensibly not looking. Tonight was unusual. Tonight, the chorus directly followed the verse.

'Hello, Editrix.' He stood at the bar, backlit to alien magnificence by an exit sign. 'I thought you might be here. What have you been up to?'

Slick. Flick. Sick. A kick in the chest, always.

'Putting out hundreds of small fires with my own blood,' I said. 'Do you have any cigarettes?'

'I hoped you might.'

'Naturally.' I shouted for a packet across the bar and lit two.

Inventing tragedies was my specialty, and The Unspoiled my best rendered to date. Enamelled green eyes, untroubled countenance, something nasty starting to harden at his jaw. A lock of red hair that brushed the creamy gold of his brow, enormous strong-knuckled hands. Both of us had nicotine rings at our fingers, and tonight we looked better than we deserved. I stood close to him, our heads near-touching as we bowed over an ashtray. We took inventory of the 7-inches and 12-inches released that week, the bands that had imploded, and the new ones who had taken their place – all called Crystal this or Wolf that, as the year's zeitgeist demanded. The Unspoiled played keyboards for the loudest and most novel, moving on the instant he got bored. That he couldn't read a note didn't matter; he was tall to the point of impracticality and imposing behind any machine.

'It's been a while,' he said, stubble brushing my ear, but I'd been working odd hours and unwell and often blitzed, so time had a new plasticity. There had been a funeral a few months ago, The Unspoiled eight rows behind me in dark sunglasses. The absinthe-crazed day I blew off my interviews so we could destroy my apartment, and an awful night at The Elysium. There had been numberless terse conversations side-of-stage, and conciliatory afternoons when I'd deliver new releases to his house, but yes, it had been a while.

'How many times have you seen Pink Fist?'

'Seven,' I said. 'None as good as the first.'

'Nothing ever is.' He said it wryly, the sound of a thousand doors slamming. Then he asked if I'd heard The Terrible Lakes, racing ahead of me towards the next thing – whatever was harder and weirder, wherever the cutest and most unhinged girls hung out, whoever he could claim to have heard first – but I wrested it back, pinned him down.

'Hey, Monster,' I said, cocking my head. 'Let's get out of here.'

He waited. A wave of MDMA broke over me, discharging flinty sparkles behind my eyes. I decided on several important things at once and set to work.

'I have a great confluence of feelings around you.' I said this standing on tiptoe so it landed in his neck.

He leaned down. 'Which is mutual, in a fashion. And impractical, as we've established at length.'

'Well, let's put a full stop to it. No more colons and semi-colons, no more drawn-out sets of en dashes, no more tortuous ellipses.'

Time arched, stretched like a cat. The Unspoiled met my gaze.

'I thought we'd done that.'

'No,' I said, plucking a flake of ash from my lip, and we regarded each other. Ecstatic suspension. He clenched his jaw in the manner I knew by rote, taking a drag from his cigarette to prolong things further. It was already happening. I was flooded with calm.

'Ok. I'll get my keyboard and meet you around the back.'

The temperature outside was still ruinously high. I ground my cigarette into a cabbage leaf and tried to text Anika, but the As kept coming up as Cs and the Js as Ks, so I leaned into the wall and contemplated the universe instead, Eno at its nucleus. In the periphery of my vision – that dim cul-de-sac of horror shows – something rustled and clinked, but tonight's kismet streak delivered The Unspoiled, blithely jangling his keys. Relief, opioid relief, the best of all feelings.

'Hey,' he said. Ice masquerading as fire.

'Oh, hey.'

We walked past dumpsters, arms brushing. His battered Trans Am was scalding to the touch. I stroked the dusty dash, the leather wheel, the pleasing symmetry of the gear. 'Stop at my apartment first,' I said, making him keep the engine idling while I went upstairs alone. Under my bed, a suitcase was packed; the $8000 I'd lifted from my ex-husband concealed at the bottom. I closed the front door hard for what I hoped was the last time.

The Unspoiled raised an eyebrow at the suitcase. 'Supplies,' I said, and we roared from the curb, now on our irrevocable way.

The Trans Am devoured yellow lines. Roads curved and straightened. The Unspoiled's jaw tightened and relaxed.

The Bookend Bridge, a string of pearls, hung magnificent in the distance. His hand rested lightly on my knee; his smile the skeleton key to the universe. As the car gathered speed, air skittered across my face in a succession of delicious dry slaps. I felt everything – magazine, apartment, writers, friends, husband, hopes, needs, obsessions – unfurl in streamers and lope into the sky. 'I adore you,' I whispered to the wind, the tunnels, the rough felt of the upholstery. I threw my phone out the window for the thrill of seeing it smash.

'Give me your phone,' I said to The Unspoiled.

'I don't have a phone.'

'Oh, that's right.' I produced two tabs and two pills from a film canister in my bag. 'Then open your mouth,' I said, placing one of each on his tongue. He swallowed without comment, eyes never leaving the road. I chewed mine, relishing the bitterness on my gums. He played Ministry's 'The Angel', an earthquake in a cathedral, the best synth-pop song made by an industrial band and the best industrial song made by a synth-pop band. Then he played a track I'd never heard – laudanum lassitude, frostbitten drums, Synclaviers that strobed through the car. We rolled onto the bridge and the music surged, echoing off the black-glass water. It was a soundtrack of epic journey: ascent and descent, towards and away.

'You do know me.'

'Of course I know you, Lucy.'

'I'm so alive I could die.' It was hard to put words to the cruel exhilaration of it all. 'A leftward swerve would do the trick – a pump of gas and clean *plonk* into the water. That, or we could keep driving forever.'

'You're nuts. Where are we going?'

I'd chosen the Camino del Sol Hotel, a painstakingly pre-served temple to '70s excess, because it was the least likely choice of anyone I knew. The valet whisked the Trans Am away. The Unspoiled checked in as Sonny Crockett, paying with my cash up front. By the time we reached the elevator, with its faceted panels of infinity glass, the second pill was bound to my sensorium, the acid's dream-logic ministrations about to begin. I leaned into The Unspoiled, into that direct green gaze, and undid his belt.

'So,' I said, rising on tiptoe, my hips now approximating his.

'So,' he said. The doors opened to a discreet chime. We barely made it out.

I'd forgotten, and hadn't, the enterprise of being locked in a room with him. The expansiveness of his hands, back and shoulders, the marble chiselling of his corded thighs, the planed severity of his jaw. What should be a procession of actions would coalesce into one, a javelin thrown a great distance and landing without sound. He was impassive and invulnerable, all possibility without consequence. Our breath synchronised as he moved in time with a noiseless beat – 'Nightclubbing' slowed to a crawl. I'd almost forgotten that internal metronome: beat, beat, beat. When his hips met mine, the door behind us melted: beat, beat, beat. It was an exorcism, a ritual sacrifice to all things before.

We stayed for three days, sustained by mineral water, room-service omelettes, and the chemistry set of substances collected from my apartment. The Unspoiled called for cigarettes, eyes glinting over the curved grey receiver. He'd answer the door in his bathrobe, the reverberation of his polite baritone through the hall striking a curious pang in me, a pang a differently disposed person might call love. We fucked furiously and languidly and furiously again, breaking away as if fleeing a car wreck only to wander dumbly back. My face, raw with stubble rash, bled at pinpricks around my lips and chin. My nostrils were numb, my waist a daisy-chain of bruises, my thighs brailed with the echo of teeth. My hipbones were chipped tiles by the second day, as were his; both of us hungry, clear-eyed, dangerous.

'Jesus,' he said, drawing back to assess the damage. 'We're going to kill each other.'

I nibbled painkillers – Mersyndol, Tramadol, Percodan, Panadol – to discourage migraines. I learned and relearned each scar on his body – the pocks of '70s childhood illnesses, the dent below his second rib where he'd been stabbed by a jealous girlfriend, with a biro, at age 15 – memorising them for a faraway time I could bear to think of this again. We sat in the kidney-shaped bathtub and dreamed up elaborate, impossible concert bills.

'Depeche Mode at the Pasadena Rose Bowl 1988, supported by *Mask*-era Bauhaus and *Pretty Hate Machine*-era Nine Inch Nails.'

'Siouxsie and the Banshees supported by Magazine and The Associates. Everyone aged 22.' I flicked the cold tap. 'Now turn around so I can watch you in the mirror,' and he did, revealing the topography of his back: porcelain flecked with the rust of freckles, muscles bisected by the infinite bridge of spine. I ran my hands over the amber hair on his arms, observing the mechanised clang of tendons against skin.

I surmised, from occasionally drawing the grey silk curtains, that it rained for the entirety of those three days. In moments of respite, we'd perch on the windowsill, draped in sheets, passing a cigarette between us, watching traffic move inaudibly 30 floors below. Nobody had a clue where I was; this knowledge a deep comfort. We lay length-to-length on the carpet, breath-to-breath, his face in my hands. 'I hope I know you for centuries,' he said, and I shifted, only by molecules, but enough; the exquisite relief as he moved again: beat, beat, beat. His eyes remained open, his tongue in my mouth, his name jagged in my throat. That vaulted state of all sensation and no feelings as the walls rippled and dissolved. The scattered cushions and overflowing ashtrays and knotted sheets became a vast landscape; the entire universe, in fact. There was nothing outside this: his red hair, his damp brow, his weight on my back. No flourish, no performance, no treble – just me and him, just bass.

For The Unspoiled, this was just one in a running total of cataclysms, enacted over successive weekends. There would always be someone to surrender their credit card for him, score drugs for him, set fire to their lives for him – for this, even a fraction of this. Always someone lending him money, accepting his collect calls from payphones, driving around with the meter running, looking for him, for a variation of this. And if not always, then for another 10 years – maybe 15. But for me, it was a onetime thing: a nuclear event. In the end, I knew him no better. In the end, I kicked him out.

I showered, dressed – observing the pleasure of this novelty – and flushed everything except the Tramadol, pocketed for the growing probability of flight. I smoked my last cigarette and repacked my suitcase, stroking the bundled 20s and 10s as one might a spoiled pet, a talisman, a treasure map. I shredded my notebook and tickertaped the scraps from the window. Then I dragged my suitcase to the foyer and hailed a taxi. To try again.

PALE SHELTER

January 2004

Robin notices her three times on the trail, nodding a friendly hello as friendly hellos are expected here, before she stops to introduce herself: Lucy. Specifically, he notices the dresses, their tiered skirts and mesh panels and big complicated bows in '80s ice cream colours of hot pink, lemon and white. They seem a strange choice, a contrivance, but then Robin walks in jeans, alternating the two pairs he owns, and given it's the blazing height of summer, this might be a contrivance too.

She slows and waits for him one day at the bridge, an unofficial marker between the national park and unclaimed craggy headland. She stands on her left leg, clasping her right foot behind her in a gesture of overstated awkwardness. Her nose is peeling. 'Nice T-shirt,' she says, gesturing at the faded Einstürzende Neubauten print. 'I gather you're not from around here.'

Robin laughs. 'Nope. You?'

'Ha! Actually, yes. I was born here,' she points vaguely south. 'I left Abergele at 14, but I've come back to take the cure.'

Chalk cliffs stripe the electric-blue sky. The ocean has a dry-ice shiver. It's a coastline of staggering beauty on a clear, chiming day. 'You've chosen a good place for it,' he says.

She falls unselfconsciously into step with him as they walk along the bluff. Rangy limbs and dead-straight hair to her shoulders, lightest around her face. An odd, sideways-skipping step, an odd looseness at the joints. They map the points where their lives intersect: she went to school with Meg, who Robin is dating, for a few years in the mid-'90s. They're the same age, save three weeks, and both studied English lit, but in different cities. They both love the new Ariel Pink record.

She tells him she's burning through an advance to expand a long-form article into a book titled *I Abject: Existentialism and Electronic Music*. He tells her he's staying with his sister to be near his grandmother in palliative care. It turns out they live on the same street, Lucy atop the hill, Robin a few blocks below. She has nicotine stains on her fingers.

They're both sweating as they pause outside her house, sun claret with 4pm fury.

'Care to come in for a glass of cold tomato juice?' asks Lucy.

Robin, who knows just one person in this town outside the handful he's related to by blood or marriage, says sure.

The house is split-level modernist. Her grandfather, her mother's father, built it in the late '50s. The front yard is a tangle of succulents, flushed with obscene flowers. There's an outdoor spiral staircase leading to a rooftop terrace. Hammered urns hold jades and agaves, the front steps are gritty with salt.

Inside it's much cooler, gnarled house plants swinging from cedar beams. The walls are the colour of mushroom bisque, the carpet the colour of peach sorbet, the kitchen the colour of avocado mousse.

Lucy builds their tomato drinks: tall glasses salted and peppered lavishly; the juice mixed to a froth with an oyster fork. 'The best thing after a walk,' she says. She motions for Robin to follow her back to the living room, a sunken nest of books and magazines. Copies of *The Face* and *Select* and *Melody Maker* and *Record Mirror* and *ZigZag* and *Flexipop!* and *Ongaku Senka* and *Careless Talk Costs Lives* are piled at the walls. A vast, misted window faces the sea. The coffee table is covered in crystal ashtrays, chewed pens, blister packs of painkillers, nail polish, more books, and apricot stones still bearing the fibrous tear of their fruit. Beneath the table is a scatter of ballet flats.

'Sorry,' she says. 'I hadn't realised how disgusting it's become in here.'

The floor is slate, smoky grey and marmalade. There's an old upright piano, a wingback chair of orange corduroy piled with dresses, and more plants: a bleeding heart that's colonised one window, a Boston fern in a water-swollen basket, a fleshy purple thing in an oxidised copper pot.

'You said this is your grandfather's house, Lucy?'

'Yes.' Her legs are curled beneath her, glass pressed to her forehead.

'His plants?'

'His everything, except the records and magazines and clothes. And some books.'

'When did he die?'

'Oh, he's not dead. He's in India for a year, meditating. He found Buddhism in his 50s.'

'As you do. How long have you been here?'

'A month. But I grew up in this house if I grew up anywhere. We moved habitually with my dad's job – every city on the east coast, the Mojave Desert, some other weird satellite towns: anywhere with an air force base, basically – so Abergele is the only fixed point in a chaotic universe. What about you?'

'I've been here four months.' Robin is self-conscious, having run out of things to ask or things that are polite to ask. He reaches for a Jenga-stack of books on the coffee table: powdery old editions of *Either/Or* and *The Ambiguity of Being*, a tea-ringed copy of *Atomised*.

'Are you an existentialist?'

'That's an asshole thing to go around declaring. But if you define it as Sartre does, of creating oneself constantly through passion-ate action, then yes. Someone I call The Unspoiled Monster calls me a weaponised existentialist.'

'What does that mean?' He doesn't ask who The Unspoiled Monster is.

'That I use it as an excuse to behave badly, or used to. This year I'm channelling Camus: *Happiness, too, is inevitable.*' She gives Robin a diffident look. 'I'm sorry, I had a Dexie this morning to write, and I'm quite talkative. I don't believe I've spoken to anyone else in days. Your sister – is she you doubled? Usually strapped beneath a baby?'

'Um, yes. That's Isabella.'

'I've seen her around. Older, younger or the same?'

'She's older, five years older.'

They are quiet.

'Well, I should let you get back to work,' says Robin. 'It was nice to meet you.'

Lucy stands, bounding towards the kitchen. 'Wait there,' she calls. When she returns, it's with a crumpled piece of card. 'I'm having a party this Saturday,' she says, pushing an invitation into his hand. 'You should come. Bring Meg. Bring Isabella. We're starting at four.'

Abergele is pitched on a fingerling of land between the ocean and a colossal saltwater lake. There's a lighthouse, an air force base, a brutalist public library, and a bowls club set in a stony plateau of a cliff. Teenage girls with rock-hard faces tear around on bicycles, diamantés glinting at their concave bellies. The bakery windows are lined with sugared buns and vanilla slice; the fish and chip shop windows stacked with pineapple rings and battered savs. Turquoise dragons stand guard over a single Chinese restaurant; black swans and white pelicans float on the lake. In the empty hours between visits to the hospital and nights watching his nephew, Robin walks, camera slung around his neck.

The whole town might be under an enchantment, time having stopped in 1986. Fastidiously trimmed lawns parked with cars and trailers and boats. Bait shacks and shimmering sandbanks and sepia arcades stuffed with breakable things. A drawbridge that parts on the hour for schooners and skiffs. You sense strange magic in the scuffed chequerboard floor of the dusty supermarket; the empty lots dotted with horses and cockatoos; the caravans on the flood plains; the giant weekday pours of house chardonnay at the surf club. Every sunset, a fine salty mist rises from the sea in an orangey-pink conjuring.

Robin had met no one in Abergele who'd appreciate the specificity of this enchantment. Until now.

He arrives at Lucy's party as the afternoon crests, Meg at his side, Isabella at work. The rooftop terrace surges with people dressed in white linen, tangerine silk and stonewash – they might have just stepped from a yacht, circa 1984. Blue Night's 'Turn Me Loose' blares from invisible speakers. Meg takes Robin's hand with certain ownership and leads him through the house, pointing out the cat-shaped orange smudge on the slate, recalled from her last visit a decade ago. Outside, the sun glistens the swimming pool, bestowing the airbrushed unreality of a menthol cigarette ad. More thrift-store glitterati throng the water's perimeter. Robin spots Lucy in a yellow dress, bound with complicated straps.

'You came!'

She's smoking, standing on one leg, a heron pose to which he'll soon be habituated. She hugs them, effusive hugs, folding Meg into her side as they exclaim over each other. She introduces them to Tabitha, her 'favourite person in the entire world', who's working on her PhD three streets away, and Harry, Tabitha's affable boyfriend. Robin meets Gudrun, magnificent in a backless emerald dress – 'the most edible human you'll ever lay eyes on', according to Lucy. He meets Julian, passing with a crate of records. He meets others, many others, but it's Tabitha, Harry, Gudrun and Julian who assume consequence in Robin's memory. They are the ones who will matter.

While Meg stashes their drinks, Lucy stands close to Robin, lighting another cigarette. 'Can I interest you in a treat?' she says, blowing smoke at the sky. He realises she's high: bottomless pupils ringed with grey-flecked blue, the endless melt into whoever she's talking to.

'I thought you were taking the cure.'

'Well, I am,' she says. 'But it's a special occasion: tonight's a blood moon, you know.'

Robin didn't know. 'Sure.'

She digs through her pockets for a Hello Kitty baggie, holding her drink to Robin's mouth so he can swallow the pill. She resumes standing on one leg, and Robin registers febrile heat in her lean.

'Tell me how you came to live on my street again, Robin?'

'Isabella moved here a few years ago to do her residency and met another doctor. They got married, bought the house, had my nephew Teddy, and burrowed in.'

'Right.'

'When my grandmother got sick, Izzy arranged for her care in town. We lived with Gran as kids, so Izzy wanted her close. I more or less followed.'

'That's very good of you, but what of your job; your friends?'

Robin shrugs. 'I worked as a cashier in the gallery bookshop.'

'Well, I'm glad you landed in Abergele. I don't know anyone here except Tabitha and Harry.'

Robin laughs. 'Yet your house is full of people.'

'Oh.' She's dismissive. 'They won't bother coming this far again.'

'You know Meg.'

'I haven't encountered Meg since high school. I kissed a boy she liked when we were 14, and that was the end of that school for me. Meg was a formidable queen bee, the whole hive at her bidding. She surely briefed you on this.'

It's true. Meg was clear she'd accompany him to the party out of curiosity alone.

'And where did *you* find Meg?' asks Lucy.

'Buying flowers for my grandmother at her shop.'

'Adorable. Well, I'm genuinely pleased you're here. You're a good egg, Robin. Perhaps we can synchronise our walks. I can test my arguments on you; the book arguments, I mean.'

'I'd enjoy that.'

'Then it's settled.' Lucy claps her hands, satisfied, then a new novelty captures her attention. 'Mani!' she bellows across the water. 'MANI!' And she's off in a miasma of nicotine.

The pill comes on as the sun descends. Robin is drenched in sudden elation – swifter and stronger than the pills of his acquaintance – and realises how unhappy he's been; the true cost of his near-solitude the past four months. 'Talking in Your Sleep' and 'Egypt, Egypt' and 'Shattered Dreams' and 'I Am Only Shooting Love' ripple from the speakers. Gudrun puts a glass of frosted pink liquid in his hand, which burns his throat with bright, tangy bitterness. Robin and Harry stand with their backs against the terrace railing, sharing a cigarette. Robin tells Harry he's a photographer, kind of, and Harry says he is too, sort of, and they talk while Harry produces cameras from his backpack, caressing their speckled leather cases. Robin, pleasurably outdone, proffers his dented Canon Rebel.

They dance to yacht rock as the vermilion moon rises and Robin pulls Meg fully clothed into the pool. They kiss on the azure steps. 'Who IS this?' she says, and it's Icehouse. 'I LOVE this.' They're dry within the hour. He walks past four girls in huddled conference around the kitchen drawers, choosing utensils with which they'll smack each other. The slaps get harder and more resonant, squeals veering from delight into hysteria. More people edge towards the drawers, taking the temperature of their want. Someone chants 'A knife, a fork, a bottle, a cork!' Those involved wear their welts proudly for the rest of the night, stroking them in a reverie of pleasure.

Robin's walking through the garden when Lucy grabs his hand. He flinches, imagining the thwack of a spoon, but he's drawn into a prismatic puddle of light to dance to Naked Eyes. 'This album is transcendent, and no one remembers it.' She is weightless, boneless, part jellyfish.

'*Burning Bridges*,' says Robin. 'I remember it.'

'Oh, you *are* a good egg.' Horizontal bruises bloom at her legs.

Meg leaves, being a person who leaves things early, and Robin surprises himself by staying, lying on an old banana lounge to breathe in the night. Someone claims the lounge next to his, a tall man with a shock of red hair hanging over one eye. 'It's Robin, right?' he says, extending a handshake. 'Julian.' A hanging question now answered – this is Lucy's Unspoiled Monster.

Julian lies back too, lighting a cigarette. He gives the impression of being even taller supine, limbs spilling over the lounge. His face, in profile, is a column of emphatic gestures: strong dimpled chin, ski-slope nose, high poreless forehead, gold brows of unexpected delicacy. His hair is cropped close at the neck, emphasising the strong planes of his skull,

'What's your take on Lucy?' he says with a Delphic smile. He points his cigarette at the terrace, where Lucy is dancing in loose-limbed pagan abandon.

'I only just met her.'

Julian shrugs. 'But you've been watching us all night. What's your impression? Are we a touch performative, perhaps?'

Robin accepts a cigarette and takes a stalling drag.

'If someone is always performing, isn't that just who they are?' asks Robin, and Julian says touché, and laughs a deep, buttered laugh.

They lie in wordless peace. At length, Julian rearranges his limbs. Robin asks if he's leaving, and Julian says, 'Why would I leave a perfectly good party when I'll be dead one day?' and it's the last lucid conversation Robin has that night. Everyone migrates inside, the true believers crowding into the sunken living room; forming piles, forming litters. There is the scramble for tobacco and papers and ashtrays. At a dizzy-makingly late hour, Robin realises Lucy is gone, and he should go as well. He opens and closes a few doors, chemically intent on saying goodbye.

She's with Julian in a study, backs against speakers, cigarettes two glowing points in the dark.

They're listening to *Nothing Counts*, the first big record Robin's father produced in 1983. Given the night's soundtrack, Robin might have expected this, but it knocks him askew, bodily askew, and his farewell lands with a stammer.

'Until next time,' says Julian, with a neat salute. Lucy bids him sweet dreams in a singsong voice, nestling deeper into Julian's side.

The sun is a flare set off in the ultramarine sky; clean, acute and potent. Robin stands at the bus stop, shoulders buzzing with insects. He's been waiting for three-quarters of an hour when an old red Fiat slows in front of him, trailing synthesised piano.

'Where are you going?' says Lucy, hair in her mouth, white sunglasses on her head.

'The hospital, to visit my grandmother.'

'Do you always take the bus?'

'Meg or Isabella usually drive.'

'Aha. Well, it's a lousy bus. That timetable might be the Voynich manuscript. Get in; I'll take you.'

She pulls from the curb with an inelegant lurch, leaning on the accelerator more than strictly necessary. They speed past Norfolk pines in a drunken waltz, a coven of yellow-beaked egrets conferring on the roof of the bait shop, the spire of the lighthouse, the grey cubes of the power station, and the whale's skeleton of a half-finished boat. 'Someone has been building that boat,' she says, pointing, the car swaying with her, 'since 1981. If they ever finish it, I'll be heartbroken.'

'Nice car.'

'My Uncle Bruce lent it to me. He has a garage full of old cars, each with a terminal illness. It's a Spider.'

'You're channelling the Wakefield twins in *Sweet Valley High*.'

'How do you know *Sweet Valley High*?'

'Isabella. Are you a Jessica or an Elizabeth?'

'I'm Elizabeth during the week and Jessica on the weekend.'

'That's what every girl says.'

'Ha!' She takes corners without slowing. Dry wind slaps their shoulders, Italo on the stereo.

'Who is this?'

'Gino Soccio, "Remember".' She turns up the volume, swerving again, and the car is engulfed in sunsets, cigarettes, silhouettes, infinity pools, swim-up bars, maraschino cherries and the libidinal throb of a TR-808. 'This burns a hole *right through me*,' and they merge onto the Pacific Highway, Abergele unfurling below them in a crescent of orange-tiled roofs hugging the lake.

'I enjoy Italo disco,' says Robin, 'but the production sounds so dated, especially when compared to the "Killing Moon"s of the same time.'

'That misses the point entirely. Italo is the shallow cut that nicks an artery. These songs are shrines to early technology: shrines to melody, mistakes, innocence, FEELINGS. Bear in mind that guitars and bass have been electrified since the '30s, but electrified pianos, i.e. synths, weren't cheap enough to own until the '80s. Even then, they were fucking hard to program, so if these songs sound vapid and crude, it's because they're essentially punk – people working things out as they go. And the reason they sound inhuman is they're *supposed* to.'

He thinks of his father. 'You're very persuasive.'

'Well, that's my job, apparently.' She adjusts the review mirror. 'Sorry, Julian enjoys arguing. I forget not everyone does that for fun.'

'Oh, it's fun; I'll just have to try harder. What does Julian do? When he's not in Abergele, I mean?'

'Oh, Julian doesn't do *anything*,' says Lucy with extravagance. 'His life is his work of art, in the manner of Dorian Gray. He plays keyboards in bands, and plays records to bright young things Thursday nights. He spends a great deal of time thrifting for suits and sleeping with a vast number of people. If you're asking what he does for money, he answers telephones.' Her gaze narrows. 'None of us are rich kids slumming it, in case you wondered. I'm eking out the advance and money I extracted from an ex. Harry and Tabitha are on PhD scholarships. And Gudrun is an adult lawyer with a proper job at the Department of Public Prosecutions. My grandfather's house is a magic trick – the only thing of value in my family. What do *you* do for money, Robin?'

'I collect an allowance from my dad – a bribe to look after his mother so he doesn't have to.'

'Well, there you go. All making valuable contributions to society.'

They drive without speaking, the traffic lights miraculously green; a feeling of controlled burnout, of drift, a feeling intensified by reaching ARP arpeggios. The afternoon has taken on a mother-of-pearl iridescence. They pass the petrol station with its inexplicable giant prawn, the Aristocrat Hotel, the Gospel Pianos wholesaler, the brutalist wedge of the police station and, almost too soon for Robin, they're at the hospital.

'Thank you,' he says.

'My pleasure. I'd wait, but I need to get to the fish markets before they close.'

'That's the other side of town.'

'I know. I'm having a dinner tomorrow – come. I'll make you an Italo CD.' And the car tears away.

In the languid balm of the following weeks, a tight constellation takes form. Robin, Lucy, Tabitha, Harry, Meg, Julian – who drives from the city in his battered Trans Am most weekends – and Gudrun, his passenger. They congregate for dinners on Lucy's terrace. Everyone brings two or three bottles, giving the illusion of endless booze and deathless, arcadian summer. The ease with which Robin is folded into their lives surprises him. He supposes, except Meg, they're all interlopers, in-betweeners. They're camping in Abergele to finish something, be with someone, to wait for someone to die. He considers Julian's quip about the group's performative affect, knowing performance needs an audience, knowing this to be his role. Robin doesn't recognise the fission that's his alone: his dark-eyed watchfulness, his soft voice drawing people closer, the romance of his slight frame and monastic rotation of five T-shirts. That he doesn't recognise it might be Robin's elemental appeal.

He delights in Tabitha's hard-bitten wit, her boyish sexiness, and the blunt instrument of her pragmatism. Following the siren call of the ocean and cheap rent, she and Harry moved to Abergele soon after Lucy. Tabitha has just started her PhD, attacking it in diligent eight-hour sittings and printing the pages each night. Robin discovers she gets a nosebleed most days and is the smartest, most disciplined and best-adjusted of them. At 23, Tabitha is fully formed, impatient for others to catch up. Harry is working on a PhD too, but now, a year in, admits he'll probably coast out his scholarship. He spends days tending to projects: reading 20 years of *New Scientist* back issues he found in Lucy's garage; collecting and repairing cameras; brewing beer under his house; trading Prince bootlegs online.

Conducting this dissonant orchestra is Lucy. She holds court, playing Italo disco and early electro and proto-industrial, pointing out passages she deems notably abject. She wears '80s party dresses and spills wine on the hems. She bakes foot-high pavlovas and conjures demoded entrees: angels on horseback, whipped bacalao dip in ramekins, céleri rémoulade, bagna càuda, cauliflower soup dusted with supermarket caviar, moulded things in aspic.

Her generosity is effusive bordering on gluttonous, a generosity that serves to heighten her own pleasure. She leaps from her seat when anyone's glass is emptying; presses plant cuttings, mix CDs, books and lists – loping addendums of conversations – into their arms as they leave. Robin knows she lives on what she calls witch food – tinned fish, tinned beans and things snipped from the garden – during the week to throw these dinners.

He takes in her reedy feet, never still under the table. He takes in her overlong fingers and chipped nail polish, her habit of biting the second joint in thought, leaving visible indents. Her tremolo movements when being watched. Her gesture of covering her face with a forearm while dancing, as if overcome, a gesture he wonders if she affects in bed. Her deficiency of proprioception; a lack of bodily awareness that sends sparks and glasses flying across the table. And the diamond-edged glint of obsession in all she does, a quality Robin recognises from his father. If it's a performance, it's a wholly committed one.

On the rare evenings Isabella isn't working or visiting their grandmother, and when her husband – the Invisible Anaesthesiologist, as Robin calls him – is home to watch Teddy, she joins them too. Robin is glad, a gladness veering on pride, to have this gift of interesting people for his sister after a lifetime sustained by her books, records, houses, and friends. He is pleased to see the old Izzy re-emerge on the terrace – red lipstick, loose curls, full glass; the Izzy who is quick to laugh or sing 'Babooshka' at the moon. Teenaged Izzy, share-house Izzy, before the grind of hospital rotations, the devotion-drunk exhaustion of tending to an infant, the bureaucratic tangle of caring for their grandmother.

Robin is overcome with feeling on these nights, a feeling that closely resembles love, although it doesn't include or exclude any one person. Love is a perfume dispersed generously on the terrace breeze.

Lucy holds him to the promise of walks. Most afternoons, around 3pm, he knocks on her door, and they set out. Robin spends the mornings with his grandmother, eating lunch with her at the hospice: nursery food – soft vegetables, potted meats. Lucy spends the mornings alone, mostly writing. The walks are a relief to them both, and – being roughly, if not exactly, the same height – they fall into step. They skirt the fat lizards lounging on concrete paths, glistening richly in the sun. They walk headland and the desire lines of the cliffs, where brown velveteen rabbits vault across the verge, making Lucy clap with delight. And then, out of breath and clammy, they cross the bridge to the national park. Beyond a tessellation of clay paths is an immense stone shelf jutting over the ocean, inset with hundreds of rockpools. It could be the surface of the moon. At low tide, with much care, you can reach a compact beach fringed with volcanic sand. Thousands of shells amass in the looping patterns of the waves, stippled with sea glass glossy as gummy bears. Pufferfish, seahorses and cuttlefish wash ashore daily. More rockpools, much smaller rockpools, corral minuscule fish and clear prophylactic discs of jellyfish. Lucy and Robin sit on the sand, collecting piles of things; far, far away from their old lives.

It's on this beach, under Lucy's guileless interrogation, that Robin confesses his father is Roland the producer, a recurrent beloved credit on her records. That things are touchy between them. That yes, he could feasibly arrange an interview for Lucy, but not right now.

'Where's your mother?' asks Lucy. Her shells resemble doll-sized urns and bleached rows of teeth. She holds a whip of seaweed, popping its pearls one by one.

'My mother died when I was four, Isabella was nine. Complications from an ectopic pregnancy. That's when we went to live with my grandmother.'

'Fuck.'

'She was from Madrid and met Roland at a gig in London: she was studying, he was a tape operator. They came here together, following some band he was producing. I can barely remember her, but by all accounts, she was a saint, just as Izzy's a saint. A prerequisite for living with my father.'

'Do you have other family?'

'I've never met my mother's family. Roland's father died before I was born, a car accident back in England. I suspect my grandmother was on the verge of a new life when she came into possession of two foundlings.'

'Jesus, Robin, that's intense. My grandmother died 10 years ago, which was sad, naturally, but I'd be sunk without my grandfather. I've been taking variations of the cure in Abergele since I was a teenager, and he's the only person who'll talk writing and reading with me – talk life beyond its basic mechanics. He gave me Beckett when I was 14, and *Of Human Bondage*, which I reread every year. He taught me the fundamentals of gardening, of propagation. When he's home, he spends days pottering and listening to Radio National, snipping at the plants, leaving me alone, and reserves proper conversation for dinner – the way it should be.'

'Well, my grandmother fulfils the same proxy-parental role, although in her own way, and not for much longer.' Sidestepping possible sympathies, Robin asks about her parents.

'They're very nice; they're just not terribly interested in me. My parents never think to call unless there's a specific reason.'

It is a brief answer for one so fond of talking. He waits.

'They've still got kids at home, twin girls who just turned 13. You could say we're giving each other space. Or you could say I've been a maniacal, monstrous cold mess the last few years, and they're steering clear lest it's contagious.'

'What type of mess?'

'The usual ingenue cocktail. An ill-advised marriage that flatlined after three weeks. Occasional trips to the emergency room Saturday nights and Sunday mornings. Martinis for breakfast, tangles in court. Nights having dark impulses on the bridge – *L'Appel du Vide*, the call of the void. As I said, my parents are very nice, and my life average for the first stretch – magical, in fact – so who knows where I got my bleak streak? A bad faerie must have stood over my crib.'

He weighs this, consigns it for now. 'You seem fine to me. Clearly, the cure is going well.'

'I hope so. Letting Julian follow me here wasn't the best idea; you don't take Iggy Pop to Berlin if you're serious about drying out. But I feel better than I have in forever. A bone and organ happiness – the inevitable kind, you know?'

Robin has no point of comparison, but Lucy's candescent with it; hair in her eyes, nose brown and peeling, shoulders loose and open to the ocean. Robin knows what she means; he feels that bone and organ happiness too.

*

Meg is a florist, in high demand amongst Abergele's summer brides. On Robin's third visit to her shop, she suggests they have a drink sometime. Why, he isn't sure. She's very pretty, a prettiness few are immune to; eyes like open umbrellas, faultless American teeth. She's simultaneously tiny and voluptuous, her shoulders muscled from hefting branches.

Variations of Abergele pixie-ring the lake, and Robin and Meg take drives to a cinema two towns over, rotating the five albums where their tastes intersect. Meg lives with her parents, so they spend evenings at Robin's house, taking turns choosing movies. She often joins him at the hospice, unflinching in the face of its terrors: the noises, the odours, the whole wing of decline. Meg is good at small talk. Her levity and practicality are a salve, so much so that Robin can ignore her tendency towards pettiness, her love of complaining, the frequency at which their conversations collapse. If she gets attached prematurely, it's because he lets her. She works hard, waking at 4am for the flower markets, and leaves Lucy's dinners before things get messy.

And they do get messy, despite the warm bonhomie of the terrace. Harry drinks steadily, heavily, with exuberance. One night he falls asleep at the table, and Tabitha drags him downstairs, bracing him roughly against her small boy's shoulders. No one is game to help. Harry gets louder and louder as he makes less and less sense. Tabitha will throw water in his face or snatch his glass, draining the contents so he can't. She'll say, 'What the hell are you talking about, Harry?' and he'll say, 'I'm drunk now – words are just coming out of my mouth!' Emboldened, Robin drinks more than he'd otherwise dare; seeking ease, seeking that hallowed, elusive state somewhere between his usual reticence and total self-vanquishment. Overdoing it renders him silent – the very opposite to Harry.

Lucy and Julian are intensely competitive, talking music and little else. The more calmly Julian contradicts her – on the year of something, the importance of something, the intent of something, the inherent value of something – the more explosively she reacts. She slaps records on the table to settle arguments, declaring, '1985! HA!' and loses three this way, including a 12" of 'Shake the Disease'. Robin wonders if she's going to cry, but Lucy just throws the fragments over the terrace wall. On the whole, it looks impersonal; a zero-sum form of seduction, of play. But occasional poison-tipped arrows suggest a lurking substratal hostility, one they're endlessly and publicly compelled to revive. One night Julian tells Lucy her self-loathing is exhausting. They're in the stairwell, Robin attempting to edge past.

'It's not self-loathing,' she says. 'It's self-awareness.'

'If you insist.'

'Oh, I don't insist. I've wasted enough time insisting things to you.'

'I believe time you enjoy wasting is not wasted time, Lucy.'

'Alright, you win, although there's little honour in it, Julian.'

Another night, Robin finds them in an ungainly embrace against the refrigerator, Julian's hand sliding into Lucy's skirt. The three regard each other with open, curious faces.

'You can come in,' says Lucy.

Robin steps forward, part pot-valour, part politeness. A new quality snaps the air.

'Oh, he *does* party,' says Julian, laughing, and Lucy wriggles free of his hand.

'Not tonight,' says Robin. 'I only came to say goodbye.' A beat, two beats. 'Goodbye.'

Lucy is never messy-drunk, not in the conspicuous style of Harry and Robin. Her party trick is a narcoleptic death drop. She'll be standing on a chair for an announcement, or setting a dessert alight, or changing the record, and submit to a sudden blitz of exhaustion, oxygen visibly draining from her blood. Once or twice she's sent them home then, but as a rule takes wordlessly to bed, reading with the door ajar while everyone else keeps going. Harry – a veteran of restaurant sinks – will do the dishes, tea towel thrown over his shoulder. Tabitha will blow out the candles, slipping the deadlock on their way out.

It's only Gudrun who's invincible, who never loses her temper or cries or falls over. She sits queenly at the head of the table wreathed in smoke; laughter tinkling with expensive materiality, stately throat a ladder reaching to the sky. In Gudrun, cool and warmth resolve in perfect tension. Her remoteness protects reserves of calm and energy far exceeding what the others have to spare. 'Gudrun got shot at a nightclub in Prague,' Lucy tells Robin, her pride in this fact manifest. 'She keeps the bullet in a glass snuff box displayed on her coffee table. On Sunday nights you'll find her on stage, gaffer tape across her nipples, but she'll be addressing court in a pinstriped pantsuit at 8am the next day.'

One evening – that summer being abundant in evenings – Robin hears Gudrun and Lucy discussing him as they coax an upside-down pineapple cake onto a platter.

'Where did you find him again?' says Gudrun.

'Near the little bridge, all dressed in black.'

'Well, he's beautiful, dying-in-your-arms-at-the-roulette-table beautiful. No one can accuse you of having a type, Lucy. Grizzled old Victor, Jules the alpha, your manic pixie dream girl, and now this wistful owl. Those gigantic eyes, always watching!

He so rarely opens his mouth that when he does, you're certain it will be exciting.'

'Shut up,' says Lucy. 'It's nothing like that. Nothing of the sort.'

'I understand,' says Gudrun, coiling her hair into a bun and uncoiling it. 'You've found another hard surface to smash yourself against. Which is absolutely fine, darling, but don't forget why you moved here.'

Robin arrives for a walk one day, ferociously sunburnt.

'Goodness! You look like a boiled lobster,' says Lucy.

He's dizzy; not sure why he came. 'I fell asleep on the beach earlier. I never usually burn.' He doesn't mention being stoned at 11 in the morning.

'I'm just untangling a knot, walking back some flawed reasoning. Come in.'

She writes in her grandfather's study, a largish room with a cedar desk built under a window. The ocean is a cube of heroic ferocity, every strike on the chalk cliffs amplified by the glass. A much smaller window frames the swimming pool's tamed wet. Shelves of irregular rectangles cover the walls, full of books, records, and biological miscellanea: a pinned scarab beetle and a mounted tiger moth; a jagged piece of malachite; succulent cuttings in anchovy jars massed with spindly new roots. A framed Swiss Design print depicts a rabbit missing a paw, a chair missing a leg, a clock missing a hand, a teapot missing its handle. Two glasses on the desk congeal with the fleshy residue of tomato juice.

Robin lies on a leather couch for a moment and discovers he's not in a position to stand.

'Oh dear,' says Lucy. She fetches a packet of frozen peas, apologising she doesn't have any ice. 'You moose around for a while,' she says, 'and I'll work,' so he picks a much-thumbed copy of *Tropic of Cancer* from the floor. The cover is a vivisected orange orb – Roland owns the same edition. Robin flips the pages, reads fitfully, then dreams vividly. He is on his father's farm, tipping a bucket of live fish into the bathtub. He is in Paris, eating a bowl of steam and gristle that sends cramping thunderbolts across his stomach. He is at a club, tinselly and dark, being pulled through smoke by a girl. Hot light needles her red hair. They bolt themselves into a cubicle and she pushes him against a wall, fucking him from behind (by dream logic this works). He surrenders to it, her pointed teeth in his neck, and Julian bangs on the door, asking if they have cigarettes.

When Robin wakes, Lucy's holding a tumbler to his mouth, uranium glass of misted milk-green. Her hair brushes his throat, and he notes the paleness of her lips, the healthy shine in the violet crescents sickling her eyes. She smells bright and outdoorsy – ocean salt and tomato juice – and has four paracetamol in her fist. They have never been this close.

'Take these,' says Lucy and asks where Meg is.

'Doing a wedding.'

'And Izzy?'

'On a double shift.'

'You have heatstroke. You should stay here.'

'What time is it?'

The light in the study is a supple, gold-flecked apricot. Sixish. He shuts his eyes again and pinballs between dreams and hallucinations, most of them disconcerting and lubricious. Lucy is still there on the occasions he wakes, typing or humming or

35

eating at her desk. The peas are swapped for a box of fish fingers, and Robin's glass of water refilled. The sea is much louder than usual.

By sunrise, marigold slicing through the blinds, Lucy is gone. She has thrown a single cream sheet over him bearing a print of Izzy's childhood – Holly Hobbie. He finds a stack of tea-stained index cards, scrawls a thank-you note, and walks home; still woozy, embarrassed. For a week afterwards, his skin peels in sheer ribbons, and Robin rolls them away with near-erotic satisfaction, a visceral reminder of the Henry Miller, the fever, the relief of the icy peas and milky tumbler, Lucy's freckled forearms against his chest.

They play a game of Top Five, excavating the vast trench of their shared obsessions. It will start in the lull between main course and dessert. Bread is torn, crusts rasping then yielding to sop the meal's last smears and sploshes. Glasses are refilled at ever-shorter intervals, a phenomenon Harry labels exponential decay, and lighters are lost or forgotten, cigarettes sparked from cigarettes. Someone will begin. Tonight, it's Gudrun, who – forgoing the bread – has just licked her plate and set it down with a satisfied G-sharp clang.

'Top five literary characters you want to fuck.'

'Dick Diver, when he was godly,' Tabitha says. 'Sally Bowles. Emma Bovary. Ursula from *Women in Love*. The teddy-bear guy, Sebastian.'

'Sebastian Flyte,' says Lucy. 'And you forgot Sonny Crockett – the most tragic of tragic dreamboats since Lensky.'

'Top five songs with harmonica solos.' Harry is a reader too but ever-impatient to move onto music, his fiefdom, where he is most agile and competitive. He regards Lucy's irrelative ad-libs as poor form, and she knows it.

'Me!' she says, standing to enunciate. 'Chaka Khan's "I Feel for You", Stevie Wonder's "Isn't She Lovely", Culture Club's "Karma Chameleon", Tom Petty's "Last Dance With Mary Jane" –'

'"Mary Jane's Last Dance",' corrects Harry.

She glowers. 'Same, same. Such a stupid contrivance, naming songs that way. 'The Eurythmics' "There Must Be an Angel" and War's "Low Rider". Is that five?'

'It's six,' says Harry. 'And they're lousy. I'll raise you "Thieves in the Temple", "Tangled up in Blue", "Heart of Gold", "Midnight Rambler" and "The Wizard".'

'If that's a joke, it's not a funny one,' she snaps. Robin also found the answer puzzling and wants to press Harry on Bob Dylan, but he's too slow. Lucy is calling for Madonna songs.

'"La Isla Bonita".' Julian volleys this in lazy baritone. '"Bad Girl", "Justify My Love", "Like a Virgin", "Burning Up".'

'Madonna is overrated.' Everyone looks at Meg. It's the first time she's volunteered herself in this way, the first time she's addressed the whole group. She has brought her new puppy, Elmo, to dinner – wheaten brown, silky, nose a just-misted cumquat – and the two have been secluded in dubious quiet all evening.

'Whether or not Madonna is overrated is irrelevant in this context,' says Lucy with a sideways look at Tabitha. She throws down her napkin, a gauntlet, a glove. 'Top Five Bowie songs.'

'"Sweet Thing", all three parts,' says Robin. Meg shifts beside him. '"Right", "A New Career in a New Town", "In the Heat of the Morning", "Sound and Vision".'

Another look passes between Lucy and Tabitha. 'Solid,' pronounces Julian. This is high praise from him, deployed with deliberate scarcity. 'Best five songs with fake crowd effects.'

'"Suffragette City",' says Robin. 'The KLF's "3 am Eternal". Pulp's "Sorted for E's and Wizz". He's warming to the challenge, drunkenly instinctual. '"Bennie and the Jets", obviously. The Juan MacLean's "You Can't Have It Both Ways". Honorary mentions to Erasure's "Love to Hate You" and Nomad's "Devotion".'

'Oh!' Lucy's hands meet in a childish clap. 'That's it, Robin wins.' Julian taps his cigarette in one-beat applause: 'Nicely done.' They regard him with new appreciation. Robin's almost disappointed it was that easy.

Meg, testing another door of re-entry, offers Lucy Elmo to hold. Robin can tell this gesture costs her. Lucy declines, a chip of ice glinting in her voice. 'Someone put a cat in my lap when I was tripping once. The shock of being responsible for another creature's wellbeing was so acute, so horrifying, that animals have made me queasy ever since.'

Meg pushes back her plate. Clinks domino; interest pricks the air. 'What the hell is wrong with you, Lucy? He's a fucking puppy.'

Whatever happened a decade ago is right back at the surface. Squabbles aren't unusual at the table, simmering dramas rising to a boil, but this one has a novel tang, and everyone concentrates accordingly. Meg tosses her hair. She wants to leave, but stubbornness blooms deep in Robin, and he refills his glass, messily. She narrows her eyes, recalculating her position. Tabitha takes Elmo gently from Meg's arms, murmuring compliments into the soft fur of his ears, and Lucy watches with open disgust. 'You and dogs, Tabitha. Honestly. I'm getting the cheese.'

She isn't gone long but returns subtly transformed, lips stained and hair brushed in a demonstration of composure, an Acapulco platter on one splayed hand.

The plate is appealingly redolent of earth. A speckled dun-skinned pear sliced thinly; a pale blue brain of a cheese, ridged and corded; a loaf of rye bread the size of a relaxed fist. Tabitha and Meg have pulled their chairs together to pat the sleeping puppy, this brief alliance helping restore halting equilibrium. Gudrun plucks a nasturtium flower from the plate, impervious to the interlude or doing an excellent performance thereof. Regardless, she has moved on. 'Right: describe your kissing style, 10 words or less.' The flower is in her mouth now; she swallows it whole. 'Mine is the Calm before the Storm. Or Storm before the Calm, depending.'

'Introduction to French Cinema,' says Tabitha.

'Good Times and Great Classic Hits,' says Harry, employing the exaggerated suave of an FM announcer.

'Elegance with a Touch of Sulphur,' declares Lucy. 'After Diaghilev.' She twists fractionally towards Julian to divine the impact of this statement, but he pays it no heed. 'Tough But Fair,' he says.

'Ha!' she folds her arms. 'I wouldn't always call it fair.'

And so it goes until Robin has sobered sufficiently to feel guilt. Meg gathers the puppy and its things. 'Come with us to the beach tomorrow,' says Gudrun, but Robin senses a tepidity in their goodbyes to him, a synthetic warmth in their goodbyes to Meg.

Meg is properly furious by the time they're outside. 'What a fucking joke,' she says, snapping the door closed behind them in an unrealised slam.

He presumes they can hear her. Every laugh and clatter from the terrace is audible, broadcast clarion to the sky. Robin tests a conciliatory arm above Meg's shoulders but she bristles and, duly warned, he draws back.

'World War III has literally just started and all they can talk about is music.'

He starts walking, thinking; trying to edge her away from the house.

'Well, Robin?'

It is a fair point, he wants to say, because Tabitha often has the same frustration: their disinterest in serious matters after dark. The situation is horrific, he wants to say, but calling it World War III is premature and possibly alarmist. But then Meg scarcely engages with the news herself; this isn't why she is angry.

'We'll go crazy if we talk about Iraq all the time,' he says.

'Oh, so we should talk Boy George instead?'

Meg walks in tight steps, the puppy held protectively to her face, her shrunken leather jacket bunching against creamy hip. 'They're so busy being clever they don't realise how stupid they sound. Lucy was exactly the same in high school – she hasn't grown up one bit.'

She's two strides ahead of him back to his house. Upstairs, the dog snugs into the pillows and Robin is exiled to the bed's far corner. It's the first in their months of nights together that they don't undress. His usual means of placation are closed off. The only thing to do is nothing.

Only when he's very certain she's asleep does he rise, locating a half-joint from earlier with the hushed vigilance of a thief. The open window admits vegetal night scents – dew-slick buffalo grass, the urinal tang of lantana, pines dashing spiny whorls against the house – and he smokes, sitting over the wide lip of the sill, blowing out all thought and feeling. When Meg's pocket alarm clock sounds 4am, he hasn't been long asleep and keeps still, eyes shut, as she noisily collects her things. Elmo protests, and Meg doesn't hush him. 'The end,' thinks Robin when the door closes, and he stretches to the bed's diagonals, sleeping for six dreamless hours.

Just before midday, Robin remembers the beach plans, weighing the notion of going on the reflexive presumption he won't. But he wants to, an urge both pronounced and mystifying, and arrives at the kiosk on the appointed hour of noon. Lucy spots him first, last night's goodbyes vaporised in a clamour of pleased hellos. Only Tabitha evinces surprise at his presence, asking after Meg in a voice that's part tease, part reproval.

They have brought many bags and towels and umbrellas, clustering around its immoderate pile to discuss where they'll camp for the day. The sun is high, the mood buoyant. But Julian, Robin notices, stands apart, his familiar gesture of rubbing his jaw assuming the demeanour of a tic. He had greeted Robin genially enough but now seems thoroughly disinterested in everyone. He wears Ray-Bans and tuxedo pants, notably pilled in daylight's unforgiving glare. Julian is hungover or bored, but there's an unfamiliar malady at play, too – unease. He announces he's leaving, that he has things to do.

'Julian is frightened of the surf,' says Lucy. She finds this hilarious.

'I have a healthy respect for the sea and a healthy distrust of the Pacific's currents.' He scowls, readjusts his glasses. 'That, and I'm part vampire. Us Scotsmen wouldn't survive here otherwise.'

'Well, goodbye then, King Night.' Lucy is conciliatory now, standing on tiptoe to kiss him. He accepts this without expression, salutes the group, and lopes up the hill.

'Bully for him,' says Tabitha. 'Now we can relax.'

The day is much like any other here, but pleasure spikes Robin's veins. The ocean is a total work of art: all periwinkles, cornflowers, picotees, uraniums. Its meridiem peaks are unsullied by foam, and a submerged chain of seaweed pulses amber. The top frequencies are susurrant with sighs and sneezes; the lower frequencies submarine bells. They unfurl their towels in a circle. Tabitha opens an orange, its tart oils setting Robin's nape into a tingle. Suddenly euphoric, he wrests off his T-shirt and sprints to the water, the salty thwack of that first soaking wave transmogrifying the tingle into a full-body assault – total, uncomplicated rapture. He swims out beyond the swell, bobs in blissful insignificance, then lets himself be carried to shore.

Gudrun watches him cross the sand.

'I've never seen you in shorts, Robin. You're very tan.'

Red bikini bottom, shoulders salted in fine grains, a paperback in her hands. She continues watching as Robin takes the towel next to hers, and he gamely meets her gaze.

'What are you reading, Gudrun?' His body still hums from the ocean.

She turns over luxuriantly, bare chest rinsed in hot light: *The Master and Margarita*. 'One of these days, I'll finish it.'

'Where are you up to?'

'Who knows?' she says, turning over again. 'Who cares?'

Abergele's 1986 enchantment is panoramic today: it's in the Tears for Fears ringing from the kiosk speakers; the art-directed scatter of striped umbrellas; the can of Coke Gudrun rests on her glisteningly brown clavicle. Men walk the shore, thrusting tremendous tanned stomachs forward to flaunt heart surgery scars and appendix scars; small kids weaving amongst their ankles. Harry complains the sand is too sandy, then attacks his pile of *New Scientist*s. Contentment.

'God, the sun is so good it might be illegal,' says Lucy. 'Temazepam and brandy beaming from the sky.'

'Correct,' says Tabitha. She and Lucy have made up, squinting as they rub sunscreen into each other's backs with care. Tabitha exudes good health from her lean muscles: a wholesome upbringing of netball on Saturday mornings, swim squad before school, summers in kayaks, Brazil nuts for snacks. She applies cream to the tips of her ears and passes the tube to Robin.

'Look at your feet!' she says, kicking one of Robin's with hers. 'They're so pretty and skinny; not a skerrick of hair. Little boy feet. Christopher Robin feet!'

Tabitha is extremely pleased with herself. They call him Christopher Robin thereafter.

It's March and the last truly hot day of the year. Lucy borrows a wonky houseboat from an uncle, one of three uncles who live in Abergele, apparently, and hires a teenager from the yacht club to skipper. They assemble on the pier. Phosphorous-tipped pylons puncture the water; the horizon is lacy with masts. A half-moon of rhomboid houses rings the lake, its balconies full of people toasting the splendour. Lucy's shoulders gleam, sundress fanning at her legs. Julian stands beside her in white linen trousers, a pastel shirt open at the chest. They're glossy advertisements for their best selves.

The boat pulls away from the pier. It's slower than Robin expected, barking smoke, furrowing the water without grace, but the mood is one of great quest; of crossing whole oceans in pursuit of pleasures unknown. This expansive, empyrean feeling is heightened by quarter-tabs of acid – 'just a taste' – Lucy dispenses from a Glomesh purse.

'I should have brought coke,' says Gudrun.

'Coke is for bankers who want to stay in control,' says Lucy. 'I don't want to stay in control.'

Robin watches as Gudrun circles the deck, filling glasses with champagne. She's in a sailor's uniform, although it's possibly a school uniform, the collar blowing back in her face. Tabitha and Harry are in matching Breton-striped T-shirts; Tabitha wearing hers with a twitchy netball skirt, Harry obscenely short shorts. Harry carries his camera and a stack of VHS tapes: *Houseboat Horror, Dead Calm, Satan's Triangle, Lifeboat*. 'If you put on *any* of those,' says Lucy, 'I'll throw myself to the sharks and take you with me.'

'Good god,' she adds her mouth against Robin's ear now. 'We look demented – a Ralph Lauren shoot gone wrong.' The boat veers left, and Lucy stumbles. Robin takes her elbow and keeps his hand there, both falling into spontaneous sway with Roxy Music.

'Smoking and dancing, hey Robin?' Her sway shifts into backwards oscillation, fingers clicking, ribcage a neat figure eight.

'Smoking and dancing – so good, Lucy.'

'Do you know what I like about you?'

Robin does not. 'What?'

'The way you learn people's names as soon as you meet them; how you address them by name in conversation. It makes one feel special.'

'I imagine I do that to ingratiate myself.'

She shakes her head. 'I think it's nice.'

'Where's Julian?'

Lucy points to the boat's bow, where Julian has commandeered the steering wheel.

'I like him,' says Robin.

'I like him too. He is pure instinct, you know. He's never wrong.'

'How is someone never wrong?'

'He just isn't. He's selfish and frequently an asshole, but never wrong; you watch. Where is Meg tonight?'

Robin coughs. After the day at the beach, he'd crawled briny and spent into bed. He woke to Meg in his doorway, a soft outline in the grainy dusk. She'd just finished work and had a bunch of tiger-striped sunflowers over one shoulder, a vase of water tucked expertly under one arm. 'I'm sorry,' she'd said, fashioning a brisk arrangement on his bedside table, then climbed beneath the sheets.

The apology came as a surprise, in part a relief. Robin viewed the dinner incident as trivial and was glad Meg now saw it that way. But later, brushing her hair in the mirror, some essential power restored, she said he was welcome to waste evenings on the terrace, but from now he could go alone. 'Understood,' he'd replied, and that was that.

Robin wonders how to explain this. 'She's busy,' he says. 'Work, family; you know. It's best when we hang out alone.'

Lucy claps her hands, that expression of glee again. 'Oh, she *happened* to you, didn't she, Robin?'

He nods without thinking. Lucy has explained things for him. 'I mean, in a fashion.'

'Meg has a powerful will for someone so petite. Well, things don't happen to me; I happen to things.' She shrugs, a freckled shoulder clicking. 'I used to, anyway.'

They're showered with a symphonic spray of droplets as Julian dives from the boat. He surfaces cleanly, a marble-wrought sculpture, and ascends the deck, white trunks low at his waist. The lake sparkles with iridescent shrimp, a smattering of which still cling to Julian's back. Robin watches, hypnotised, as Lucy rubs the cords of his neck; the veins at her wrist magnified coral, a nimbus of light ringing her hair. Robin remembers the acid.

'Not so afraid of the water today,' says Gudrun, cheeks flushed with mischief.

Julian turns, a salty pendant suspended tremulously from one brow. 'That's not just water, dear Gudrun; that's the Golden Pond of Eternal Good Life.'

The sunset is pink and orange, a light leak tearing the sky. Violet jacaranda smears the distance, the bunting of blue and yellow sails hangs over the lake. Robin watches Harry snap photos in his casual, near-negligent way, camera held high in unfocused clicks. Julian cuts a pineapple into a saucepan and adds rum, portioning out bowls with a Bakelite ladle, their cocktails gritty with spines. Harry and Lucy dance to 'Glittering Prize' in lightning-bug unison, having found the hinge where their obsessions most joyfully coalesce. Lucy hands out more quarters and turns up the stereo and things get soft around the edges. The sunset goes on forever, the day gradually snuffing itself out: an '80s Sunkist sunset, an orange Tab sunset, a Pepsi Tropical sunset, Robin decides.

They dance. *Young Americans* begins at colossal volume, and by the time 'Fame' rolls around it's dirgy and melted, much slower than usual: the fourth day of a Quaaludes bender, the last day of the '70s.

'On that side of the boat,' says Harry, pointing at faraway mangroves, 'it's the Mississippi. And on that side,' he gestures to the shore, 'it's the Riviera.'

'Liar,' says Tabitha. 'That side is silver things and goblin sharks, while *that* side is violet things and fauns.'

Their skipper, newly 18, drinks bowl after bowl of pineapple rum and abandons his duties to lurch moon-eyed after Gudrun. She's inexplicably dripping, leaving a brackish trail, and utterly ignorant of his attentions. The floor is glassy, wet with water, wet with rum, and soon their dancing has assumed the glides of ice-skating. The boy sits on a pile of damp towels and succumbs immediately to sleep.

Robin is struck by how beautiful everyone looks in the sky's humid matt-black embrace. He mustn't forget this, he thinks; he mustn't forget how young they are tonight. Lucy, pale as a dandelion, is imploring them to go onto the roof where it's dry, and a new sensation strikes Robin; a blunt roil of nausea spreading across his stomach, violent as a slow-motion punch. He holds onto the railing, waiting for it to pass, while the others file to the upper deck. Vomiting seems prudent, but when he leans over the lake, it spits at him like a cartoon witch's cauldron, so he backs away.

Cautious steps to the kitchen, edging along the walls. There's a narrow bench piled with bags, and Robin clears it with a shove to lie on the striped mattress. Better. He closes his eyes, but the badness returns, so he keeps his gaze fixed on the teak ceiling, registering every shudder and stamp from above. They're deep in AM radio territory now, Lucy singing the opening couplet of 'Boys of Summer' in a thin, rapturous voice. He follows her through the verses and the choruses, as familiar to him as hymns, and the nausea subsides. It seems later, much later, when Tabitha discovers him.

'Robin! You poor egg, are you ok?'

'Maybe. A bit.'

'Oh god, first the teenager, now you. I have Maxolon – Harry gets seasick sometimes. Do you want one?'

'I'll take anything.'

Tabitha prepares the water and Maxolon, helps Robin to sitting. He thinks longingly of his weed, which Harry borrowed earlier.

'Do you have any downers?'

'I'll check Lucy's medicine chest.' Tabitha finds Lucy's purse, inspecting a handful of blister packs. 'Temazepam ok? Or –' she says, unbuttoning the pocket of her netball skirt, extracting a joint, 'there's this.'

'This. Definitely this.'

'Clearly, you're not that sick.' She locates matches above the camp stove, lights and inhales daintily, then passes the joint to Robin.

They smoke. Everything is much better.

'You should go back,' he says.

'My nose is bleeding; I need to sit for a bit.' He notices the splatter on her T-shirt, and Tabitha begins her ritual of pinching and dabbing. 'I didn't even realise you were gone, Robin. You must think we're monsters.'

'I think you're swell.'

'Ha!' Tabitha tilts her head. 'Well, hang onto that sentiment.'

It is very pleasant, her perching here. 'If you're sure you don't mind staying.'

'I'm sure, babe.' She folds one of his hands into her small rabbit's paw. 'My acid has fizzled, anyway. I only had a quarter.'

'We smoked the monster out.'

This is funnier than it should be. They both snort and giggle, Robin choking on his own spit, Tabitha grasping for her tissue to staunch a fresh trickle of blood. She resumes her pinching.

'Remind me of your PhD topic,' he says when they've recovered.

'Repressive desublimation and the aesthetics of excess in music video – the liquidating of art's transgressive and transcendental properties into value propositions, hollowed of original meaning. Once all pleasures are allowed, all pleasures are controlled, blah blah blah. Basically, I'm watching a tonne of Mark Romanek, Janet Jackson and Puff Daddy videos, and filling myself on red herrings instead of tackling the main course.'

'Genius. Although you're the least excessive person here.'

'That's why I'm the only one capable of analysing it as a phenomenon – pragmatic remove has occasional benefits. And I do succumb to peer pressure from time to time, as evidenced by tonight's houseboat horror show.'

'I did my honours on consumption in *On the Road*.'

'You were smart. You kept it contained.'

'Only because I couldn't use terms like "simulacra" or "libidinal economy" with any confidence. What are your parents like, Tabitha?'

'Oh, we're doing this, are we? Well, they're very nice, very cuddly, very tweedy academics, born at precisely the right time to have good lives. Harry's are less straightforward: hopeless, really. Poor Harry.'

'And Gudrun's?'

'They're hippies-made-good, and they're crazy for each other. Crazy for Gudrun, too, as you can imagine.'

'You can tell. About your parents and Gudrun's, I mean. Lucy says you're both fully-formed people as a result.'

'Well, that's sweet, although I'm not sure it's true. What else does she say about me?'

'She worships you.'

'She does that. It's a problem – with Julian, especially.'

He thinks of Lucy on venerative tiptoe. 'Could I have a Temazepam, after all?'

She rolls her eyes and hands over the pack. 'There's much to appreciate in Julian,' Robin says, popping a tablet.

'Sure. Julian is ok. He has excellent taste, but Lucy treats this as a moral virtue. He's using taste as a lazy way to navigate the world, making decisions based entirely on what he rates and doesn't; who's fuckable and who isn't. Even worse is his masculine habit of discovering a band or a director or movement, colonising the territory as if it's his own, then getting sulky when others discover it too. Middlebrow tastes are unpardonably awful, according to Julian. If you made him choose between the Beatles and the Stones, he'd choose the Kinks. If you made him choose between John and Paul, he'd choose George, just to be obtuse. The Kinks are great, but did Ray Davies write "For No One"?'

'He did write "Waterloo Sunset", and many other excellent things, too.'

'Silly Robin.'

'But don't we all do that: navigate our lives by our obsessions?'

'Well, I don't. Lucy does, but in a binge-and-purge cycle so deeply rooted it's unconscious. Harry's obsessions are the result of intellectual curiosity. He values things in their whole context – the time, place and circumstance of the art. Julian just snatches the spoils, discarding the husk and seeds. And Julian, you'll discover, has many stupid rules. Once a cult song has peaked, you can't play it in a DJ set for 12 years. You can't spend more than one consecutive night with someone, although it's a rule he breaks with Lucy because she feeds him so well. That fucking in beds is bourgeois. All very tedious. I doubt Julian has ever picked up a newspaper. It's fun getting blitzed with him, but breakfast the next day is a nightmare. I, personally, will be glad when he's gone for good.'

'Interesting. What does Lucy say about me?'

At that moment, Harry appears, crossing the kitchen in curious undulations.

'Harry, my love, what are you doing?'

'Dancing.' He holds the ladle aloft triumphantly, a pheasant he's just shot.

'That's not dancing; that's shuffling on acid,' she retorts. After much clattering, Harry crabs sideways and up the stairs.

'Lucy adores you,' she says, turning back to Robin. 'Meanwhile, I think you want to go to bed with us – all of us.'

'That's no secret to me.'

'You minx, I knew it. She wonders why you're with Meg. Which, to be fair, I don't understand either. She's gorgeous, a triumph of symmetry and dentistry. But I don't get how it fits together. What do you talk about? Are you the type that just needs a girlfriend, Robin? That thinks they can't function without one?'

'Ooof.'

'Well?'

'Possibly. You're not the first to say that. It was only Isabella and me growing up. I used to sleep in her bed when I had nightmares, and she walked me to school every day; supervised my homework. I attached myself to her friends like a limpet, and my teenage years were spent riding around in carfuls of girls, the place I've felt most comfortable since. When I left home, I lived with a girlfriend – one of Isabella's friends, actually.'

'Then what?'

'After that ended, I lived with my dad for a stretch, and then I moved in with another of Izzy's friends.' He coughs. 'Who became my girlfriend.'

'Robin!'

'I realise that's rather shameful and pathetic; now I'm saying it aloud. So you may be right. And now I'm back with Izzy, living in her attic.'

'Lucy is obsessed with incest as a literary trope: *Flowers in the Attic, Ada Or Ardor, Cassandra at the Wedding.*'

'You're getting fixated on the attic bit, Tabitha. I don't want to fuck my sister.'

'No, but the mere suggestion of it makes you fascinating to Lucy.'

'Well, this has been illuminating,' says Robin, and it has. 'Thank you. I'm much better. Sleepy, very sleepy.'

52

'Good.' Tabitha kisses him on the forehead, enveloping him in musky cinnamon perfume. 'Sleep tight, Christopher Robin. Let's hope the skipper recovers and we make it home alive.'

Months pass, and Lucy leaves the door unlocked for their walks. One day, Robin arrives to find her cursing into the telephone. One day, she's conducting the waves to 'Wuthering Heights'. On another, she's playing the piano, a halting child at a recital. Robin wonders if these are performances for his benefit, faintly repelled by the idea while still hoping it's the case. He finds himself fixing things around the house without being asked: a leaking tap, a flickering dimmer. He helps Lucy move the heavier plants in their seasonal pursuit of photosynthesis. He re-screws cupboard doors, relights the water heater after a windy night, replaces fuses. Each bedroom has a porthole window, compounding Robin's sense of being adrift, the tracery of his old life growing ever-more distant and nebulous.

'How are you so handy?' Lucy asks.

'I'm part orphan. There was nobody else to do these things.'

'That makes sense. I'm the child of hyper-competent parents: a high-strung perfectionist of a home-economics teacher and an obsessive aerospace engineer. That's probably why I'm so useless.'

Lucy, in turn, gives him small gifts. A dubbed Essendon Airport tape. A dried seahorse, its exoskeleton preserved in salt. A slab of cultured butter from the farmers' market.

Autumn deepens, and so do the walks. Lucy still wears party dresses, but layers old trousers and scarves of her mother's. An oversized fisherman's jumper is wrapped at her shoulders one afternoon, and from then she's rarely without it. The jumper gets caught in bushes; her ballet slippers splattered in clay. She points out cabbage-tree palms, nodding wildflowers, and pale grasses like strings of gold bells. She points out a clump of petrified dog faeces. 'You *never* see white dog shit anymore, just like you never see yellow cars. They both perished with the '80s.'

Robin loves the big daffy heads of pampas grass and is reaching to pluck one when Lucy shoves him back onto the path. 'They're full of rats,' she says. 'Hiding under the clumps.' 'Mice, surely,' says Robin. 'RATS,' says Lucy. 'And pampas are weeds. But I agree, they're darling.' By May his lungs have expanded, and his blood pumps with new economy; more of it reaching his organs, his limbs, his brain.

They discuss her book endlessly.

'My argument is weak,' she says. 'It's undisciplined, as I am.'

'Set it out for me.'

'But I can't! It's a soufflé, a chiffon cake. With any prodding, the whole assembly deflates.'

'So set out what the music *means* to you, then.'

'It means *everything* to me, and that's the issue. Tabitha thinks I mistake feelings for opinions and opinions for arguments; excusable in an article, perhaps, but not a book. Still, it's very important to me that Charlie's "Spacer Woman" sounds like wet slaps in the dark, piping the promise of rough sex through nightclub speakers with the demented power of a spell. It's important that Eleven Pond's "Watching Trees" was recorded in a derelict swimming pool, that it reconciles pastoral urges with mechanised abjection before that monolithic bass solo destroys everything like a great war. It's important to me that the Human League's "Rock 'N' Roll / Nightclubbing" is deliberately dinky – as if recorded on a child's Casio, in a washing machine – in defiance of rock's postured authenticity and contempt of all good taste. That it taps into the utter doomed pointlessness of going out hoping to find a good time.'

She stops, snapping a branch of wild blackberries and crushing the flowers in one hand. 'It's important to me that Das Kabinette's "The Cabinet" evokes the chilling promise of early cinema, that they pronounce Dr Caligari four different ways in one song because it delights Das Kabinette to do so, or because they simply *don't care*. It's important that Throbbing Gristle recorded on top of Victorian plague pits. That Cabaret Voltaire recorded in a former air-raid shelter. That the "just" in "Just Fascination" is crucial; as if one flimsy word could undercut the fascination that's so viscerally, obviously overwhelming. That "just" is the punctum of my feelings for Julian. It's important that Kraftwerk could've sprung straight from Satie without the influence of rock 'n' roll; that Dr Dre could've directly followed Kraftwerk without the influence of guitars. That the (Hypothetical) Prophets' "Person to Person" predicts the transactional nature of internet dating over a decade before internet dating was invented. That this cold, cold, cold electronic song has the best vocal melodies the Beach Boys never sang. And the lyrics! *Iron fist in a velvet glove / Elegant young lady with decadent inclinations is seeking an older man to cosset and amuse me.* Jesus Christ! How glorious! But being important to me doesn't mean it's important to anyone else.' She pries a thistle from her jumper. 'You see my problem.'

'I do not, Lucy. You should be home writing right now.'

She ignores him.

'I know Tabitha is annoyed at how much I fixate on this, seemingly at the expense of anything serious. I spent a chunk of 2001 writing closed captions for the 7pm news, a task so stultifying and bleak I tapped out of headlines and haven't found a way back in. But this music isn't escape for me – it's total immersion. I'm with Heidegger: art sensitises you to the world, opens you to it. It's a gateway drug to the truth of living: your brief physicality and its interplay with everyone's brief physicality – your *being-there*-ness. And the music I love was created in direct relation and opposition to the politics of its time: Stalinism, Thatcherism, Reaganism, whatever fresh hell we're in now. It faces down the cruelty of the world and *just keeps going*, the only form of protest you can summon sometimes, and, to my mind, inherently uplifting. But not too uplifting – the edge keeps you hungry, alert, angry.'

She stops and pulls a pocked milk bottle from her bag, drinking gustily and offering it to Robin. It's water, not milk, she assures him, so he takes a swig.

'I'm most alive listening to nihilism.' Lucy returns to her argument at a pitch that demands they walk faster. 'Admittedly, this can tip into grimness, especially if I burrow too far into Liaisons Dangereuses or Nitzer Ebb. Which is another problem, given I've been compiling lists of reasons not to kill myself since I was 14.'

She says things like this. Robin has learned not to be alarmed. 'You haven't been a teenaged boy, Lucy. It's the exhilaration of pure noise that gets you through.'

'I get it. That's the whole point of noise – that it's loud and ugly and unlistenable. It's *supposed* to be transgressive. It's supposed to destabilise, make you feel tough; it's supposed to scare your parents. To the point of hilarity sometimes – I mean, "The Anal Staircase"! But noise is infinitely more subversive when it's charged with real sensitivity. That's why Nine Inch Nails are holy, occupying a locked chamber in my heart. Trent Reznor understands provocation is cheap; the real game is paralysis by melody. He understands that if you wanna make girls wet, your voice is your most important instrument. You need to let everything else fall away, get right into the mic, and *whisper*.'

They're moving at a rapid clip now, cheeks flushed. 'I'm impressed, Robin, that you genuinely love Einstürzende Neubauten – you're much tougher than me. I enjoy the *philosophy* of Einstürzende Neubauten, the *idea* of being tied up by Blixa Bargeld, but I'd prefer to listen to Depeche Mode.'

'Depeche Mode were once described as kink-play disguised as religious yearning.'

'Ha! I read that too. And by extension, "Head Like a Hole" is kink-play disguised as anti-capitalist protest. Lately, by way of palette cleanser, I've been thinking about hymns. Not in the religious sense, but songs you know so intimately they *become* hymns, or nursery rhymes.'

'Piano songs,' says Robin. 'Parlour-room songs. Torch songs.'

'Exactly,' says Lucy. 'Mazzy Star. Magnetic Fields. Scott Walker. "Islands in the Stream".'

'Very nice. I love songs that compress a Russian novel's worth of plot and pathos into four minutes. Which overlaps roughly with your hymns.'

'Such as?'

He motions for the milk bottle, thinking. 'Scott Walker's "The Old Man's Back Again", of course. 'Pulp's "This Is Hardcore". "Sundown, Sundown", both the Hazlewood/Sinatra and Salmon versions.'

'Yes!' She claps her hands. 'Oh god, the pathos of Kim Salmon's "Sundown" could put you in the *ground*. Does "Rattlesnakes" work?'

'Absolutely. And "Unfinished Sympathy". "Wicked Game".'

'"In the Air Tonight"!' Lucy stops, catching her breath. 'But look what happened: I've fallen to the rapture of making yet another mix-tape instead of making a book.'

They emerge from the bush, one street beyond their usual. The sun is low; the day evaporated of warmth. Lucy grabs his hand. 'Robin!' she hisses. On the balcony of a mission-brown brick house sits the most exquisite boy; 16 or 17, sun-whitened hair, devastating scowl. He takes a gulping drag of a cigarette and passes it to his mother. She is leathery, leached out by life, but certainly his mother. The air between them is incendiary.

'There you go,' says Robin. 'There's a whole Russian novel contained in that scene.'

Holy Saturday on the terrace: French onion soup with sourdough croutons and volcanic strands of Gruyère. A changeable mood, nerves right against the skin, possibly because Gudrun – the alkaline to their collective acid – has been delayed. Lucy tells Harry she loves him, but if he brings another Prince bootleg into her house, she will feed it to the garbage disposal. Then she tells Tabitha she resembles a sexy grasshopper in her '60s dress, and Tabitha, in misdirected smarting, then accuses Harry of eating like a disobedient horse. Harry stalks off in a rare fit of ill-temper, clattering down the stairs toward home. Later, Tabitha attempts to move the conversation to the looming federal election and, finding Lucy's response wanting, calls her a champagne socialist, which Lucy denies in a furious little outburst that does nothing for her case. 'Besides,' she says, in huffy closing. 'If I'm anything, it's a romantic liberal dunce, like Flaubert.'

Robin goes to the bathroom, loitering by the study in the hope this storm will pass quickly. When he reclaims his seat on the terrace, Lucy and Julian are at opposite sides of the table, a nasty vibration between them.

'I know you want to fuck her.' Lucy delivers these words slowly, unusual for her.

Julian's jaw tenses. He shakes his head, says nothing.

'I know, and I don't care. I'd watch you. I'd watch you do everything to her that you do to me, and it would be *boring*.'

Julian sits straighter. Robin has seen this many times: his animal arousal, his feline habit of conserving energy then stiffening to sudden attention, preparing to pounce or bolt.

'Really.'

'Really,' says Lucy. 'I'd watch you, and I'd smoke three or four cigarettes, and it would mean nothing, because you're terrifically boring, and who you want to sleep with is terrifically boring. You'd tell me to cross the room, get undressed, get in the tangle, but I *would not*.' Her hand moves across the table until it meets a glass. Robin watches as she pushes it, inch by excruciating inch, towards the edge, never breaking eye contact with Julian. With a pixie flick of one finger, she sends it to a smash, her face betraying nothing.

Tabitha yawns. 'Alright, Christopher Robin, it's time we went home and let these lovebirds do whatever weird thing they're working up to.' So they leave.

Robin returns the next day with books he'd borrowed from Lucy: *Charlotte Sometimes*, *The Easter Parade*, *The Kandy-Kolored Tangerine-Flake Streamline Baby*. Gudrun has arrived. Julian is still there. The study is flushed with autumnal sunshine, syrupy light through the dirty windows giving the afternoon a mellowed bronze lustre; a petition to indolence.

Each of them occupies distinct, cordoned-off territory: Gudrun in full recline on the couch, silk palazzo trousers spilling around her; Julian kingly on the armchair in last night's tuxedo pants and a Mr Mister T-shirt; Lucy standing at the bookcase, pulling out records, wearing what might be a child's white party dress with white tights.

'More books,' says Julian.

'Ignore him,' says Lucy. 'Julian is illiterate.'

'Yes, and you're film illiterate. Now, Robin, I thought I'd roll something. Do you have any weed?'

Robin is hungover in the right measure: enough to be liberated from action, from thought, from dread, so he sits. The three monitor lizards who live in the sacred basil thatch press their snouts against the glass. Lucy sits too, and the bottom of her tights are dirty, the feet of a white rabbit. Time passes in its elastic way, Julian breaking apart his cigarettes to roll tight orderly joints, while Lucy puts on song after song, pointing out the passages that mean most to her – the baroque middle-eights and the soaring pre-choruses better than the choruses themselves – becoming increasingly dejected at the breviloquent response.

'It's pointless,' says Julian, passing a joint to Robin. 'You're ultimately alone in your obsessions, Lucy, just as we're ultimately alone in life. No one will ever care as much as you. And if they do, it's as rare and brief as a shared hallucination; a simultaneous orgasm.'

'A simultaneous orgasm! How curious, Julian. And disappointing. I thought this stuff was important to you.'

He pulls her in, arm hard around her waist. 'It is, my petulant one, just not today.' She looks as if she may cry, though Robin knows she won't. He has plenty of thoughts on these records, things they might discuss on their walks, but he doesn't want to express them here. 'We should go outside,' he ventures instead, ever the peacekeeper. 'There aren't many of these days left.'

'Oh, but it's so chilly,' says Gudrun from the couch, her voice a knife on a crystal highball. 'We do have enough people for an orgy – there's an idea.'

Julian turns over with the dangerous arithmetic of a panther uncurling. 'A decent idea,' he says, melting into his new position. 'Though who could be bothered right now?'

Robin puts the books away. Julian strokes a hand across the red needles of his stubble, watching him.

'Hey, Robin, where is your Meg? We haven't seen her for a while.'

'Meg's at a baby shower.'

'Pity.'

'Why is that?' says Robin eventually.

'Well, it's freezing, which I suppose is crummy for a baby shower. And the music needs shaking up – I'm curious to hear what she'd play.'

'Jean-Michel Jarre,' Robin lies.

'Really?' says Julian, not believing this. 'Cute as fuck *and* excellent taste – you are a lucky man.'

'Can everyone please shut up?' says Lucy. 'I'm getting a headache.'

'You don't have to be so rotten,' retorts Julian.

Robin closes his eyes, entranced by the counterfeit chime of house piano, the reliable pull of his inertia, the comforting hum of close-by conversation to which there's no expectation he contribute. 'Rhythm Is a Dancer', 'Rhythm Is a Mystery', and 'Rhythm of the Night' follow each other as they were always meant to. It's a shift in tonality, not words, that at last suggests action. There's a party in the city. Julian wants the girls to come with him, but they won't. Julian can't find his wallet because Lucy has splayed her goddamn records everywhere.

'You know I can't go to parties anymore, Julian,' says Lucy.

'Only throw them. Control them.'

'Correct.'

'C'mon, Gudrun. I'll give you a lift back. You don't want to be stuck on the train tomorrow.' Robin opens his eyes. Seeing Julian forced to negotiate is new.

'No, thank you, Julian.' She is clipped, professional. 'I've had a massive week at work.'

'Fuck work.'

'Well, you're welcome to fuck work, but mine is important to me.' Robin closes his eyes again, and there's a segue from SWV into Haddaway. The door slams, and the Trans Am growls toward people, parties, the world.

'Finally,' says Gudrun. She prods Robin with her bare foot. 'Get up, Christopher Robin. It's Easter Sunday: time for a resurrection. We need supplies.'

Lucy, always anticipatory, always the host, is calling a guy who, for a price, delivers booze and groceries. She'd called the guy who sells her Dexies that morning, but he hasn't yet materialised. She opens a desk drawer and produces a fistful of 10- and 20-dollar notes, patting them into a neat pile. Gudrun positions glasses on the desk, the short crosshatched ones they prefer. It's nearing night, so Robin closes the blinds and turns on the lamps, his gesture toward usefulness.

The groceries arrive first. Fish fingers, a Viennetta, a block of cheddar for cubing, a jar of lurid pickled onions, a capsicum for their health: nursery food; stoner food. Gudrun dispenses piccolos of Henkell Trocken and pushes a bottle to her sternum. 'One *sip* and the possibilities of the universe expand radically,' she says, rolling back her shoulders.

'Indeed,' says Lucy. 'Although they won't expand to my satisfaction until the pills arrive. We've been waiting all day. Gamins under a tree, Waiting for Drugot.'

'You pick your tree; you wait. I'm sure Paris Hilton has picked her tree and climbed to the very top, and she wouldn't be wearing underwear, either. That's the tree I fancy waiting beneath.'

Robin, still stoned, imagines they're stocking a nest: cushions brought in from other rooms, ashtrays washed and returned, cloth napkins demarcating place settings, the soothing noises of plates against plates. *Off to sea in a beautiful pea-green boat*, he thinks. He cuts the capsicum into uniform strips. Gudrun puts on Luther Ingram's 'If It's All the Same to You Babe' and aching piano-as-bass fills the room. She crosses the slate in a loose Northern Soul stomp, snapping the fingers of her left hand, a sound as resonant as the first church bells of morning. 'See, things are better already.'

'Because Julian's gone,' says Lucy.

Gudrun shrugs. 'Maybe.'

'I'm always so itchy to get him here. I'm sick with want; sick with the hatching and plotting and waiting. I'm sick when I go to sleep and sick when I wake. I'm even sick on the days when I roll over to find him lying next to me: sick, sick, sick. I'm sick with the thought next time might be the last. And yet lately, I can't wait to get rid of him.' Lucy lights a cigarette. 'If it's exposure therapy, it's slow going. I want it to be over.'

'No, you don't, darling – that's why you're still doing it. He must have an enormous dick.'

Lucy snorts. 'Who cares about that? Anyway, you play stupid games; you win stupid prizes. Words to carve on my tombstone.'

The pills arrive, and the fish is ready, and they assemble their goblin tea on the rug, sharing one fork because Lucy had taken the rest outside for polishing. 'Polishing!' Gudrun is aghast. 'They were my grandmother's,' says Lucy. 'She always took care of her things.' And they eat, passing the fork to each other with great seriousness, crushing black salt over the fish fingers, admiring the Dexies dotting their plates in expensive garnishes, the origamied Viennetta folding in on itself.

'I forgot the Count Chocula,' says Lucy, standing suddenly. She's off in a blur of white.

'Sit, Lucy, eat!' calls Gudrun.

Lucy is back with a box of cereal. 'I come from a long line of women whose defining characteristic is jumping up from dinner for one last thing.' She sprinkles chocolate vampires over the Viennetta. 'There, perfect.' She sits again, visibly content.

'This could be a midnight feast at boarding school,' Robin says. They're his first words in what might've been hours. 'Not that I went to those feasts.'

'I didn't know you went to boarding school,' says Gudrun.

'For the last two years. It was good for Izzy, so my father rationalised it'd be good for me.'

'And was it?'

'Not wholly. It made me very tolerant of my own company. Possibly too tolerant.'

Gudrun smiles, the sad smile of an icon in repose, laying a hand on his forearm. Lucy fills her bowl with ice cream, oblivious.

They are drunk, then swiftly, loudly blitzed. Lucy jumps from the rug and sends the leftover pile of 10s and 20s flying. 'Good!' she says, kicking them further, an outraged Tinker Bell in her urchin dress. 'That's Victor's dumb dirty money, and that's what it deserves. Good day, sir!'

'Lucy, we must take care of our things,' says Gudrun, but Lucy says the money is keeping her from engaging in real life, and perhaps she's trying to dispose of it; she'll be glad when it's gone, anyway. Robin enquires as to Victor's identity and is informed, with patience verging on condescension, that he's Lucy's ex-husband. They play more records, taking turns this time; the interstitials now ectoplasmic with meaning. Robin puts on Pat Benatar's 'We Belong'. Lucy dashes off, returning with a tangle of old opera gloves which they roll up their arms to howl the chorus, and she's away and back with more clothes – a Max Headroom T-shirt, a bridesmaid's dress of stiff grapefruit taffeta, a kimono beaded with moons and stars, a bolero shedding fishy gold paillettes, a silk bomber in '80s deco print, and worn leather skirts in white, periwinkle and zebra.

They change, not without difficulty, and Lucy says, 'Wait, wait, wait, I have just the thing; swap gloves, THEN I'll play it.' She drops the needle on 'Song for Guy', and it's precisely the right thing – the dry-ice fizz, the synthesised wind in synthesised wind chimes, the bossa nova soft-shoe shuffle, the galaxy of pathos in the schmaltzy piano-bar affect. They sway in increasingly close circles, charms jangling on a bracelet, and Robin says, 'Richard Clayderman, yeah?' And Lucy shakes her head, forearm across closed eyes. 'No, it's Elton John, but it's what Richard Clayderman *should* be, so it's clever of you to think that, Robin; it's a very correct thing to think,' and they return to swaying.

The song vaporises, and they sit, overcome, sticky in Lucy's thrifted finery. 'Quick, what's your kissing style, Robin?' asks Gudrun.

He thinks. 'The Price of Liberty is Eternal Vigilance.' It doesn't land, so he tries again. 'I Love You But I've Chosen Darkness.' Gudrun claps twice, satisfied, and proposes they take a bath, a chaste bath, the Georgian kind in white smocks. Lucy agrees but first, she says, turning on her monitor; first, I must read you this.

'I found it yesterday. It's Richard Hell, and it ruined my life.' She takes a gulp of air, as if planning to swim to a great depth.

The Sex Pistols famously screamed, "No future!" at the end of "God Save the Queen" . . . the noteworthy thing to me about the "No future" subject isn't the Sex Pistols' anger about their boring prospects as citizens, but rather that the lack of a future is an unacknowledged foundation of rock and roll. There is no future in being an adolescent, and rock and roll is the music of adolescence . . . Rock and roll is about natural grace, about style and instinct. Also the inherent physical beauty of youth . . . You just have to have it, to get it. And half of that is about simply being young, meaning full of crazed sex drive and sensitivity to the object of romantic and sexual desire.

'That's my central thesis right there,' she says. 'No future in being an adolescent. No future in me writing about music because there's no future in music for *anyone* except the rich guys at the tippity-top. Music's apparatus sucks the best ideas and most tender sensibilities straight from your bones when you're cradle-fresh, and next year's class will step on your neck to claim their place. As I did! As they should! But it's no wonder I'm so tired: I'm 24, burnt-out, used-up, all my marrow squandered, THE END.' She removes her kimono; dashes it to the floor. 'Let's have that bath.'

When the tub is precipitously close to full, Gudrun empties in eight doll-sized bottles of coppery liquid, branded with the crest of some hotel. The bubbles rise in glacial formations, misting rind and seeds. Lucy and Gudrun take opposite ends; baptismal muslin fanning around them and water sploshing the tiles. 'We forgot the cigarettes,' says Gudrun. 'Robin!' He is halfway down the stairs already, bringing them to her dutifully, understanding the role he fulfils here. She is the proper degree of grateful, soapy hands clasping his as she accepts a light.

'Come in, darling.'

'There is no way I'll fit. You're both quite tall – we're all quite tall.'

'No, I suppose not. Stay with us, though. It's the day of resurrection, after all.' And so he fetches the plush vanity stool from Lucy's room and an old issue of *The Face*, something to hold.

'Now, Lucy,' says Gudrun, turning the cold tap to a trickle and pushing her big toe into the spout. 'I saw Julian at the bottle shop last week, glued suggestively to a girl. Nothing out of the ordinary, but this seemed more serious than usual – it was early in the afternoon. He was looking especially yachty.'

'That figures – the yacht, the seriousness, the girl. What kind, though? Goth girl? Art girl? Indie girl? School girl?'

'The kind that gives blow jobs to Tori Amos.'

'I won't hear a word against Tori Amos. What do you give blowjobs to, Gudrun?'

'"Gimme Shelter".'

Lucy splashes her, delighted. 'My new year's resolution was to give Cabaret Voltaire blowjobs to people who weren't Julian. Hypnotic, devastating blowjobs; delirium-inducing blowjobs; critically acclaimed blowjobs – it was time I took them to a wider audience. Instead, I'm in self-imposed exile, taking the cure.'

'But I thought you were spreading your affections far and wide! Whenever I saw you last year, you were in ardent clinch with someone different: Julian, James, the rest.'

'That was my demivierge year. I made out with hundreds of people, but The Creep and Victor turned me off fucking around. They're not the worst that can happen, and they were pretty bad. It's obvious Julian is a bust, but at least I can trust him, vaguely. What did the Bush Tetras say? "I just can't pay the price of shopping around. No more!"'

'It's the worst!' says Gudrun. 'Too many creeps! YEAH!' She pitches her full glass at the wall behind Robin, where it explodes in a cherry bomb of froth and shrapnel. She does it with the same polish she does everything, but Robin is surprised it misses him, assuming he'd been forgotten. 'Clean cup!' Lucy bellows, now White Rabbit and Mad Hatter at once. 'Clean cup!' She pats around the sink for the wine bottle and fills her toothglass for Gudrun. 'It's annoying because I love fucking – above all life's recreations. When I suddenly got cute at 14, I thought I'd have lots of fun, but things just got fraught and weird. When I took over the magazine, I thought I'd *finally* have fun, top-notch perverted fun, but things got acutely weird. Can't a girl capitalise on her youth and promise by sleeping with an assortment of interesting people who are filthy and generous in bed without worrying she'll get strangled afterwards? Or during?'

'I've heard it's possible,' said Gudrun. 'Come here and give me a little puff of your cigarette, Lucy. Mine's all wet.' She draws deeply, smiling. 'Now – who would you like to fuck?'

'Nigel from Slow Release. Sebastian from Gorge. Phaedra from Boarding School. The head gardener at The Plot. The guy who works Tuesdays at The Record Exchange. The drummer from Picnic, Lightning. The singer from Petrol Rainbow. But only if there was equal want. Conquest is squalid business – my objective is communion.'

'I'm afraid that list of prospects contains scant opportunity for communion. I have this on good authority, Lucy; the greatest authority being mine. Still, there's probably an orgy at that party of Julian's, if you wanted to roll the dice.'

'A KISSING orgy, Gudrun. It's always a kissing orgy these days, with the new people we don't know and one random guy getting grubby.' She's angry now, phosphorescent with it, arriving at the state she's been hurling herself towards all day. 'I want to obliterate myself in pleasure; I want to fuck through new portals of experience.' Her hair is wet, giving off a chemical shimmer.

'How, exactly?' Gudrun moves, sending sheafs of water over the side. It's a duel now, each inciting the other to reach ever-higher notes. Her collarbones are exclamation points turned on their sides.

'You know, the sex you have eating acid and ecstasy – candyflip fucking. Bones, organs, teeth, thoughts and emotions all melting away to leave pure sensation. Caverns opening off caverns off caverns; total hallucinatory descent for six hours. Kissing with such persistence, such ferocity, that your chin bleeds for a week afterwards. Someone gathering your hair in a bouquet and holding it *just* tight enough while they obliterate you.' She takes a rapt drag from her cigarette. 'Someone you trust spitting on your asshole, *helpfully*, sending you both completely nuts before you even begin. Alison Moyet saying she wanted to *penetrate* Vince Clarke. Or just holding hands with someone you shouldn't – furtive hand-holding in the cinema, under a restaurant table, in the back seat of a taxi.' She shrugs. 'That whole thing.'

'And what do you think of this?' says Gudrun. She turns her full attention to Robin with what he imagines are her interrogatory airs of court. The women are drenched, ecstatic, furious. He makes a calculation of the distance between him and the bathtub, barely 20 centimetres, and the complication crossing it would entail.

'It sounds exhausting,' he says. 'You must both be exhausted.' He stands and finds the walls are moving. 'I'm wasted. I'm going home.'

'Poor Robin,' says Gudrun, her voice bouncing along the hallway. 'I wonder if one girl is too much for him, let alone two.'

DRINKING ELECTRICITY

August 2003

I woke that morning to James's ponytail prickling my face, pins and needles flaring along one arm. She was leaning to ash in my water mug and had likely been there for some time.

'Who is Julian?' Her voice was bright and cloying, traces of ground glass.

'How are you smoking now? What time is it?'

'Eight. Who's Julian?' She had milk on her upper lip.

'Someone,' I said, and motioned for the cigarette, because how else to confront the spectre of Julian so early in the day? 'It doesn't matter. He's dead.'

James shook her head, taking a showy drag. Embers fluttered and floated, settling leisurely on my pillow. 'You're a liar, Lucy Lux,' and I was. I said he might as well be dead and to please get off my arm.

'I bet you like him more than me.' She play-acted a pout. 'Now get out of bed, Lucy: I'm bored.'

A few months ago, a lifetime by current metrics, James dropped her demo at my office. As a rule, I avoided the unsolicits, but I'd just come back from an interview and noticed her at the front desk, James being a type I'm hardwired to notice. Hard eyes, hennaed hair in a horsy ponytail to her waist, a full stately fringe convexing over the lashes. Mid-height, not a mark on her – no veins, no freckles – and strikingly small kitten-sharp teeth. I promised to listen to her CD and didn't, but she returned the following week with zines and giant stickers of sad-eyed girls holding cats. Without my explicitly agreeing to it, she started spending Fridays in the office, transcribing my interviews and leaving exclamations in the notes. She was always hungry, so I'd buy her lunch at the place next door that did triple-breaded sandwiches for truckers, and we'd talk, or she'd talk, and I'd pitch in occasionally, worried about the office's accumulating bonfires. Her stickers and stencils multiplied throughout the neighbourhood: the cats, always the cats, but two-colour renders of Rimbaud and Verlaine as well.

She fronted an all-girl band called Goblette (a nod to Goblin's soundtracks; they were Dario Argento nuts) who wore swimsuits and capes onstage, ripping through punky Au Pairs-esque torch songs at deafening volume. Her bubble-gum sprechgesang would've made her instantly iconic in 1978 and might make her proper-famous yet. One song was just James screaming, 'Traitor! Crater! Alligator!' over and over for two minutes – and it absolutely bristled with hooks. Goblette were devotees of Live Journal, where James posted one-act plays and lithographs. There, she also recounted stories of Tuesday and Wednesday blowouts that ended with skinning her knees, or losing her bag, or being caught stealing, or getting her car towed, or waking hungover to self-penned graffiti across the walls. She told these stories with the triumph of one who'd found a diamond in the gutter or delivered a breached lamb. Her recklessness had a pointed quality to it, as mine did – an accusation buried in every stunt – but James was still having fun. She was 21, a semester off graduating from a degree unrelated to her plays, music or lithographs.

She was fascinated by the office, pecking through its detritus to find 'treats'. Clear vinyl, hot-pink vinyl, silver vinyl, signed posters, keyrings, pencils stamped with the insignia of breakout post-punk bands I hated – it all went into her backpack. She'd riffle through the filing cabinets of obsolete press shots, exhuming Ani DiFranco, Cyndi Lauper, Lydia Lunch and Lene Lovich, and crumpling them into her pockets. She claimed a Sophie B. Hawkins promo tank – 'Damn I Wish I Was Your Lover' embroidered on the chest – which she'd wear braless with an inside-out denim skirt and mesh gloves.

She found the stack of letters from The Creep, the ones written in nauseant upright cursive, the ones I'd sorted by date for the police. She found the pile of gifts, the ones always delivered by night, waiting dew-damp and limply ribboned on the doorstep when I unlocked. For years The Creep was just static – a detuned radio, a hiss only unnerving in the feeble hours or those muzzy first minutes of wake. But the signal intensified exponentially and now broadcast high-fidelity, near-constant alarm. I hadn't moved closer to the transmitter; it had moved closer to me. I told James not to touch in a voice that startled both of us and served to double her attentions.

She'd flutter over to my desk – blister packs of painkillers, dictaphones and back-up dictaphones, precarious towers of cassettes – to bequeath trinkets. Tin badges she pressed out at home: Virginia Woolf quotes, more cats, my name in bubbled capitals. Expensive pots of lip-balm to replace my apparently poison tub of Vaseline. She left an open document on my computer titled 'Nine Things I Love about Lucy Lux.' Number two: 'The yellow dress with the crazy straps that makes her look like a just-hatched chick / Easter duck.' Number seven: 'Great at kissing?'

One night, walking home from a show at the old museum – there were never any cabs that year, hence the uptick of deaths-by-beating in cab lines – I found myself on a five-pointed corner, its angles unfamiliar. I'd been standing there a while, cold fire working along my arms, when a pack of girls in short skirts, stripy socks and ballet flats (calves shaped by 17 years on ponies, hair glossy with 21 years of the best shampoo) moved as one from a Chinese restaurant. James was headmost, a handful of helium balloons in her hand.

'Luxi!' she said, enveloping me in a proprietorial hug, the balloons smelling of kerosene. 'Are you lost?' She shed the girls, walked me to her car, and sent the balloons skyward.

I'd assumed James was a broke waif, but her apartment – her parents' apartment – occupied three floors in the financial district, windows framing the river so the rooms appeared swimmable. Parts were tiled in tobacco brown, others carpeted in champagne shag, and every space – even the honeycombed nothing-rooms for dressing, powdering and storing wine – was overstuffed with furniture. There were satin love seats and low Chinoiserie tables covered with old copies of Italian *Vogue* and Memphis vases; oversized black-and-white portraits of James's mother shot by a Helmut Newton-type in the '70s; and grand, lacquered expanses of turquoise and red. It was my first orbit through money, or real money, anyway.

There were two sets of bunk beds in her room, a relic of childhood slumber parties, where a pile of plush animals still lived atop. Her parents were overseas – her father had work, her mother had shows – and a stern woman in her 50s called Susan came twice-weekly to put together what James tore apart. James believed Susan was spying on her, reporting back to her parents, but I couldn't imagine any parent going to the effort.

And so that night we smoked and I paced, and she showed me more of her work, work entirely free of self-consciousness, a quality I envied. I was fumbling through my pocket for a light, cursing Julian as if this was his fault, when James peeked out from under her fringe, a peek surely practised in the mirror most nights of her teens. I gave in, gave up, gave over to it. She had a frantic way of kissing that recalled fish pecking through aquarium gravel, or a mammal biting its offspring's face to establish the order of dominance.

On Fridays, James drove me to the apartment after work, which I let her do because of The Creep and general weariness. That things were bad with Julian and bad with Victor made it easy to stay whole weekends. We smoked weed and fucked around in every room of the apartment. We did lines watching daytime television (*Ricki Lake*, *The Real World*, endless reruns of *Married with Children*), piped in by satellite. We ate cross-legged in front of the always-stocked refrigerator, pulling out shiny fruit and cold cuts wrapped in wax paper. We'd spend Friday nights writing with angora blankets over our knees, a long-married couple, and Saturdays in compensation, breaststroking across the chequerboard tiles of the main bathroom after soapy hits from an eyedropper labelled Unicorn Sneeze. 'Oh, I LOVE you, Lucy Lux,' she said once, powder glistening in her nostrils, and I said love is knowing you could be killed in your sleep any time. Luckily both statements landed as jokes.

I wore her clothes and fishboned her hair and became deeply fond of the baltering way she rode a bicycle. The way she stubbed out her cigarettes when they were only half-smoked. The way she sawed the hems from her dresses to leave a frayed edge – the more expensive the dress, the more careless the cut. I found many things about James endearing. Her heedless way with punctuation. Her inexhaustible passion for banana splits and American cereal eaten from mugs. That she became enthralled with a new cultural theorist each week, but always mispronounced their names. That everything she owned was covered in stickers over stickers over stickers, a gummy patina of impulses dating from 1989. And her lies, non-stop trivial lies; lies so obvious they functioned as meta jokes or elaborate forms of flirtation.

Less endearing was her habit of chasing the cats through the apartment and wearing them as stoles. The way she enticed people – bartenders, delivery guys, strangers on the street – to confess things, a ploy to comfort them with treacly concern afterwards. I confessed nothing, but she'd dug Julian's name from somewhere. Still, I let James stand proxy for every best friend lost to moving vans between 1985 and 1994: those sainted best friends who disappear at the height of your attachment, before you know each other too well, before the gradual erosions of growing up and falling out. If our sprees amounted to rock-bottoming, at least I was doing it in a fortified building; at least I wasn't doing it alone.

So when the landline rang through the apartment that

morning – James answering with the actressy voice saved for her parents, bellowing, 'Lucy, phone!', and shoving the receiver at me – it had the violence of a door being kicked in. Familiar acid bloomed in my chest, that cold fire branching outward.

'It's Anika.' The phone was bronze and ivory, its heaviness lovely to touch. The fire retreated. 'Are you ok?'

'Periodically,' I said.

'You sound odd.'

I told her I'd felt old lately. Everything louder or softer than it should be. The sense of organs being replaced with photocopies of organs; of the furniture being rearranged in the night.

'That's congruous with derealisation,' Anika said.

'What does that mean?'

'Detachment. Dissociation.'

'Well, that sounds useful to me.'

'The very opposite. It's time you came back to us, Lucy. Pink Fist are playing tonight.'

I knew. I'd interviewed them last week, marking the show in my diary. It was a terrible idea, but protons of rightness charged at its centre, the way of most terrible ideas.

I half-muffled the receiver against my stomach. 'Wanna come and see Pink Fist, James?'

'I'd rather eat razor blades.' Her tastes lay elsewhere.

'I don't want to go out,' I told Anika.

'I heard the exchange. But things are hardly going to improve by re-enacting *Performance* with James every weekend. Forget her. Forget everything. It will be fun; it will be *fine*.'

'Maybe.'

'My feelings are gravely close to hurt, Lucy. Look, I'll make us dinner at mine first.'

Cheers roared from the television as James laid out mugs of Lucky Charms. A cat, spying me, diverted its path to swish its tail on my ankle, leaving a puss-moss-caterpillar sting. If Anika could find me here, anyone could, I supposed. It was time to leave.

Anika made gnocchi with fresh sardines. In the snug chaos of her apartment – busts draped in costume jewellery, medical textbooks and crumbling Victorian anatomy books, full-wall canvases and palm-sized pieces by her friends, jars of glitter, a drift of incense ash across everything – the universe tipped back toward rightness. She recounted the week's horrors in Accidents & Emergency, and my anaemic sorrows paled. She opened the balcony doors so we could smoke, inadvertently admitting the first wattle-y portents of spring. Things were better; things were fine. We decided to walk to the city. As we were locking up, Anika pressed the residuum of our last spree into my bag: a gridded Rollbahn notebook, a film canister of god knows what, and my grandmother's cocktail ring, the one I'd been sick over losing for weeks.

'Where are things with Julian?' she asked. Anika walked in neat locomotive steps. Her black skirt, made entirely of ribbons, trailed behind her, the tail of a fast-moving bird.

I said I hadn't seen him since the funeral, the funeral of one of my writers, a few months ago. That Julian had been eight rows back – black T-shirt, sunglasses, narrow trousers, Agent Crockett at another wake – but we hadn't spoken. When she asked how the divorce was progressing, I told her stalled – Victor wouldn't sign the papers, palpating his last lever of control. When she asked after The Creep, I reported his mother had started calling me at work – tearful, baffled – so at least two people were questioning his sanity. That the hearing for the restraining order was scheduled for next week. I narrated a recent dream: hitting him with a fence post – his back, his shoulders, then over and over at the head – until his skull yielded with the crack of marzipan icing and liquefied.

'The ooze was radioactive lime,' I said. 'Very B-grade; very schlocky. I was both horrified I could do such a thing and gleeful *someone* had finally done *something*.'

'You'd never do that, Lucy. Unless you had no choice. Besides, you wouldn't use a fence post; you'd use a chic industrial machine part.'

'Usually, in nightmares, I just curl up like a hedgehog – better to be caught than endlessly pursued – so it counts as a breakthrough, of sorts. Anyway, I don't think he's going to hurt me, like kill-me hurt-me, but a girl never knows, ha!'

'Ha!'

'It's just so *boring* – the sleeping with the lights on, the chain-smoking, the rashes.' I showed her the new spray of hives on my arms. 'They itch like the devil, Anika.'

She takes my hand; inspects them. 'I'd wager you got these at James's – those boho debutantes never change their sheets. She's very cute, Lucy, but the unhinged cute that ends in tabloid headlines: "Party-Girl Editor Dies in Heiress's Hot Tub", etc. If you don't want to stay at your apartment, then stay at mine.'

'Under your loving diagnostic observance.'

'Exactly.'

'That's a whole other category of terrifying, Anika. But thank you.'

We were nearly there. The fluorescent arc of the Bookend Bridge cast a petrol-spill reflection across the river, each elementary particle of the sky trembling against the next. I stopped to breathe it in, then sat.

'What *are* you doing?'

I didn't answer. The cold fire started again.

'Are you crying?'

'I'm thinking.' It had just occurred to me that the interview for Monday's cover story hadn't come through, that I'd have to cobble a piece together in the next 14 hours. I dumped out my handbag, trying to find the Rollbahn, trying to find my notes, and the canister bounced on the ground with three neat plonks.

'Remind me how that poison quote goes, Anika?'

'*Poison is in everything, and no thing is without poison,*' she recites. '*The dosage makes it either a poison or a remedy.* Obviously, that's a bastardisation of the original Paracelsus, but pithy when delivered at parties.'

I shook the canister. 'Amuse-bouche?'

She looked at me, calculating.

'Only if you get up. Only if you stay up.'

So I stood, an overshot giraffe, while Anika lit us cigarettes. 'That's better. Now it's your turn to ask me things, Lucy,' and, chastened in the nicest way possible, I did. We set back into the night.

Young Nun were finishing a chaotic support slot as we arrived, spraying beer over Pink Fist's keyboards. Inky, Pink Fist's singer, stormed onstage – defilement of keyboards being the owners' privilege – and a mood approaching mutiny surged at the front.

This was Young Nun's town, and Pink Fist were parvenus on the ascent: bands had been glassed here for less. I turned away, knowing the feud would play out for years, knowing it would be impossibly dull. Too bad. Anika got us tumblers of Chartreuse and butterflied through the crowd. She talked with people we knew and I hung close to her ribbony skirt, sheltered by the glitter at her shoulders.

By the time Pink Fist came onstage for their proper entrance, my bones and sinews had knitted themselves back together. Inky leant over his Oberheim and pounded two bass notes in thundering alternation: gut, groin, gut, groin. The air's composition shifted – more hydrogen, more neon, more nitrous, Pink Fist largely forgiven – and I pulled Anika to the room's centre. It was hotter there, and the pounding continued: gut, groin, gut, groin. Fred battered the kick drum.

'It's "Baby's on Fire",' Anika said.

'No, it isn't.'

'It most certainly is. Listen.'

They doubled, tripled, quadrupled the first two bars, stretching them to infinity.

'Oh!' Anika was right. Inky lifted his head from an outstretched arm, cast a blazing glower into the dark, and licked the mic.

An occult ecstasy took over the room, and there was a crush towards the stage as if a collective ache propelled us, because a collective ache did. Pink Fist had no guitars, but a noise of equivalent brawn tore the air, then a blunt, monstrous beat demolished everything – lurch and churn, churn and lurch. 'Now is now is now is now is now,' I whispered, the same thing I'd been whispering in dark caves since I was 15.

Minutes or hours passed; baroque metronomic repetition urging us through tunnels of flickering exit signs. Pink Fist had discharged a distress flare from behind the velvet curtain, a flare we all recognised. It announced stunted romance, love turned septic, vampiric yearning, pastoral longing, loss of sensation and the slow contamination of our childhoods. It warned of disease in the demi-monde, the robotic crippling the erotic, and the second-hand daylight that would eventually invade our safe cave like a strobe. It was a flare that said rescue me, but please don't come too close. Songs collapsed into each other, now one torturous tap dance through the minor keys; loud enough to constrain the body and muzzle the mind. I thought of Simone de Beauvoir on her first visit to New York, wanting to take bites from every neon sign she saw. I considered how I got music and fear and lust hopelessly confused, although what was love but conflation of the senses? Slick. Flick. Lick. Sick. Sick.

Inky's Korg issued a shower of sparks and smoke, and then it started raining. We opened our mouths, baby birds, to swallow. Sprinklers were responsible, it transpired, but it may have been the beginning of the flood. Vapour rose from our skin in a witches' conjuring. Water ricocheted off the drum kit and piano keys, making them sickly resonant. Inky swung the mic stand across his shoulders, hair plastered to imperial cheekbones. Another keyboard moaned and failed, and he pushed it over, screaming WASTE WASTE WASTE WASTE WAAAAAASTE. Never-ending echo, pinballing around ceiling, ribcage, skull. He stalked offstage. Fred shoved his snare backwards, and it was over.

'I do declare!' said Anika.

'The poison is the remedy is the poison.'

A stupefied hush had overtaken the room, but with the house lights came buckets and mops, and everyone began returning to themselves. I pulled Anika onstage for a wet crush of embraces with Pink Fist.

'How's your gear?'

Inky was drenched, thrumming with the cold luciferase of a firefly.

'I can only hope it sounds better this way.'

We got more drinks, and Fred dropped 'Tonight She Comes' onto the turntable, its heartbreaking chords stabbing the tenderest parts of my stomach. Gudrun materialised at the crowd's fringe, and I pulled her onstage too. 'Hey dollface,' she said, her hair a soaking rope. We fell into easy step and sway; the music-video dancing of our childhoods.

She asked after The Creep with a glissando roll of her shoulders. Step, sway, snap.

'The hearing's next week. Any advice?'

'You need to communicate damage for the judge. You need to communicate distress.'

'I assure you that will be no problem – my hair is falling out with distress. But at this precise moment, I'm a dandelion clock: a wonderful downy puff of nothing.'

'Good,' she said, extending an arm over each of my inferior shoulders, pulling me in. We kissed and danced and smoked, and I tapped out percussive stabs of piano with my cigarette. The hem of my dress caught fire, and Gudrun extinguished the flames with three tranquil bats of her hand. Fuck The Creep. Fuck The Unspoiled Monster. Fuck my husband. Fuck everyone not in this room. The tech, having his knock-off beer, swung the spotlight so it lit Gudrun and me alone. We were Queen and King of the prom; we would never be younger. We danced to Mr Mister's 'Broken Wings', belting out the chorus as synths promised deliverance and resurrection. We danced to Lionel Richie's 'All Night Long', Inky swinging me in a bearish hug and knocking over Fred's halfway-packed drumkit. A hand from the crowd grabbed my ankle, but I kicked it away as hard as I could, and Fred put on Foreigner's 'Urgent' to collective writhing,

'What's your kissing style, Gudrun?' I asked. 'Ten words or less.'

'Attention to Detail, Lucy, Attention to Detail. As required of any good lawyer.'

Pink Fist drove ahead to a party at The Elysium Hotel, site of a rumoured secret set by Jacques Lu Cont. Anika, Gudrun and I set out by foot. The sky was spilt ink, congealing in denser formations; the pulse of the city infirm, berserk. People leant out of club lines to shout things at us, Gudrun daring me not to shout back. We passed signs and their gaudy offerings: 'NOODLES', 'XXX GIRLS', 'KARAOKE', 'SMOKES'. We walked through cobbled backstreets and laneways, and laneways off laneways; massaging each other's hands, sidestepping evil-smelling puddles. Anika explained the prefixes and suffixes of biology – the blasts, thrillingly responsible for building and producing; the clytes for maintaining; the clasts for destroying and breaking down. 'Which begs the question: why do we have iconoclasts, but not iconoclytes or iconoblasts?' We walked past the casino where the same man had been playing the same songs on the same Calypso steel drums since we were teenagers – a ceremony we held sacred. At last, we reached the hotel. I waved the others ahead to find a bathroom. There was one tucked in the foyer's corner, a cube of smoked glass with unbroken views of the skyline. My eyes were overlarge in the mirror, and I looked dangerous, consumptive, unbreakable, myself. This was what I did. This was what I was.

Midnight in the conservatory of The Elysium. Indoor swimming pool emanating steam; the verdant musks of lust and decay. There was a DJ in the corner, head gold under the lights – maybe Jacques, maybe not – and leggy kids in dayglo stilettos danced like they'd been awake for a week. They danced to Can and Colder and Colourbox and Das Kabinette and Deux and Fad Gadget and Gay Cat Park and Grauzone and Kazino and Krisma and M83 and Mu and Vicious Pink and Vitalic; an alphabetical trawl through the abject. The room had its own pulse, unconnected to the city beyond.

Pink Fist were at a table in the farthest corner, smoking and sawing through steaks. Inky motioned at the seat beside his. I was half in love with him, but he had thick hair that hung fetchingly over his eyes and heart-shaped lips, so it was hardly an original desire. He'd been a piano prodigy and still moved through the world as if it had plans for him, which feasibly it did. When he smiled, he displayed two rows of boundless teeth – more teeth than lesser humans – and his arms were ropy and capable, fingers strong with recursive sustain and release.

He pulled me into an expansive hug and smelled wonderful doing it. I registered stubble, absinthe; melted into him.

'Holding anything interesting tonight, Lucy Lux?'

I dumped out my electric-blue handbag: painkillers, cigarettes, telephone, notebook, badges, lip-balm, lighters, a role of Anika's bondage tape, sunglasses – and the film canister. I confettied the contents into my palm and we divided its mysterious spoils around the table, saving the best for ourselves.

'I enjoyed your article,' he said. '*Pink Fist make you wanna crash your car and cheat on your girlfriend.* I hope so.'

'I possess neither a car nor a girlfriend, but the sentiment remains. Gorge should do a remix.'

'Fuck yes.'

'I can introduce you. It needs to be nine minutes; say 9.34.'

'Tell me more.'

'It should be a pagan, mechanistic death-rave, with drums like a heart, a metronome, a steam valve. It should be the best 12" that Flock of Seagulls never wrote: waves, birds and cicadas synthesised to wet lustre and processed so heavily they tip from real to fake, then back to real. It should be a knife slitting water; tantamount to hearing Bach or "Father Figure" for the first time. It should have the combined urgency and languor of a speedball. It should be Simon Le Bon playing "November Rain" on the piano, in a cabaret bar, at the world's end.'

'That's quite the specific fantasy, Lucy.'

'That's what I'm here for, Inky.'

The walls, in due course, throbbed. The palm fronds throbbed. The floor – black glass – crackled. The lilies in the swimming pool throbbed. The mosses in the room's secret groves throbbed. Inky took my hand, the beat at his wrist precise and persistent: throb, throb, throb.

'Ah,' he said. 'That's very nice.'

'Yes.'

'I behave myself, though,' he said, and he did: St Inky of the Invulnerable Girlfriend. I drank it in: leather jacket zipped against monumental jaw; the type of person I'd move to the country with, given the chance. 'Don't worry,' I said, 'I've ruined my life enough lately. Let's just sit here quietly.'

And so we did, holding hands under the table. I breathed as slowly as I could without stopping; mosses colonising the walls, lilies gambolling in the swimming pool, devil's ivy twisting around my legs, music travelling the floor in crisp currents that trailed sparks. I lit a cigarette, but it flopped, a piece of cooked spaghetti, useless in my hands. So there was acid in the canister. 'You smoke too much,' said Fred, leaning in, a pocket-sized Animal from the Muppets. He took a cigarette for himself. 'It'll kill you – death by a thousand puffs.'

'I don't care what happens to me,' I said.

'Maybe you should start.'

'Why? Not caring untethers you, makes you powerful – it's my edge on everyone here.' I gestured broadly to the room. More people kept arriving – people I knew, people I liked – but I didn't talk to them because talking was useless and I never wanted to do it again. I rested my head on Inky's shoulder, ready to sleep, but the music segued into The Human League's 'Sound of the Crowd'. Everyone stood to dance in sculptural movements; syncing with the ruinous cacophony of descending Linn drums. I stood and danced too, snapping straight into its keening synth ostinato, elastic pulled to its utmost tension without breaking. The song was too good, too important, for sleeping. Everyone was there, but when I closed my eyes, they weren't.

I fell through disused factories, vacant apartment blocks, rusted gilt plazas, burnt-out museums, shipwrecks and floodplains.

I fell through abandoned tract estates, abandoned phone booths, abandoned swimming pools, and abandoned train stations. I fell into caverns into caverns into caverns, deeper and darker and aromatic of earth. First, caverns of hollowed-out hedonism, disordered noise, piano-bar paranoia. Caverns lined with dusty amber bottles. Then I fell into the good ones: the caverns of opalescent stalactites, bluebells and croquet courts, fruit and fish, malachite and marcasite, mandolins and harpsichords, the caverns of spangly lilac pools. A list crystallised: Instructions for Living.

> Take big bites out of neon signs
> Drink electricity
> Scrapbook: Dutch still-life paintings juxtaposed with '70s cookbook still-life photographs
> Jaeger eye charts embedded with secret phrases; 'Oceanic Feeling'
> Live in New York's natural history museum with the minerals and bones
> Live inside Japan's 'Quiet Life'
> Live inside the flamingo sunsets of Abergele forever
> Live by describing things with great specificity
> Ride through monochromatic fields on a grey horse, velvet cloak whipping in the wind
> Find The Unspoiled Monsters who hammered these drums into form, ask how it was done
> Find the new in the old and the old in the new
> Stamen, pistil, sepals, petals, nectar glands
> Polaroids of faces post-orgasm
> Random acts of senseless beauty

Minimal wave and electroclash as feminist protest against
existential nausea; the music is cruel and ridiculous
because life is cruel and ridiculous
Polka-dot toadstools and umbrellas to match
Pastel days and neon nights
Sunday Reed's kitchen garden
Lobster Newburg and Bombe Alaska
Your Honour, I abject!
'Rhythm Is a Dancer', 'Rhythm Is a Mystery' and 'Rhythm
of the Night', all in a row
Take the cure
Just keep driving
Smoke the monster out
More, more, more, so there's always enough

I opened my eyes. In the doorway stood Julian, backlit to
unseemly perfection.

Anyone alive long enough knows relief is the best of all
feelings; that it's relief that matters most. Relief is the altar at
which you'll sacrifice everything else. I filed the list for now and
walked to him, brushing off the wet fists that grabbed at my
dress. I took his hand, flooded with relief; wantonly transfused
with the scorching blood of it. We walked without speaking,
rounding a hallway of identically closed doors.

The first opened onto a ballroom, tables resting under
starched cloths. A pale breeze tinkled through teardrop
chandeliers – Debussy. Julian pushed me against a wall, and
we kissed roughly, our bones fusing with brittle symmetry, as
always. He enacted this as one might a foregone conclusion
because it was – we both lacked imagination and could think

of nothing else to do. He tasted of salt, ash, arsenic, ice, the ground, the end. He tasted of iron, carbon, sulphur – the whole periodic table of elements. He braced me to his chest, and our pulses synchronised with a distant beat; all sensation and no feelings.

A grand piano, Lucite and gold leaf, occupied a far corner of the room. We walked to it, a crossing in which whole continents shifted; icebergs splintering and melting into the sea. I motioned for him to sit, which he did, lifting the lid obediently. 'Astonish me,' I said finally, 'I'll wait for you to astonish me,' which Diaghilev once bid of Cocteau. Julian readied his alabaster hands over the keys, and after two breaths began. He sang of highways, overpasses, underpasses, cigarettes, car cassettes, headlights, midnights, white lines, yellow lines, lines of flight. Julian of the salty eyelids, forever Unspoiled. Julian, pure instinct, utterly sure of himself and his place in the universe, which right now was this ballroom. Julian, my idée fixe, both the poison and the cure. 'You do know me,' I said.

He closed the lid, a full stop.

But it wasn't a full stop. Julian produced a baggie, and the world swiftly reclaimed its old contours, cocaine being the iconoclyte of drugs. We reclaimed our old contours too. Julian said he could always pick my bad weeks from the magazine, and I said I could always sense when his natural urge towards politeness was being outpaced by his urge to be a cunt. I told him I was leaving town, for New York maybe, to which he replied wherever you go, there you are; along with your neurosis, Lucy. I said he could ignore everything between us, but he wouldn't be pretty forever, so what then? A bedsit with the other men who thought jobs too bourgeois? Who'd buy the drugs and pay for dinner? And Julian declared this hilarious, given I was currently mid-sniff of his coke.

He tucked in his shirt.

'You're just going to go.'

'Yes.'

'Well, goodbye, Julian.' It came out almost singsong, more flippantly than I'd meant. It occurred to me to try making him stay, but I felt suddenly tired and for once couldn't be bothered.

I waited, measuring out enough time for Julian to get comprehensively gone. He'd left a demi bottle of whisky on the carpet, which fitted just-so in my dress pocket. A fire escape opened onto the swampy gloaming of the mall: raiders, rogues, looters, drunks, heaving in a doomed ship. I counted my cigarettes – three – and joined the line outside a convenience store.

Extraterrestrial light surged from the doorway, holding us in mute paralysis. Nobody talked, nobody moved. When an arm circled my waist, I observed it with abstraction. The arm had none of Julian's coiled power, so by reasonable elimination it must belong to The Creep. The arm gripped and lifted, and I observed this with abstraction too, or perhaps amphetamine lockjaw.

'Hello,' said a man.

'Oh, it's you.'

Not The Creep, then. A lower-case creep, one of my writers; Jack. He gestured at the pizza bar next door. 'I was just having a drink – care for one?'

'No, thank you.'

'You'll be in this line forever. C'mon.'

Cold fire. I felt my pocket for the whisky, but it was gone. The line hadn't moved.

'One drink only.'

We sat. An exhausted waiter, captive of the doomed ship, asked for our orders.

'You strike me as a girl in need of a peppermint tea, Lucy.' Jack said. 'We'll have a peppermint tea and a pint of stout.'

'Don't listen to him – I'll have a house red.' I coughed. 'Please.'

Jack was mid-30s, immune to all social cues. He had Disney-princess hair, fastidiously conditioned, of which he was excessively proud. Supposedly, his hair set him apart at the government agency he worked by day, where the women had made a pet of him. He was a prodigious bootlegger, a grammar pedant, and obsessive about his copy, polishing it to beautifully pointed missiles. He had a perverse fondness for most genres but was a populist at heart, believing he could divine qualities in the nightclub bangers, stadium fillers and café soundtracks that no one else could. This amounted to being an excellent writer, and I overpraised him, loading him with CDs, tickets, and the best jobs so he'd keep filing for what little I could pay. I accepted his bootlegs and invited him to parties, but I didn't like him, not one bit. Especially right now.

'How is your evening?' he asked, and I shook my head. Jack said it looked that way. He talked at length, describing that night's gig, the interferences in his recording, while I sat dumb. The drinks arrived.

'Interesting choice for the cover last week,' he said. A lure, a bait. 'Can I suggest Terms & Conditions were a touch esoteric?'

A headache helixed my left eyeball. 'Can I suggest tonight is not the night for this discussion?'

'I'm not trying to be critical. But just because *you* don't think a band is cool doesn't mean *nobody* thinks they're cool. Put The Killers on the cover! Give the people what they want!'

'Did you say, "Give the people what they want"?'

'Gentle advice from your resident genius.'

'Who anointed you resident genius?'

He laughed. 'You called me that last week.'

This is true. 'Well, that demonstrates how poor my judgement's been lately.'

He smiled and sipped his drink, enjoying the game, his game. 'Clearly. I put an Easter egg in my piece last issue, a mistake, to see if you were paying attention, and you missed it.'

I stood, holding my glass in line with my shoulder and letting it fall. Three bouncers were on top of me in seconds, yelling, 'You, OUT.'

Out I went; I'd never wanted to be there to begin. Jack – not entirely ignorant of social cues, then – didn't follow.

There were no taxis, a fact governed by classical mechanics at this hour, so I started walking home, stepping over rancid lettuces and cabbage leaves. 'I love you but I've chosen darkness,' I tapped out to Anika, then sent it to another 11 people. 'Time to go home,' Mani replied. 'Excellent band name, shit band,' Harry texted. Anika called.

'Where did you go?'

'I had a fight with Julian and then a fight with Jack.'

'Jack! People like Jack get an instant erection if they even *sniff* an opportunity for an argument. You don't fight with people like Jack.'

'Apparently. This job is full of Jacks, and they're all having more fun than me. I knew going out was a terrible idea.'

'Perhaps. I'm sorry, Lucy. The question, now, is what do you want? And then what will you do?'

'Buy more cigarettes.'

'I mean philosophically; broadly. You can't keep throwing good energy after bad.'

The whisky had been in my bag the whole time. *Cherry tart*, I thought, drinking. *Custard, roast turkey, toffee, and hot buttered toast.* Better. 'I wanted Julian,' I said, recapping the bottle. Three fingerlings of liquid, the correct amount, remained. 'It was pure and hard and propulsive, that want – a magnetic compass for the universe. Now it's unequivocally over and I, unprepared as ever, have nothing else to navigate by.'

'It was propulsive, Lucy, but proportionally corrosive. Eros plus danger equals chemical fire. I think you'll find that you're left with less than you started with.'

'You adore Julian!'

'I adore Julian as I adore vampires and Eminem and snakes – from a distance. You don't keep them as pets.'

'It stings. Horribly.'

'My point exactly: they sting. And the sting won't stop until *you* stop. Lance it. Cauterise it. Beat it back because it's useless, Lucy. Tell me again: what do you want?'

'A divorce.'

'Good. More.'

'I concocted a whole list of things at The Elysium, but I've forgotten them. A restraining order, I suppose. Seven hours sleep in a row. A town without Creeps. An office not infested with rats. A cottage garden by the sea. No more Julian, no more James, no more trouble. An internal compass all my own.'

'I'm pleased. Do you mean it this time?'

'I wish I was dead, Anika.'

'No, you don't. You wish you were unconscious and dreaming of little fluffy clouds. You wish for ego death, not death-death.

Come over, sleep it off, and we'll discuss everything in the morning.'

'I did have a nice talk with Inky tonight. Imagine if Gorge remixed Pink Fist.'

She ignores this. 'If you walk to the end of Ann Street, you might get a cab. You're a very silly rabbit, but I love you.'

I was well past Ann Street, so I kept walking toward Anika's, using the bridge as a beacon. I left the labyrinthine laneways and shattered spectacle of the casino behind. I walked past empty lots garlanded with chains, past whole blocks of once-lovely houses that had been razed and dug into gargantuan pits, only useful for trapping giants now. I walked past bulldozers and diggers; their insectoid-dinosaur claws poised in the air. I walked past bundled newspapers splashed with the worst news of the week; past the bridge, its reflection vanquished. I walked past new buds of frangipani, early sprays of inflorescent wattle, and into the yellowing dawn. My list, new instructions for living, was in the ether, somewhere. Anika texted to say she'd left the key in the fuse box, and there were crumpets and lemon curd for breakfast.

JUST FASCINATION

July 2004

It's Lucy's birthday. Lunch is being held inside, the terrace now occupied with the squalls and rages of winter. Robin and Isabella are last to arrive – Teddy had resisted his nap – but despite Robin's punctuality anxieties, their timing is perfect. The living room is a sunken stage, a riot of carnations. Heaving jugs of apricot blooms have been set atop the furniture. The window frames an apocalyptical king tide, thunderous whitecaps coiling then savaging the shore with barely a breath between sets. There's gala in the air, along with the powdered-clove smell of flowers and a heady alloy of perfumes.

Robin finds Lucy in the kitchen, prodding meringues. Every drawer is open, every implement splayed across the bench. A Perspex stand, identical to his grandmother's, displays a hand-written recipe stained with decades of iterative cooking, of enjoyment.

'Robin! You're here!' Metallic blue dress with lavishly puffed sleeves, the skirt hacked short. Lucy – with her spangled socks, stacked gold boots and lashings of mascara – is pitching for 1980, he thinks, or 1981.

His gift is a slim volume of out-of-print Updike stories, a treasure of the arcades. Lucy opens the book instinctively to his inscription.

Lucy,
I think you, me and Updike can agree that part of being human is being on the verge of disgrace.
Happy birthday,
Robin.

She hugs him in that crushing way, puffed sleeves completely obscuring his vision. 'Thank you, Robin, thank you,' she says through the gauze, voice fluttering at his ear. 'May we all be on the verge of disgrace within the hour.'

She steps back, still smiling. 'You brought your camera – good. Are you here alone?'

'No, Izzy is around somewhere. The Invisible Anaesthesiologist has a few days off, and Izzy bought a tin of formula, so I suspect there's a spree brewing.'

'Excellent. And Meg?'

Robin coughs. Meg has been sidestepping him all week.

'Never mind. Get yourself a drink. And send Tabitha in here. Once we finish making lunch, I'll be out.'

He hovers in the doorway to the living room, watching; Lucy's message for Tabitha forgotten. The house has been tidied, giving him a new appreciation for the '80s hand across its

'50s bones, the renovations Lucy's grandmother oversaw in her final decade. Chrome, glass, cork, leather and slate, animated by the peacock sprawl of today's party. Lucy's orchestra is already in full tilt: glossy limbs, waterfall laughter, the clinks and chimes of their ever-shifting anomie, their aesthetic protests, their terror of boredom. Tonight's cast is Isabella, between Tabitha and Harry; Julian and Gudrun; and three others Robin hasn't met. He is shy of the house all over again, wondering how to broach the room, when someone rises on tiptoe to kiss his cheek.

'You're Robin.'

He bends his head to meet hers, blank. 'Anika,' she says. 'Has Lucy not told you about me?'

Lucy has told him lots. Robin knows she's a doctor, midway through a residency in A&E. That she and Lucy co-wrote a column called 'Nine Things' for the magazine; Anika's contributions always the best and smartest, a repository of beautiful information. That they'd been to hundreds of shows together, Anika possessing a matchless ability to get backstage, to the hotel, wherever the real fun waited. That this year Anika has been interred in double shifts at the hospital, concurrently grinding through exams. Lucy likened their forced separation to all the world's champagne going flat at once.

Robin had imagined another Gudrun but sees now the ways he was wrong. Gudrun – the weekend Gudrun he knows, anyway – is lush, imperturbable; a hothouse heliotropic bending instinctively to the nearest amusement. Anika is high energy, high focus and high vigilance; a meticulously calibrated instrument. She wears a bustier of cameo-pink bondage tape and matching platform sneakers; violet contacts, black ringlets, rubber leggings.

'Well, I know plenty about you,' Anika says. 'Not enough, though.' She touches his forearm, motioning they should sit on the leather cushions near the window. There, he submits to her grilling, which – as far as he can judge – is born from genuine interest. When did he move to Abergele? Who is his favourite writer? At which hospital does Isabella practise? Who is supervising his grandmother's care? What music is he into? But what hip-hop? Who'd win in a fist fight between a synthesiser and a guitar? Did his mother speak Basque or Catalan? Does Robin speak any? What does his girlfriend do? Is his eye painful?

Robin touches it, self-conscious.

'No, don't touch! It's a cyst – it needs flushing.' She tips out her bag; sifts through make-up, gauze, antiseptic, cyanoacrylates. 'I thought I had eyedrops, but no. When you're home, ask if Isabella has any.' Then she says he must meet Sasha, her boyfriend, the best of humans, and heaves him up to join the table.

Lucy and Tabitha bring out champagne risotto with grilled peaches. There's very good bread, excellent butter, and a boggling quantity of wine. Everyone is soon incandescently drunk, the rare and wonderful kind of no shouting, no hurt feelings, and no falling down the stairs; at least not yet. The doctors have found each other and talk at a galloping clip throughout lunch. Robin is seated between Sasha and Harry, ensnarled contentedly in their ping-pong of shared obsessions: Afrika Bambaataa, Grandmaster Flash, Big Daddy Kane. After dessert, Eton Mess, they drift from the table, and Robin finds himself back on the cushions with Anika.

'Because the root of placebo is "I will please",' she tells Robin, 'whereas "nocebo" means "I will *harm*".'

Robin laughs. He doesn't know how long they've been sitting but feels relaxed, expansive.

'What's your kissing style, Anika, 10 words or less?'

'Oh! I love this game!' She lights a cigarette, narrows her eyes. 'Ok – Proportional Forces. No, hang on – My Idols Are Dead and My Enemies Are in Power.' Seeing Robin raise his camera, she shifts fractionally so the glitter at her collarbones catches the light.

Lucy looms above them, towering in her boots.

'I just told Robin my new kissing style, Lucy: World War III edition.'

Lucy smiles. In three boneless moves she's recumbent, head in Anika's lap.

'You can't sleep!'

'Just for a minute.'

Anika puts out her cigarette and strokes Lucy's eyebrows in a course of soft, curative gestures. 'Lucy Lux: falling asleep at parties since 1979.'

'Only because it's so fun,' says Lucy, voice cottony. 'It's what I miss most about parties. I love when the chat rises in filmy *puffs*, and I let it drift away, zero compulsion to join in. It's like pretending to fall asleep after a late drive so your parents will carry you to bed; the sense of being cared for without needing to say a word.'

'Lucy! You never *stop* talking,' says Robin.

'That's not true! Well, I don't stop talking around *you*.' But conversation is a high-stakes game with Anika and Gudrun, says Lucy, clever things lobbed like shuttlecocks, and it's difficult to keep up. Gudrun uses her voice with great skill and self-possession to send bad men to jail. Anika has a photographic memory; arcane medical facts landing as punchlines. 'And

James!' Whoever James is emerges, a dryad in jazz shoes. 'James sings torch songs at cyclopean volume, reducing audiences to a puddle. What could I possibly add?'

Gudrun is there now and they form a kittenish pile, unquestioningly folding Robin into the centre. James produces a tray of whole glacéd fruits, filched from her parents' larder, and passes it around: cherries, clementines, angelica and shrunk-down pears, candied to hard, sticky translucency.

Robin is lulled into the feminine trance of his teenage years, of Isabella and her friends; the trance in which he's always been happiest. The sorority air of slouchy boots, ceramic deer, beaded cigarette cases, mohair mittens, Virago classics, Art Deco mirrors, lush houseplants, leaky pens, and tinkly 1960s lamps hauled home from thrift shops. Their sloped shoulders and soft arms; the casual ease of their physicality. Their entwined ink-stockinged legs spidering out from couches, their smells of lemon rind and bergamot and just-washed hair. Their occasional blowouts where grievances are aired aloud. Their early mastery of life's essential skills: how to bake a soufflé, take up hems, find off-script antibiotics for UTIs, and sprint in heels if necessary. How to shop for gifts overseas (duty-free Sobranie cigarettes, miniature tins of Fauchon tea). How to find an abortionist in states where the profession isn't strictly legal. How to stage a wake or tribute show for a friend who dies unexpectedly; what to say after a miscarriage, a break-up, a suicide, a bad review.

Robin thinks of these women: St Isabella, St Gudrun, St Tabitha, St Anika, St Lucy, and all the other fallible saints. Isabella, who clamps people together after car crashes, expanding her last reserves of energy to safeguard Robin. Gudrun, who, in her second year as a lawyer, distinguished herself in a case forging new rights for sex workers. Tabitha, who gave her debut lecture last month, now vigilant to plagiarism, disengagement and disorder in her students. Anika, who – in less-than-optimal circumstances – just defibrillated her first patient. The subject was shocked back to life; Anika sufficiently exhilarated to make a nice breakfast when she got home, instead of falling asleep in her clothes. Lucy, who took on the care of two infants when a kid herself, who still feeds people far more than she's ever fed. Who ground out the magazine in 16-hour stretches, having stand-up fights with the publisher to ensure her writers got their cheques. Even Meg, with her diligent 4am wake-ups, hauling massive, spiked bundles across her shoulders to fashion fairytale posies for hungry would-be brides, never rising to meet their tempers. Robin thinks of how little he does, what little he's done, amazed they allow him in the litter.

He listens and builds an imaginary picture of their life, Lucy's life before this – the sybarite life to which she'll no doubt soon return. The parties in hotel rooms and warehouses and fire escapes; the sotto confidences in silk-lined elevators and plush interstitials between concert hall and foyer; their country weekenders raiding flea markets for satin bedjackets and feeding apples to horses; their ironic mint juleps in rooftop hot tubs; their stealth strategising by text message; the quiet simmer of their ambition; their hushed Sundays under a shared blanket drinking Earl Grey.

Lucy sits and rubs her eyes. 'I'm getting the mushroom caps.'

She hands them around, three apiece, transparent membranes exposing the peaty moss of their interiors. They wash down the caps with blackish port. Julian sits at the piano, rumbling the bass notes, and Gudrun lies atop to sing 'Ain't Misbehavin'', trying to writhe without falling. The room is coated in holographic light, thrown out from the Aurora Borealis sequins of Gudrun's slinky green sheath.

Afterwards, Lucy crash-tackles Robin from the side.

'You're awake!' he says.

'I'm very awake now!'

'That was smashing. I've always wondered what that piano was for.'

'Oh, but you don't know the half of it. I dreamt the whole thing when I was 10. A nightclub in a cave in a field; low lit in intimate browns. A celluloid phantasm of a woman sang "Ain't Misbehavin'" from full recline on a piano – although a grand piano, naturally, not an upright like mine. I took it as a premonition of adulthood and everything it should be. And clearly, I've never shut up about it.' She shakes her hair, rapt. 'You can live an entire life in your head, but occasionally – very occasionally – you find sympathetic characters to take it into the world.'

'You're very lucky.'

'I am. It's your birthday soon, isn't it, Robin?'

'Three weeks exactly.'

'Oh! What are you planning?'

'Nothing! Maybe I'll celebrate early tonight.'

They dance to a mix of saxophone songs Tabitha made for the evening. Glenn Frey's 'The Heat is On'; The Waitresses' 'I Know What Boys Like'; Glass Candy's 'Life after Sundown'; Hall and Oates' 'Maneater'; Sisters of Mercy's 'Dominion'; Sade's 'Smooth Operator'; Aretha Franklin's 'Pink Cadillac'; Sheila E's 'The Glamorous Life'; Grauzone's 'Eisbär'; Guru Josh's 'Infinity';

Tina Turner's 'We Don't Need Another Hero'; Don Henley's 'All She Wants to Do Is Dance'; Laid Back's 'Bakerman'; Bruce Springsteen's 'Dancing in the Dark'; Wang Chung's 'Dance Hall Days'; Screamin' Jay Hawkins' 'I Put a Spell on You'; Robbie Nevil's 'C'est la Vie'; Sad Lovers & Giants' 'Things We Never Did'; Playgroup's 'You're So Gangsta'; Romeo Void's 'Never Say Never'. The mushrooms lend the songs a hymnal quality; they're exaltations, offerings to a louche god.

Lucy stands on a chair. 'Harry! Harry!'

He looks up from across the room.

'Go on, Harry, play it; I know you're dying to.'

'Play what? You'll have to narrow things down.'

'Play Prince's "Girls & Boys".'

He claps his hands. 'Oh, now it's *my* birthday.'

Harry dances, limbs thrown out in freewheeling gestures. Anika dances on the toes of her platforms, arms around Sasha's neck. James embarks on a snakelike pas de deux with the lamp in the corner. Tabitha dances alone in stylised patterns, eyes darting fetchingly to the side. Isabella skates in and mirrors her, fully committed to the wild rumpus.

Harry puts on Bryan Ferry's 'Don't Stop the Dance', and Lucy and Gudrun fall into a rhapsodic slow sway, heads on each other's shoulders. Halfway through, Lucy ducks from under her arm, crossing the room in her undulating backwards manoeuvres. 'You're always dancing away,' laughs Gudrun. 'Oh no,' says Lucy. 'I'm dancing backwards in the style of Billy MacKenzie – I'm dancing *towards* oblivion.'

Julian appears beside Robin just as 'Hit Me with Your Rhythm Stick' begins. Black leather harness over a Hypercolor T-shirt, darkly pink under the arms. Up close, he smells of smoke and soap; beneath that, heat and something animal. He keeps immaculate time with his right hand, fingers poised as if holding a pencil. 'Have you seen the video – Davey Payne playing two saxophones?' asks Robin, and Julian says of course with a beatific smile, clapping Robin on the shoulder, and their glasses splash port on the slate.

It's decided that they will go out – karaoke. Lucy calls a guy she knows with a limousine because it's reputedly cheaper than three taxis. They descend the winding cliff road and speed along the Pacific Highway; Moroder and Cerrone on the stereo, knees touching, laughter pealing through the windows. Lucy props her boots against the glass, and her legs, chiselled from long walks, inspire loud jealousy and delight. Beyond the skylight, stars jangle like money.

They stop at a hotel perched on the silt banks of the lake, not far from where their boat disembarked all those months ago. A blinking sign – 'Cocktail & Keys' – throws an acid-green spill across the water. They have arrived.

The private rooms are upstairs. They cram inside; legs draped over legs over legs. Harry passes around the bag of mushroom caps and Lucy orders a tray of martinis served in aggressively triangular glasses. 'Here's to the pleasures of human intercourse and the enjoyment of beautiful objects,' she says. They raise their drinks.

Anika sings 'Like a Virgin' as a bored German model, electroclash at its peak.

James sings 'You're So Vain' with unglued Streisand flourishes.

Tabitha and Harry sing 'Kokomo', spinning a dinner table contrivance (prescription drugs replacing tropical paradisos) into a fully realised canzonet.

Sasha recites 'Ice Ice Baby' with breakneck prowess, one powerful arm arrowed out and back to bring the mic right to his mouth.

Lucy snatches the microphone and cues 'Is That All There Is?'. She dubs in the Cristina lyrics, hissing them through the rasp of her hair.

And when I was 16 years old, I went to my first nightclub;
I was REALLY excited
And there were bored-looking bankers dancing with
beautiful models
And there were boys with dyed hair and Spandex
T-shirts dancing with each other
And as I sat there watching, I thought there was
something missing; I don't know what
But when I headed home, I said to myself
Is THAT all there IS to a disco?

'Goodness!' says Gudrun, who'd been holding a cigarette to Julian's mouth. In a slow-fast panther manoeuvre, Julian captures Lucy and rends her taut, laying her prone form across his and Gudrun's laps. She relaxes, then melts, forearm across her eyes.

'I don't imagine you can smoke here,' Harry pipes.

'What?' Gudrun is holding the cigarette to Lucy's mouth. 'How could anyone possibly know?'

'There will be cameras. Or smoke detectors. Or both.'

'Bah humbug,' says Gudrun. 'You may as well do as you wish in life, because you'll get into trouble anyway. Besides, did you clock those shady guys in the foyer? I bet they're running illegal gambling and dirty massages out of every other private room. They don't care.' This seems, for the time being, true.

Julian rises then for 'Orinoco Flow', and it's as if a vial of poppers has spilled, the room dissolving into unhinged pagan hysterics. The hotel has snapped from its footings; they are floating out to sea. It might go on forever, pinned helpless beneath those harps, but then Sasha stumbles backwards into the tray of empty glasses and the spell, mercifully, is broken.

'You're up,' says Julian and passes Robin the mic, a baton.

A peculiar itch surges through him, a charge of synthetic bravado. Implausibly, between the David Bowie and the Duran Duran, Robin finds Dramarama. And so it goes. He belts it out, just four dumb chords, chords majestic with deranged love and anger. They are fists in his guts, always. Robin is soon drenched beneath his jacket and tries to wrest it off, becoming stuck and smashing hard into the wall. There's a thrilling crunch of bones on concrete. He slides to the floor, skull and shoulder a symphony of pain, and screams the chorus from the sticky carpet.

I'll give you candy, give you diamonds, give you pills
Give you anything you want, hundred-dollar bills
I'll even let you watch the shows you want to see
Just marry me, marry me, marry me

He pitches the mic with spent flourish, a liberty only accessible to the very drunk, and collapses back into the carpet;

throat hoarse, eyes wet, breath ragged. Gudrun leans over and plants a smacking kiss on his mouth, sparks flying. Julian applauds with giant hands, brow hitched in one of his appraising late-night looks. Isabella shakes her head. Robin stands unsteadily and goes in search of a bathroom.

Lucy intercepts him at the bar, backlit by a tropical fish tank. The puffed sleeves cast a sapphire hue across her face; her expression frightened, aggrieved. 'Who the hell are you, Robin?' She swipes his brow, showing him the blood. 'Who are you, looking as you do, singing as you do, materialising in Abergele? You're unknowable.' She hands him her drink. He sniffs it: gin and indeterminate viscosity. 'I am SLOSHED,' she says, 'STINKO.' And she walks off. Everyone is gathering their things. He has ended karaoke.

MDMA in the limousine home. The murdered remains of lunch await them: plates smeared with berries, Belladonna rings of port residue, crumpled napkins and prawn tails everywhere. Robin snaps the accidental still lifes. The pewter scallops of the ocean are just visible, waves thunderous as ever. They sprawl on cushions, but Lucy stands on the chair and demands they come to her bedroom. She makes Harry move the speakers and then ferry beers and water. She sends him back for a jar of mussels. She kicks away her gold boots and directs where everyone should huddle, so she has Isabella to her right side, Anika to her left. Against logic, they fit. Lucy takes the mussels from Harry, spearing them with a miniature brass trident.

'That is disgusting,' says Tabitha. 'You are the only person I know who can eat on drugs.'

'I can eat on drugs,' says James. 'Is there any of that bread left?'

'Oh, but you can't eat carbs,' says Lucy. 'You need salty things, briny things, things that will keep you alive.'

Julian goes out for the bread anyway and puts on 'Caribbean Queen', engendering a noticeable lift in mood. Gudrun dances from her perch, one arm fishtailing above her. Everyone is smoking, even Isabella, she and Lucy in furious, whispered conversation, and the floral covers are littered with ash. Julian rests his arm on Robin's shin, keeping impeccable time with his shoulder.

'Julian, darling, tell them the name of your new band,' says Lucy.

'Sex Nest,' he says proudly. 'It is the nest that's created when you fuck, rumpled sheets and ash, not unlike this situation here, and what happens to the back of your hair after you've been at it for a while.'

'And they told me you were just a pretty face.' She beams. 'Not as good as my band names, though. Dirty Magazine. Private Lesson. Cold Mess Hotline. Business Model. Beach Witch. Gush. Infinity Pool. Follow the Anvil. Heatstroke Heart. Felt & Hammers. Just a Minute. Slow Release.'

'There's already a band called Slow Release,' says Harry.

'Yes, because I fucking named them! How soon people forget.'

'It's true, she did,' says James. She has nestled catlike against Robin, trying to engage him in conversation, but he's well past that.

Time passes. He hears Julian ask Anika what her leggings are made of, and she says the skins of my enemies. Anika asks Julian what his kissing style is this week, and he says The Mind Is a Terrible Thing to Taste. Gudrun posits cum smells the same as wattle blossoms to very loud dissent. Tabitha says why must we half-kill ourselves to prove we're alive.

Cabaret Voltaire lurches through the speakers, and Robin, hitched to 'Just Fascination's 4/4 amphetamine throb, listens, really listens. Every fourth beat is an anvil on which the previous three are obliterated, a recursive pattern engineered to hold you in terrifying thrall. It paralyses you with melodies as much as it does with machines; the horrible ache of that stifled *just*. Here the logic of pop lyrics is inverted: the eyes know things, but the body lies.

Across the bed, Lucy moves in her serpentine circles, arms bending where they shouldn't, veins bright. Her cigarette has carbonised to her fingers, but she hasn't noticed. Robin's about to yell that fire burns, put it out, put it out, but James leans in and kisses him. He kisses her back, the sounds of the party retreating as he submits to her pointed teeth, the blunt ends of her hair, her patchouli embrace. 'That's my cue,' says Isabella distantly, and there's a chorus of no, no, don't go, don't go, and Robin opens his eyes, and someone upsets a bottle of wine, red gushing across the sheets, and Izzy's gone.

'Shall we find another room?' says James, sitting on her haunches. Her eyes have a mean faerie glimmer, sharpened arrows.

'I probably shouldn't. I have a girlfriend.' Robin glances at Lucy. She is watching them. 'Ah,' says James, seeing this. She flicks her ponytail. 'That's fine. You know Lucy doesn't like boys, though. Not really. Which is dumb because you're adorable. Unlike nasty old Julian.'

'What are you up to, James?' says Lucy. 'I hope you're being nice.' James meows.

Robin decides to leave, which takes forever on account of pins and needles and everyone grabbing at his legs and yelling. He takes the stairs, murmuring *inky pinky ponky, drinky dranky dronky*, a nursery rhyme to stay upright. He hopes Isabella might still be there to help him navigate the hill, but she's not. He spends pointless centuries searching for his jacket, treading on a record, and by then, he's beyond walking home. He lies on the leather cushions and pulls his jacket over his head.

When he wakes mid-morning, he finds that someone has put two blankets over him and tucked the edges under, a gesture of tenderness so deliberate it hurts his chest. Tabitha and Harry are in comatose nuzzle on the couch, one of Harry's legs resting on the rug in a sprinter's crouch, Tabitha's hair flattened against his chest in a big tawny quiff. James is curled sleeping on the wingback chair under the pile of Lucy's dresses, ponytail looped around her neck.

Robin limps to the kitchen. Broken glass, broken eggshells, broken meringues, broken plates. The record he trod on last night is shattered cleanly on the floor: *Gentlemen Take Polaroids*. This will be unpleasant to confess. The drawers are still open, and Gudrun, wrapped in Lucy's kimono, is rifling through cupboards.

'Morning, Christopher Robin,' she says, kissing his cheek. 'You ok?'

Robin shakes his head.

'Me neither. Now, where does Lucy keep her painkillers?'

'Everywhere,' says Robin. He looks on the bench: a Glomesh handbag, a transparent Perspex handbag, Gudrun's battered half-moon Chanel, his camera. Isabelle's bag is there too, and he hopes she got into the house without incident. He reaches around the top of the fridge, locating a box.

'Perfect,' says Gudrun. She walks back upstairs to Lucy's bedroom. The door closes with a LinnDrum snap.

Meg goes on a skiing holiday with her family. Robin skied for years with Roland and Isabella – semi-annual jaunts unusually enjoyed by all – and Meg asks, once, if he'll come. Robin demurs on the grounds of his grandmother, and she doesn't ask again.

He and Lucy leave for their walks earlier, staying later. Robin brings his camera now, sufficiently comfortable to use it in her presence. She points out native violets, tea trees, bottlebrushes, a stray sunflower that must have sprouted from spilled trail mix, the rotting coconuts at Stinky Point, and the invasive blackberries Lucy calls bacon-and-egg plant because of their yolky pool on crimson. They break into the old quarry, and she shows Robin the death-trap piles of coal where she played as a child. She shows him the wooden footbridge where her parents got married. She shows him the concrete igloos on the crest of the cliff where soldiers kept lonely guard during World War II. The light inside the igloos is paranormal, as Lucy promised, but she declines to join him while he explores. She can't anymore, she shrugs, citing real and imaginary rats. They climb higher and higher and arrive at a clearing, both breathless. The ocean, elusive for hours, is right there, a hunk of pyrite framed between cliffs. Lucy stands to admire it, rocking on her swayback spine.

They're crossing the last verge back to their street when she asks to see his photographs. It occurs to Robin she's never been inside his house. He leads her to the attic, knowing what awaits, knowing he's inadvertently let it assume the weight of a reveal: a four-track recorder, an eight-track recorder, a polyphonic Korg PS-3100, an E-mu Emax SE, and a candy apple Fender Jaguar.

'But of course,' Lucy says, taking inventory.

'Of course.'

'Well, this explains a lot. You're so annoyingly secretive, Robin. What do you make?'

'Noise. Grim noise. New buildings collapsing, a factory floor after the flood.'

She stands over the Korg's sloping bulk, stroking a D-sharp as if assessing its corporality.

'How long have you had this?'

'The Korg and the E-mu are recent acquisitions – your influence, Lucy.'

'It's heartening I still have some influence. Wherever did you find them?'

'Online. There's a guy who must be stockpiling gear for a very specific doomsday scenario.'

'Do you know how to turn them on?' Distrust pricks her voice. Robin had misestimated the degree to which his secretiveness might read as deception.

'I played trumpet at school. And oboe. And double bass. I'm versed in prying sound from recalcitrant instruments, I guess.'

'A prodigy then.'

'Burnt out, all promise squandered.'

This mollifies her. 'My favourite kind. I bet you read music. Asshole.'

Robin is embarrassed, which oddly goads him to continue. 'I was a champion trampoliner when I was 12. I wrote a piece at 14 that got toured with a youth orchestra. For a while, when I was seven, eight, tennis was a real thing, coaches and competitions. My grandmother was very accommodating.'

'That sounds nice. I went to 13 schools, so extracurriculars didn't figure. I can barely spell – I can only spell the good words, anyway.'

He pulls out shoeboxes of photos. Suburban roadside signs in various states of decay from the outskirts of Abergele shouting, 'Glamour Pools!' 'Cardiff Fish!' 'Baby Town!' 'Gospel Pianos!' A compendium of old barbershop windows, ancient combs and jars of pomade displayed with old-world care. The gutted interiors of factories and substations being gradually reclaimed by nature. And at the bottom, photos from his father's studio: bands smoking in the overgrown kitchen garden, bands drinking Roland's celebrated tea in the control room. Lucy sits unselfconsciously next to Robin on the bed, sifting through the prints, methodical. He is agonisingly aware of his possessions: his watch, the pile of Japanese handkerchiefs accumulated over many Christmases, an old sewing machine, a tincture for mouth ulcers, eyedrops.

'Why don't you do more of this?' she says.

'I do it all the time.'

'But as a vocation. For money. For work. They're excellent, Robin.'

'I don't know. I'm not good at going after things; I've learned too well to go without. It feels unnatural to want things, painful.'

'I want things so much I'm constantly in pain. You get used to it; then you start chasing it – the pain as much as the things. Freud had many stupid ideas, but the Pleasure Principle wasn't one of them.'

'I suppose I've ascribed a pious value to keeping life low. I've made passivity an extreme sport.'

'You're lucky. Because you're so pretty, people just think you're deep and mysterious.'

'I am deep and mysterious.'

'Ha!'

She finds his shelf of tapes – Systematics, Primitive Calculators, The Slugfuckers, Voigt/465, Los Microwaves, Nervous Gender, Belle Du Soir – and appraises them as one would evidence. Having hit some vague limit for the day, Robin induces Lucy downstairs by telling her Isabella might be home.

Izzy is home, but only just, squinting at the stove while Teddy protests on the floor. Lucy claims him with the affectionate growl of one used to subduing infants. 'You're quite right, Teddy. Why should you sit on the ground with the hoi polloi when you can be carried, VIP style?' She walks him to the window, murmuring into his head.

Isabella raises an eyebrow at Robin, its meaning unclear. 'Will you stay for dinner, Lucy? I'm making my bolognese, which I've been told is edible.'

'Oh! I'd love that, Izzy, but I borrowed a mower from my cousins ages ago and promised I'd return it today.' There's new ease between them since the birthday party. A pleasurable jealousy flits across Robin.

'Dinner is still an hour away. At least. Both of you go – hopefully, there'll be a meal of sorts when you're back.' It is decided.

The mower is a hulking beast of a machine, frills of grass sprouting from every crevice. It takes half an hour to heft it into the Fiat's back seat, Robin sweating by the end, Lucy in fits of laughter. 'How the hell did you get it out to begin with?'

'With great obstinance and minor flesh wounds, Robin, the same way I do everything.'

'Did you say it's your cousin's mower? I didn't know you had cousins in Abergele.'

'I have lots. My dad's one of eight kids, all prodigious breeders. Half of my cousins are here, and the other half are in a former commune town up north – a bunch of the siblings drifted there in the late '70s.'

'And you never invite these cousins to your parties?'

'Separation of church and state, silly – one of the most important ideals of the Enlightenment.'

'Your family being?'

'State.'

They set off in the opposite direction of town, parts uncharted by Robin. A drop sheet of mist covers the cliffs and they pass an old cemetery; stone angels veiled in clouds, aphids sounding ritualistic alarm. They glide along the sinews of a bridge, hugging the cliffs and curving with sudden ceremony over the ocean. Lucy pushes in a burnt CD and announces the songs to Robin – Night Moves' 'Transdance', Mount Sims' 'No Yellow Lines', Oppenheimer Analysis's 'The Devil's Dancers' – but is otherwise quiet, concentrating on the road.

'Your driving is different, Lucy. Better.'

'I was reading about Cristina this morning.'

'Do I know Cristina?'

'*Cristina* – No Wave Cristina. I sang her at karaoke.'

'Oh, *that* Cristina.'

'Anyway, she called herself "Madame Bovary of the Highway", a description I might borrow for myself. Cristina's mother said, "You were always a brilliant writer. A good artist, a good actress. How could you be so self-destructive as to *sing*?" What a line – total devastation.'

He watches Lucy, her slight arms on the steering wheel, her implacable expression. She's wearing a 'Life. Be in it.' sweatshirt, one of her tattered favourites. Robin has the vertigo of ascent, of rising to approach the unknown, the music acting as amyl nitrate on his blood to slow everything down and turn it right up. In the dazzling reveal of new vistas, he smells bloodwoods, blue gums, ironbarks and close-by rain. He smells rusted-out train tracks and the decaying boat cleats up and down the coast, now fused irreversibly into the rocks. He smells drying grass from the back seat. He understands now what Lucy's trying to conjure by dissecting and cataloguing this music. A life where limitations become advantages by necessity. How centuries of human folly can be conveyed in a radiant, four-minute reduction. How 'Transdance', with its homemade handclap machine, is shorthand for both the Blitz of 1940 and the Blitz Kids of 1980, for the ravages of Thatcher and the plague alike. How Cristina's ennui is the pierced and chiselled key that unlocks a new life for a particular person: the sardonic and hyper-literary kids, eyes overlined in black, who've seen everything by 17 and want more, more, more.

They're right on the skin of the night when Lucy pulls up outside a house and honks. Her cousins, three of them, descend on the car and together haul out the lawnmower. They're suntanned, wholesome late teens and early 20s, full of good humour and promise. Lucy becomes one of them, shape-shifting into another leggy coast girl; tragic air evaporated. Strange.

*

The next afternoon, Robin arrives for their walk, not noticing the Trans Am until he's at Lucy's front door. Magazine's 'Permafrost' rattles at the windows. The window is a diorama: Julian supine on the slate, Lucy astride his chest – legs bare, pale hair a curtain, fisherman's jumper voluminous – holding a cigarette to his lips. Robin leaves.

The day after, Lucy takes Robin to the cemetery they'd passed on their drive. The sleeping grounds slope to the water, meeting a crumbled pier where coal once shipped out and smallpox shipped in. The oldest graves, covered in dinosaur-spined agave, are simple – the dead buried in haste – but grow increasingly ornate as the salt-crusted earth inclines to the bush. They walk, quiet, Lucy pointing out her favourites occasionally: Celia, tendons in her neck pulled forever taut, 'Eternally 25 while the rest of us keep getting older,' she says. And Isabella, blightless arms embracing a marble crucifix, ringlets thrown back in what could only be ecstasy, the fabric of her robes clinging to the cleft of perfect backside, one ankle crossed chastely over another. Sunlight bathes the statue's bare feet.

'Goodness!' says Robin.

'I know. That' – Lucy gestures to the crucifix's hand-wrought inscription, *Rock of Ages* – 'completes the perfection. As you can imagine, I pay my respects here often.'

'I have to show this to Izzy.'

'Oh, *your* Izzy – yes! It was so nice of her to come to my birthday. I was delighted that she stayed so late. Smoking in the nest, even.'

'She's a secret hedonist. You remind me of each other sometimes.'

'Really? I wouldn't call my hedonism secret.'

'No, I mean in energy; a spiritual dimension. A crash-tackling-life, getting-things-done dimension.'

'Well, I'm pleased you think of me in that category, with Izzy, an actual grown-up, no less.' She smiles, turning her head, almost shy. Her gaze lands on another headstone, and she stabs it accusingly with one finger.

'Look! Look at that! *Here also lies Charlotte.* And right next to her: *Also Mary.* For every Celia or Isabella, another 50 women are mere postscripts on their husband's tombstones. Once you notice, it's all you can see.'

'I'd be happy to subvert that paradigm. I'd be content with *Also Robin.*'

'Now you sound like Eeyore. I've been thinking about what you said the other day; that your passivity is an extreme sport. You're a Stoic.'

'Oh god, that's depressing. Without passion, you mean.'

'Without suffering *or* passion, Robin. An enviable state, in certain respects.'

'Oh, *in certain respects.*'

'Don't be cross. I was going to say your music – your musique concrete – is the exception. I mean, if you're making anything as loud and discordant as those tapes you hoard, you're being engulfed in the world of the senses; totally subservient to extreme noise. All bass, no treble, just *drowning* in white mass – what de Beauvoir might call *enclosing oneself in the pure instant.*'

'Is that quote in the book?'

'Naturally.'

'So, it's a space where I relinquish control, then.' The cemetery is emboldening, salt blowing off the water like pink frost, sea fizzing like lemonade. 'And in that freefall, find hidden depths to life – claim some ownership for myself, even.'

'See, I wasn't being a dick. Freefall is a good word, Robin – we're both in the thrall of that devastating, lovely, lovely freefall. Except I take it too far. The same itch that makes me keep pecking at Julian is the same itch that makes me listen to the same song 30 times in a row, for as many days or months as it takes, until I'm finally tired of it; the thrall over, the wound cauterised. It's a prolonged journey of supplication to get to the endpoint – which in my case *is* control.'

'Kink-play, then.'

She kicks his foot.

The monuments start repeating themselves: the same anchors wreathed in the same heavy chains, the same filigreed hands in unending handshakes, the same weeping maidens with their unmoving locks of hair and unmoving dresses, all reaching toward taffy clouds. *The limits of forever don't lie specifically with love*, reads one; *Back to the things themselves*, another. Robin and Lucy are spat, abruptly, into a thicket of tangled lantana awash with the call of bellbirds, terrain similar to that of their regular rambles but more sheltered, more sequestered.

They walk the old Pacific Highway, an unused grown-over stretch on its way to becoming track again. A symphony of scents follows them, heavy and resinous: the needled teeth of she-oaks, bearded moss tendrilling from taller trees, acrid heads of three-cornered leek, the jagged upheaval of the earth's crust.

'What happens if you keep walking?' he asks, drunk with it.

'I haven't the faintest. Let's find out.'

So they walk, on and irrepressibly on, vehicles of pure proficient movement now, until the path splits into two: a quarry on one side, a pedestrian bridge on the other. They take the rickety bridge over the highway, giddy, the sun getting low, the trees thinning out, the sky dimming. Ahead, wreathed in fairy lights, is a restaurant with a deep balcony sickling over the sea.

'Aha!' says Lucy. 'That's the Scarlet Ibis. We'd go there when I was a kid for fisherman's baskets. The baskets were made of potato, deep-fried like life's best things, and you'd eat them last: a sleight of delicious gimmickry. Are you hungry?'

They take seats on the balcony, the lapis lazuli of the sea below them, its incessant puckered wet all around. Lucy orders a basket to share – still miraculously on the menu; still edible, they're assured – and a bottle of the second-cheapest wine.

'Did you visit the hospital today?'

Robin nods.

'How did it go?'

He begins to say fine but stops. Lucy watches him, chin in hands. It takes time to assess this stuff of his feelings, with a further lag as he weighs what can be spoken aloud. He knows she must find this maddening – most people do – but Lucy has learned to wait, mining a private reserve of patience.

'Different,' he says eventually.

'In what sense?'

The wine arrives then, another minor miracle, and he pours for them. 'More intense, but quietly so. The forced cheer and relentless administration of those early months have fallen away. I was always grateful to have Meg there, but I think it sustained an artificial normality; the collective performance of being ok. I've been going alone this week, and the conversations have been looser, more . . . profound. I don't mean that philosophically; we're not doing The Big Questions. But my grandmother's been talking about growing up in Kent: the dresses she made for Saturday-night dances, the button shop where she worked as a teenager, the pageantry of mid-century English life – all fairytales and Kinks albums to me.'

'Village green preservation. Strawberry jam, Tudor houses, China cups.'

'Exactly. The church and the steeple. Custard pies, willow trees, puffer trains. She's been talking about my grandfather in a new way. That she snatched him from a biddable girl called Gwendoline at one of those Saturday-night dances. That they married in a spring shotgun wedding five months later. That Roland left home under cover of night at 16, his goodbye note largely instructions for feeding his pet cockatiel. That my grandfather and the bird, both gifted and prolific whistlers, were from then mutually devoted. Things I never knew about; the oddments and scraps that roughly make up life's essentialism.'

Lucy says nothing, chin still in hands. 'I feel lucky,' Robin continues. 'Lucky to have this time with her. But there's also a feeling that's occult-adjacent, as if I've been granted admittance to a roped-off realm.'

'Do you mean The End?'

'The End, and what comes before; the definitive last lap of a life.' He coughs. 'If you know what I mean.'

She shakes her head. 'I don't, actually. I'm all goosebumpy hearing you describe it.'

He refills their glasses. He is finished. 'When did you first come to The Scarlet Ibis?'

'Who can say?' They're quiet for a stretch, Lucy surveying the room. 'There used to be a white baby grand in the corner,' she says at last. 'The tables made up with peach carnations and peach napkins folded into swans. My parents had dinners with their friends – '85, '86, so I must have been five – the kids beneath the table in the sway of stilettos and painted toes, falling asleep to glasses tinkling like tiny bells. I've been trying to recreate that mood ever since.'

There are no carnations, but a vase of frosted lilies is set upon their table, divesting powdered saffron and an intense basal scent. The rust flecks on cream petals remind Robin of blood poisoning, an effusion that coursed up his arm once after meeting a rusty nail on the farm.

'There were nights like that at Roland's,' he ventures. 'Those nights go on forever when you're a kid. But I don't remember flowers or napkins: just lots of smoking and loud music, people necking on couches.'

'Including Roland?'

'Not that I recall. I read this interview with Ian McCulloch from Echo & the Bunnymen where he described the process of writing love songs. He said he used those experiences to fantasise about a greater, more powerful life. You're in the throes of infatuation, but the actual love-object isn't the woman; the love-object is the song itself. That's Roland – that's his whole manifesto, as far as I can tell.'

'Are you ever going to let me meet him?'

He has held her off for six months now. 'I'm working up to it,' he says. 'Separation of church and state, etc. If you want me to talk about my father, then tell me how you came to be married at 21.'

'Oh, that,' says Lucy. 'Are you sure? It's rather grubby and demeaning.'

'You have my full attention.'

She lights a cigarette and exhales. Victor was her editor, she says. When she was 17, she used to slip her fanzine under the magazine door. One day, he caught her in the act and gave her a stack of singles to review; because she was cute and eager, she supposes, and because the last reviewer had gone AWOL. This became a regular column, and she'd cut school to spend whole days at the office, transcribing interviews, arms loaded with promos. Heaven. When she turned 18, she started reviewing shows and would take the last train – the 12.58 – home to her parents afterwards.

'Except one night I missed it, so I stayed in Victor's spare room. He lived in the loveliest old terrace house; walls covered with books, records, and CDs. His girlfriend Celeste was a costume designer who collected old corsets, standing ashtrays, modernist vases. I was enraptured by their things, their house, their life. But then my flight to the adult world had started much earlier.'

She gives a précis of her mostly only-childhood: Strawberry Shortcake birthday cakes with homemade dresses to match; note-perfect Alice in Wonderland costumes for book week. Being taught to read with flashcards as a toddler. Being hoisted on her dad's shoulders after Chinatown dinners, surveying the world from a temporarily safe vantage. And then a sudden reorientation at 12 when the twins were born two months premature. The girls had been ok after a few anxious months but had colic and asthma, then a cascade of autoimmune problems. No one in her family had coped very well; Lucy's mother especially.

The waitress arrives with their seafood basket: mussels, oysters, a disk of dubious pink. Lucy extracts a prawn, swings it by the tail, and lets it drop. 'Nothing compared to losing a parent, obviously, but being abruptly left to my own devices was still rather a jolt. Because by implicit agreement, I was an adult then, with the attendant freedoms and responsibilities. My initial reaction – the correct one – was diligence, taking over cooking and night shifts with the twins. Taking plates to my mother in bed. I've talked about this before, but I enjoyed the rituals: the baby-soothing and bottle-boiling while MTV hummed in the background. I enjoyed being self-sufficient and helpful. Just the same, after two years, I progressed to covert revolt: turning feral and staying feral. Minor insurrections at first – ditching school to read in the library; Updike, *Prozac Nation*, *Praise*. Ditching school to haunt record stores; poring over liner notes and edging towards the goths, trying to see without being seen. Smoking weed in cars, smoking Beedies at university parties. But then I saw Pop Will Eat Itself and Nine Inch Nails back-to-back at 15, and it rearranged the furniture of the goddamned universe.'

'Alternative Nation. I was there too,' says Robin. Ecstatic suspension, sheets of light, the taste of smashed keyboards in his mouth. 'I think everyone was there.'

'Or claims they were.'

They've finished the bottle. Lucy motions, near imperceptibly, for another. 'It was transcendental, right? Going through the mirror and never coming back. By the time my parents had the energy to tap back in, I'd found a whole other life: friends with cars and share-houses, art openings and gigs and dinner parties. I'd been electrified by demoniac blue-black want, and I was *done* with parents.'

The atmosphere changes shape. Inside, a piano appears from nowhere, then deflates: just a tablecloth in slow shake and release. Robin puts on his glasses. The wine has gone straight to his head, lungs, legs; blood thickening. Lucy takes out her earrings and works off her rings, arranging them on the table. She's wearing an oversized cardigan covered in raised snowballs of yarn, hair pulled messily into a top-knot. There's a snaggle-toothed imprint on her finger. She looks alarmingly young.

'So from baby goth to child bride, then.'

'Not intentionally. Victor and Celeste were nearing 40 when I met them, impossibly adult. They were very kind, very parental, but behaved as if we were equals – an irresistible combination. It was the days of milk and honey when record companies still had cash. Victor would call a different rep every Friday to take us to lunch, and we'd stay at the bar 'til late: drinking, talking, chain-smoking. I'd drink until I literally fell off my stool; 45 kilos, trying to match these big guys, being put to bed by Victor and Celeste afterwards. The idea that he was purposefully getting me drunk didn't occur until much later; the idea I'd been put on lay-by at 17.'

'Gross.'

'Yes. Naturally, I got crushed-out too – Victor had this white denim jacket that killed me. But it was the attention that wore me down, and we slept together when Celeste was away. I'd told him once I'd never fucked anyone, a cheap lie designed to foster intrigue, but it had the unfortunate effect of making him infatuated.'

Robin pushes his plate back. '*What do you call a bad man? The sort of man who admires innocence.* It's a weird thing to find exciting.'

'Yes, but clearly, I had his number. And off we went, sneaking around, disgracing ourselves. Victor's teenage girlfriend died when they were both young, so shades of Nabokov there; I was

21, doing my dream job and perpetually wasted – significant fumes of obsession fuelling us both. He left Celeste and rented an apartment. By then, I was at uni. I couldn't get a student allowance because of my parents, but by a bureaucratic quirk would be eligible – emancipated, ha! – if I was married. Victor suggested this, jokingly at first, then not. Insane, patently, but neither of us possessed especially good judgement. It happened at City Hall, a party at the pub afterwards – no family, all industry, including Julian, weirdly. He'd started doing sound at gigs, becoming part of that scene. Victor got blotto: I had to drag him up the stairs afterwards.'

Robin refills his glass, making a mess of it. 'How did your parents react?'

'They didn't, really. Probably because I didn't tell them until things ended with Victor. I think they'd have preferred not being told at all: everyone was mortified, especially me. I realised at once I didn't want to be married, even for administrative purposes. That Victor repulsed me. That I'd only wanted someone to teach me about serial commas and pat me on the head; tell me I was talented occasionally, tell me I was doing a good job. People can positively *sniff* when you've been under-parented: you're easy fare.'

'If I have children,' says Robin, 'I will protect them with every sinew in my being. I'll smother them. I'll . . .' He grasps for an intensifier. 'I'll *microchip* them.'

'Me too,' says Lucy. 'Because we moved so often, I'd developed the habit of using my refraction across others to figure out how I fit – a useful strategy. But then I started using that refraction to judge who I *was* – the looking-glass self. What did Victor think of me? Julian? Tabitha? Gudrun? You?'

She empties the bottle into her glass. 'It's a stupid way to live. That contortion and recalibration is exhausting, causing you to behave in absurd ways: either being over-accommodating or making yourself repellent so people will leave you alone. It ends in narcissism.' She fixes him with a brittle, unyielding look. 'I know, Robin, in case you wondered. I know I'm a narcissist. I know I'm unbearable to be around.'

'Only occasionally. Like when you call me Eeyore.'

She smiles briefly. 'Anyway, Victor's drinking became problematic, or I saw it had always been problematic. Falling-down-stairs, sleeping-at-work, coughing-up-blood problematic. He quit the paper and took a shit-hot government arts job, putting me forward as editor before he left. *What trust*, I'd thought then. *What affirmation.* As it turns out, the magazine was bordering on bankruptcy, so why not give it to a 22-year-old girl with everything to prove; a force of mania who'd plough her entire being into the job?

'Victor, too, realised he'd made a grave mistake in marrying me. He started going to Celeste's at night and telling her as much. Our relationship was predicated on me revering him, and him fetishising me – feelings that fell over fast. I stomped out of our last dinner because he was extinguishing cigarettes in the lamb and walked across four suburbs to see Pink Fist – they'd just released their first EP. Julian was DJing, and we barely knew each other, but I let myself into his booth with two beers. Inky was so magnetic, so angry; the words of "Very Good Advice" landing like grenades. Julian and I edged closer in holy-shit incredulity because it felt like Siouxsie and the Banshees' first show at the 100 Club, or our imagined version thereof. It was a nuclear event. Afterwards, I went back to the apartment and packed my stuff. I took eight grand from this stash of Victor's: money he used to skim from the magazine, his rainy-day money. I told him it was tax on an ill-advised investment.'

'Your drawer of 10s and 20s.'

'The very same. And that Pink Fist show *was* honestly a nuclear event, Robin. I set fire to Victor's canon and finally had my own agenda. The record company guys we'd been drinking with were made redundant. There were new indie labels, new bands forming every week, parties in condemned factories and old toilet blocks, outfits sewn for every event – total delirious opulent deviance. People dismiss electroclash, but it was my first experience of omnisexual music, of omnisexual life. At school, even the suggestion you mightn't be 100 per cent straight would get you punched in the face. The paper was full of typos because everyone – the writers, the office – was high or exhausted or coming down, but it felt vital: the opposite of Victor's manicured mortuary for guitars.'

'Was Tabitha around then?' Robin can't quite picture her in this milieu.

'Oh, yes. Tabitha was right in the messy thick of it, braiding everyone's hair at parties, burrowing to the middle of the make-out piles. The Tabitha you know is largely reformed – unlike Gudrun and me.'

'And Julian?'

'Julian was our patron saint. Jules, the Byronic ideal with his bottomless crate of records.'

'And how did you conquer this ideal?'

'I didn't – we conquered each other: at the beginning, anyway.' She tells him it was a slow build, stretched over agonising months. The low drone of portent as she taxied to a party. Of whipping through the gamma flashes of the Eastern tunnel, emerging with the conviction her life would soon attain substance. Julian answered the door, and she'd never been so happy to see anyone: *never*. He'd said he'd been hoping she'd materialise all night. There had been pills and dancing, then they took possession of a bedroom, doing everything but fuck while people came in and out, asking for cigarettes, or apologising, or stopping to talk, or giving them more pills. By morning – sitting against the refrigerator as the sun rose, a crocheted blanket over their knees, knuckles bruising knuckles – she was gone, ruined, utterly possessed.

'How do you eat so many pills without dying, Lucy?'

She regards Robin. This is the wrong question.

'How do you drink as you do without dying? How do you smoke all that weed without your brain turning to mush?'

'Fair.'

'You get wasted to dull life; I get wasted to intensify it. Evading the world of the senses vs being engulfed, as our friend de Beauvoir would say.'

'That's not entirely true. Often, I'm getting wasted so I have enough guts to join the intensity – the engulfment, as you call it.'

She tells Robin that he's smarter than she is. That engulfment should be a sometimes-thing. That it's a volatile state, composed of unstable compounds. She tells him about The Creep and his sudden lurch from weirdness to psychosis. She tells him about the writer – the sweetest sprite-raver of a boy – who died, an overdose Lucy wonders if she might have intercepted were she not so fucking wrapped up in Julian. That by then, the paper was haemorrhaging money, and she outright loathed herself; all previous want collapsing to a single impulse – the easiest line of flight. She'd drafted the book pitch in better times and emailed it to a contact one manic 2am. Luckily it landed, because she'd decided it would have to be the book, New York or the bridge, and New York would have been a disaster.

They sit. 'Sorry, Robin. I realise you didn't ask for most of that story.' He lights a cigarette, passes it to her, and then lights one for himself. Just beyond the balcony, the ocean balters and batters, its lonely rollers milling rock, shell, quartz, husk, skeleton, mica, feldspar, and mollusc into powder, bearing it into the ground. *The fresh bloodless wetness*, thinks Robin. *To have the superb icy electricity of a fish.* He asks if she got a divorce.

'I did. Victor moved back in with Celeste. As far as I know, they're still together, but I don't believe his new job lasted.'

'You must hate him.'

'Sure, but I knew what I was doing. I used Victor to leapfrog into a new life. I just didn't correctly calculate the personal cost beforehand.'

'Do you still feel that way? The bridge, I mean?'

'Not right now. It's impossible to be unhappy in Abergele.'

'Well, it's an impulse I know well, Lucy. Only an illogical person doesn't consider killing themselves in the suite of options.' Robin thinks of Tchaikovsky, walking into the freezing Moscow River after a disastrous nine-week marriage, his pockets full of rocks. Of what was nearly voided, but for Tchaik's brother diving in to rescue him. Robin summons a page from his Philosophy 101 textbook, a passage he'd aggressively highlighted.

'*Do you ask what may be the way to freedom? Ask any vein in your body.*'

Lucy regards him blankly. 'Who sings that?'

'Seneca.'

'Oh god, you really are a Stoic.' She plucks a flake of ash from her lip. 'Julian never considers it. Julian's the happiest nihilist you'll ever meet.'

'And here you are, two nihilists in love.'

'Wouldn't that be a nice ending?' She waves for the bill, her movements brisk and businesslike. 'I'll get a taxi and drop you home.'

Robin dreams of the igloos that night. Lucy's wearing the fisherman's jumper, and they fuck noiselessly against the concrete wall, her waist cold and blueish in the low light. He wakes overheated, cursing. It had been there the whole time, but distant, abstract. Now it contracts, droplets of water cohering to form a pool: not a fleeting want but a chest-crushing need. He calls Roland first thing, understanding this is akin to pitching a safe over a cliff; an action acquiring momentum of its own.

The day is one to be endured. He walks Teddy to day-care and tidies the house, anticipation needling his guts: the very sensation he's spent years garrisoning himself against. He turns on his gear, resents the expectant hums and flickers, and turns it off again. When he lets himself into Lucy's that afternoon, she's lying in the doorway of the study, silver ballet flats propped against the frame. The Chameleons play.

'I've hit a patch of black ice,' she says. 'I dreamed last night the moon fell out of the sky. I haven't written for four days, and I've run out of Temazepam, so I haven't slept much either.' Through the smaller window, the swimming pool has taken on a gangrenous hue. It rains.

'I've got weed,' says Robin.

'That will have to do.' She puts on The Modern Lovers' 'I'm Straight', which Robin guesses is a stab at humour, while he rolls. 'Poor Jonathan Richman, he always sounds like he has a cold,' says Lucy, resuming her prone position. 'Which makes me love him more.'

'He can take this place, and take it straight. Good old Jonathan. I can't take it straight.'

'Neither can I.' She exhales. 'Jesus, Robin, this stuff is strong. Where did you get it?'

'A guy at the hospital.'

'How often do you smoke it?'

'Every night.'

'You're nuts.'

'I need to be on the edge of exhaustion to achieve anything worthwhile.'

'And I need to be on the edge of anxiety. The trick is not going too far over.' Lucy puts on Television Personalities' 'A Family Affair', and Robin lies on a couch, a flash of the summer's heatstroke – that uranium glass tumbler – strobing over him. He keeps very still, enjoying it, occupying it wholly, snapped into reverb-soaked bass.

'Do you have any Neu?' says Robin when the side finishes.

'I have the one on tangerine vinyl.' She makes a vague gesture at the bookcase. Robin puts on 'Hallogallo', and then 'I Love the Sound of Breaking Glass' and 'Everywhere That I'm Not' and 'Making Plans for Nigel', things intended to cheer her.

'Do you have any Felt?'

'Holy shit.' She sits up. 'You're testing me!'

'I'm not!' He is not and stung she'd think it.

'You are! Do not test me, Robin – it won't end well.' She

studies him: his owly eyes flecked with orange, the thick fringe of lashes bleached transparent at the tips, his mended glasses, the violent angles of his narrow shoulders, his faded blue T-shirt, his fine wrists and thin veined hands, the worn strap of his watch, the gold band of his mother's wedding ring. He has the sense, once again, of his nerves turning on one by one under her scrutiny.

She reclines, lights a cigarette. 'What's your favourite song, Robin?' He is forgiven.

'I don't have a favourite song – that's impossible.'

'Julian's is "Harley David (Son of a Bitch)" – I always think of it as being by Serge GainsBourgeois because I can't spell Gainsbourg. Mine is New Order's "True Faith". It's so simple, and the lyrics so inane, but oh god, it's affecting. It made me nostalgic for my childhood at six years old. And I loved Bernard to distraction, his unthreatening schoolboy shoulders. My parents used to have date dinners in the good room Sunday nights, letting me watch *Countdown* in the kitchen while I ate mine. Hence my fixation with any track featuring keyboards from that time. You're so pliable at six – maybe if they'd put on nature documentaries, I'd be a marine biologist. Maybe it's less a case of being what you do repeatedly than what you *think about* repeatedly.'

'You honestly have just one favourite song? That's rather prohibitive.'

'Of course. New Order lost what Peter Hook thought was the best version of "Blue Monday", you know. Stephen Morris was using a tea-kettle cord for the mixer, and it fell out mid-recording. Imagine!'

'Lucy?' Things are getting away from him.

'Yes?'

He hesitates, his swan dive crumpling into a kick ball change.

'Do you have any chicken?'

'I have chicken. I bought it yesterday.'

'Could we make chicken burgers?'

'I only have English muffins.'

'That's perfect.' And so they stumble around the kitchen, frying the chicken and the muffins, hacking slabs of cheese and frying it too, giggling with the ridiculous effort of the endeavour.

Lucy, pale and crooked, eats standing on one leg.

'Why do you stand that way?'

'Oh.' She's embarrassed. 'I broke my foot jumping from a brick fence after sneaking into a public swimming pool one New Year's. I'm supposed to stand on the bad one to strengthen it, but I don't believe it's working.' She rubs her eyes, a plain child now with blotchy skin. 'Tell me why your glasses are held together with sticky tape.'

'I fell asleep wearing them. They snapped when I rolled over.'

'Cute. Well, I feel better, thank you, Robin, or at least I feel different.'

'What should we do now?'

'I should sleep, and you should go home.'

He thinks of her bed, her old floral coverlet, of burying themselves there, a crush of bones, pushing away her dress to get to her ribs; the skeleton of the world. Limbs knotted, ensnared in her hair, entombed in sleep, hiding together until it's safe in the world, or never having to leave at all. It's an urge that's murderous in its intensity. He tells Lucy he's arranged the interview with Roland, then lets himself out.

SUBSTANCE

The day they're supposed to drive to Roland's, Lucy calls Robin with a list of terse instructions. She needs him to break into her house and get the car key from the enamel bowl. She needs her dictaphone from the study. She needs him to get her from the city. And so he sits behind the wheel of the Fiat for the first time, the seat creaking, hoping he can remember how to drive. He plucks a CD from the back seat full of misted jewel cases and coaxes the car through two hours of rocky highway cuttings, the clutch protesting the duration.

As promised, Lucy is waiting outside a petrol station, overnight bag on her shoulder. She slams the passenger door and looks straight ahead.

'Jesus, Lucy, what happened?' Three strips of medical tape along her right cheek cover unfresh dressings. There's a sick mauvey bruise around her eye.

'I went to The Terrible Lakes show, in defiance of my better instincts,' she says, throwing her bag in the back seat, scattering CDs. 'The one with the glassing. Did you hear about it?' Robin has not.

'I swear I'm done with shows. They're overlong and mimetic at the best of times: the unbending formula, the redundant encores. But it takes just one minor grievance, one disproportionate reaction, one broken bottle and – surprise! – full-scale melee. This one was bad: a roomful of barely-contained bloodlust sparking better than kindling would. Real rapey overtones, too.'

'You weren't the one who got glassed, were you?' He flinches at the word rape.

'No, I just got caught in the middle.' She folds her arms by way of punctuation.

'Well, we'll need petrol,' says Robin, and Lucy is opening the door, and he says no, you always pay, and she says it's fine, and he says it's not, and by degrees she relaxes, submits.

Robin buys water, sandwiches, painkillers, baby wipes and potato chips, which Lucy accepts with a thin smile. She gargles water and spits out the window. She wipes her hands. She pops four pills from the blister pack and swallows them in one gulp. She eats.

'Was Julian there?'

'I haven't seen Julian for three weeks. He's out wandering like a ginger tom, a more protracted wander than usual, which I suspect is because he's about to turn 33. He's making a point to himself.'

'I imagine he'll wander back soon enough.'

'Ha! So do I. Julian always comes to Abergele to regenerate; when he feels old and hungry, not certain his life can continue on its charmed path forever. And then, having slept off this uncertainty beneath clean sheets, he's gone.' She presses her cheekbone experimentally. 'Well, too bad for Julian because I've had enough. Julian is a drug that has *worn off.*'

They sit. 'Do you want me to drive?'

'Yes. Yes, please, Robin. And thank you. For collecting my stuff; for collecting me.'

He puts on Boards of Canada and points the Fiat towards the mountain.

The last hour is perilous: the hairpin turns, the Vantablack drop so near to the road, the wind shrieking through the gaps in the soft top. Robin's whole leg cramps with the effort of keeping the speedometer in check; such is the urge to go as fast as he can, so it's over. He wonders if this was a terrible idea, if it might kill them, but he gets to the iron gates, a filigreed pattern of interlocking keys. Opening them takes forever. His hands are numb instantly, his leg still convulsing. Through the windscreen, in the milky light thrown back from the headlights, Lucy is chewing at her finger. The car shudders over a cattle grid, then skates in disconcerting freeform across the soft gravel of the driveway, but they're here. They walk the last stretch, struck with the always-strange feeling of reaching a destination at night.

Roland meets them at the door, opening a gold lozenge of light to the evening. 'Come, come,' he says, clapping their shoulders. 'It's bloody cold out there.'

The house reveals itself unhurriedly: the uneven slabs of sandstone, the worn Persian rugs, the buttery leather furniture crouched to the floor, the topographic swirl of the panelling, the tectonic stone of the fireplace, the Blackmans and the Prestons, the aurelian glow of the lamps. Lucy trails Robin closely as Roland leads them to the kitchen, motioning they should sit. He bangs around, making his venerated tea and offering whisky, both of which they accept. Robin watches Lucy watching: slate benches of a similar vintage to Abergele's slate floors, olive cupboards, heavy beams, a smear of stars through the skylight, an ancient Aga radiating heat. Roland joins them at the table, a hunk of tree trunk pulled from the river when the house was built. Lucy traces the initials carved into its surface, marks of musicians who've eaten there.

'So,' says Roland. He is handsome but mildly so, preserved by 30 years in dark studios: full lips like Robin's, greyed sideburns, heavy-framed glasses, bony fingers, nails cut scrupulously short, sleeves rolled to expose pale, almost hairless arms. He wears frayed Converse high-tops, an old leather jacket, a pressed flannel shirt.

They are polite, not exactly knowing what to say. It has been three months since Robin visited, three months since he's seen his father. Lucy's hand keeps moving to her cheek. Roland asks after Robin's grandmother, Isabella and Teddy, and Robin answers in a rehearsed, formal tone Lucy hasn't heard before. After a civil duration, Roland excuses himself and returns to the studio.

'Excellent tea,' says Lucy.

'Ha,' says Robin. 'I can make it too. It's Assam, always, and strong. Lots of milk and not much sugar; enough to add bass but not enough to taste sweetness.'

Lucy peers into her mug. 'Thank you for bringing me. The wind at Abergele was driving me nuts: those giant windows make you feel like a moth in a glass jar. I promise I'll be in better form tomorrow.'

'We've missed dinner. Are you hungry?'

She shakes her head.

'Me neither,' he says. 'Come on; I'll show you your room. I think Toni Halliday slept there once.'

They wind back through the lounge room to a smaller sitting room beyond. Hexagonal club chairs in orange, two wall-height portraits by Anton Corbijn, a pencil cactus scraping the ceiling, a paper lightshade hovering like a hot-air balloon. He is grateful that Lucy, in her depleted state, doesn't exclaim over these things. He nearly has them to the hallway when she stops. On the sideboard is a four-foot terracotta horse, front leg eternally bent, head cocked so terracotta ringlets curl over its brow – the guardian of Robin's childhood. It's what's next to it she's interested in, though; a photograph.

'Your mother.'

'Yes.'

'She's beautiful.'

'Yes.'

'Isabella got the Spanish name; you got the English.'

'Correct. I was named after Robin Guthrie.'

'Roland's a Cocteau Twins fan, then.'

Robin coughs. 'Big Robin, as he's called here, is my godfather.'

'Naturally.'

They walk through frigid, low-ceilinged passages to the farthermost of the house; a wing of bedrooms with the clubby air of a Swiss boarding school. He has chosen the nicest for her: bookshelves built into the headboard, a huddle of Depression glassware, a rattan desk. The bed has been made up with soft checked blankets, stiff sheets, hospital corners. Her face is uneasy as she closes the door. Robin takes his usual room further along the hallway, trying to read as the gas heater clanks. He waits, sick.

She knocks 10 minutes later. 'Heya,' she says from the doorway, chewing at her finger again. Fisherman's jumper, black tights, blood on her cheek. 'Could I maybe sleep here? It's been a fresh hell of a week: a cocktail for nightmares.'

'Lucy, your face.'

She touches it; examines her fingers. 'Curses.'

In the en suite, Robin directs Lucy to sit on the bath's edge while he rakes through the cupboards: bars of soap that had been there since the '80s, filmy bottles of cologne. The dressings are soaked through, and he asks if he can remove them. Underneath is worse than he'd expected; an angry tear the length of a sardine. He sets about cleaning while Lucy surveys the bathroom: the Lucite backsplash of primary blue, the red crosses of the taps.

'Do Roland and Isabella get along?' She rolls her wrists in circles, wincing.

'What? Look at the ceiling and stop moving.'

'I asked if Roland and Izzy get along.'

'They do – because Isabella's a much nicer person than me.' He retapes the cut and dabs the slow leach at the edges. 'It's bad, Lucy. You might need stitches.'

'It's fine. I'll be fine.' She sweeps past him to the bed, taking the side where he'd been reading. She smooths blankets around her into a casket shape, a shroud. Robin climbs in opposite, leaving a monastic distance between them. Her hair smells faintly of cigarettes and under that apple-y shampoo. Pupils like swimming pools, a worried tautness at her jaw. Noticing Robin watching her, Lucy snaps out the lamp. Their eyes adjust. 'Was this your room?' she asks, brushing her fingers over the wallpaper, crumpled palm trees.

'Kind of. I lived here for a few months when I was 19. Before that, I had a room next to Izzy's in the main part of the house.'

'What did you do here?'

He turns, fractionally, towards her. 'Washed dishes at a restaurant in town. Took photographs. Learned to ride a horse. Learned to cook by taste. Learned to drive. Learned to identify pine mushrooms and magic mushrooms. Learned not to hate Roland quite so much. Fed the chickens. Missed Isabella. Missed my grandmother. Missed my ex-girlfriend. Read Roland's Sartre and Maugham and Henry Miller and D. H. Lawrence. Found baggies forgotten by bands under the studio couch cushions and dispensed with their contents; tearing down the hill on a bicycle and swimming in the creek, blitzed out of my mind, amazingly not coming to a bad end. Occasionally slept with waitresses. Occasionally did drugs with waitresses. Slept with keyboard players. Slept with a singer. Slept with a bassist.'

'You fucked all The Dandy Warhols, didn't you?'

'Totally. I might have played some guitar and piano; recorded some stuff. I was certainly miserable, a real monosyllabic asshole, dreaming of meeting people like you and Gudrun, Tabitha and Harry.'

'The bands who stayed here – were they obnoxious?'

'Always.'

'No, I mean, you must've been a hopeless temptation, big-eyed and 19 years old, locked atop a mountain. I don't imagine you were doing the pursuing.'

He hesitates. 'Occasionally, they were obnoxious, yes.' She reaches for his hand. It's distracting: her cool fingers, the ridge of her cocktail ring, the glint of the safe in the water below.

'Are you ever embarrassed that, despite our insane privilege, insane by any comparative measure, we find it so hard to be comfortable in the world?'

'Constantly,' Robin says, and destroyed by the drive, by the week, they fall into sleep, fingers interlaced. In the morning, she's gone.

Breakfast smells coming from the kitchen. The easy choreography of Lucy scrambling eggs and Roland cutting bread, making tea. Robin sits and watches them, unsure of what to feel. The bruise around her eye has spread, the dressing ragged, but Lucy is a blue flame turned right up. She has her interview; she has Roland onside. After they've eaten, Roland and Lucy shut themselves in the studio, and Robin does the dishes. He lies on the couch for a while but, stirred by his own blue flame, craving industry and toil, he goes in search of his old books, spending a satisfying duration in appraisal and sorting. After three hours of this, Lucy and Roland emerge.

'Ok?' he says as he passes Lucy in the hallway. Roland is back at work.

She nods, flush with triumph.

'Shall we go for a walk?'

After Lucy has put the tapes in her bag, tucking them away with the care of one swaddling an infant or concealing treasures from customs, they pick through the hall cupboard for coats and scarves. Robin takes an olive oilskin, buttoning it over his camera. Lucy takes a nylon raincoat that trails brash ingenue perfume. It is crystalline cold outside, entirely still. They start up the hill, steadying each other on the slippery grass. Robin points out the goats, Steven and Lloyd. He points out the well from the cover of *No, Nothing, Never*; the cattle jump from *Under an Empty Sky*; the lichened rocks, imposing as shrines, from the cover of *God Without a Church*. He takes photos. As they walk, the countryside unravels around them: the copper verdigris of the church roof, the weeping willows tracing the curve of the stream, a copse of unmatched trees resembling a hastily gathered bouquet; black flecks of faraway cows to one side, white flecks of faraway sheep to the other.

The hilltop is saturated in yellow: the grass, the sky, Lucy's hair. Patchwork fields are showered in the day's last flinty light. Lucy sits suddenly, saying she's woozy, good woozy, and Robin knows what she means. He sits too.

'I haven't seen that camera.'

'It's Roland's old Leica. He said I could keep it.'

'Film?'

'Yup. There's a whole shoebox of the stuff, likely still good.'

'Do you know, Robin, I'm never sure what colour your eyes are.'

He turns away from her without thinking, then forces himself to look back, to hold her gaze.

'They're a bit of everything – segmental heterochromia. Izzy's are the same.'

'I bet there's an album being named *Heterochromia* right now.' The ground ripples in front of them, and Lucy claps her hands. 'Oh, look, a rabbit!'

'I thought you hated animals. Rodents especially.'

'You know I love rabbits! They're the exception to animals that proves the rule. Anyway, bunnies aren't rodents; they're lagomorphs.'

And they're quiet again, sitting side-by-side on the dampening grass. Only when their fingers are numb do they set down the hill again, half walking, half sliding. The house is alight, ludicrously inviting even to Robin, but as they step onto the patio, Lucy snatches the end of his oilskin and tugs him back.

'I'm going to have a cigarette.'

'You haven't smoked all day.'

'I don't smoke when I'm walking – it's the only time I'm not anxious. Also, my lungs can handle walking and smoking, but not both at once.' She shakes her hair from her scarf. 'Have one with me.' Robin acquiesces.

'So tell me why you hate him,' says Lucy, engulfed in her familiar cloud.

'You're going to say how charming and clever he is.'

'No, I'm not. I'm used to people in music being charming and clever. The cunts are especially charming and clever – not that I'd put Roland in that category.'

'Well, I don't hate him. But he left me and Isabella with my grandmother the week our mother died, and we didn't see him for six months.'

'Not once?'

'Not once. And perhaps he was grief stricken, or whatever, but he managed to produce three big albums that year, the albums everyone knows. Isabella has gone through the whole therapy regimen; she's the rational one. In her view, he loves us but wasn't capable of caring for us – still isn't capable – and did the kindest, most sensible thing by giving us to his mother. All true. Except he obviously could have afforded help, or even better, moved my grandmother here.' He pulls his collar higher. 'I had accepted the situation, but lately, all I can see is Isabella looking after people: Teddy, my grandmother, her patients, her husband, me. And I'm trying to look after Izzy and Teddy and my grandmother. Roland, meanwhile, isn't looking after anyone: he's on his toy farm, making albums and doing interviews for *Q* magazine.'

Lucy slides down the wall; crumples to a dramatic sit. 'That's horrible.'

'It's ok. This visit is one of the better ones, and I'm more favourably disposed towards Roland as a result.'

'You must think I'm a total dick. All that hand-wringing at The Scarlet Ibis. You should have told me to fuck off when I asked to interview Roland.'

'I didn't want to; I wanted you to come.' He helps her stand. 'Stop gaping at me like I'm a wounded deer. Let's find something to drink.'

They had decided, without real discussion, to stay another night. Roland makes reservations at the Hungry Hunter, where Robin used to wash dishes, and they retreat to their rooms to get ready, a Saturday-evening vim in the air.

'Robin!' she calls up the hallway. 'Could you do that thing to my cheek again?' She skates into his room without waiting for an answer, black lace flicking at her cream woollen tights. Robin's bathroom is still full of steam, a fact he finds excruciatingly intimate, but Lucy doesn't notice, taking her seat at the bath. This time she moves her wrists in figure eights, hitched to some melody in her head.

'How does it look?' she asks, eyes trained obediently to the ceiling.

'Terrible! How does it feel?'

'Like a story that will hopefully be funny one day.'

The Hungry Hunter is as it's always been; an elegant defiance of time. Plush beige carpet, pools of lilac light coming from nowhere. Roland is shown his usual table by the fireplace and orders like it's 1983: devils on horseback, garlic scampi, Beef Wellington and tiramisu, all catnip to Lucy. She eats with great appetite, dusting the table with damper crumbs, leaving impressionist wine pools around her plate. A shared sensibility crackles between her and Roland. They talk of Delia Derbyshire, Lizzy Mercier Descloux, Fern Kinney, Nona Hendryx, Anna, Vivien Goldman, Vivien Vee and Valerie Dore, but she has pulled her chair closer to Robin; she has chosen a side.

The whole of *Histoire de Melody Nelson* plays, then *Dummy*. People stop by the table and say hello. Roland orders Burgundy, brandy. Robin feels drunker than he should, in rude high spirits, and declares so loudly. Lucy excuses herself.

'You're very warm,' says Roland, touching Robin's forehead.

'It's the fire.' Robin ducks away and Roland smiles.

'Are you ok for money?'

'I am.'

'And so I'm clear, Lucy is not your girlfriend. Your girlfriend is a Meg, who is in New Zealand skiing.'

'Correct,' says Robin.

'Lucy's very articulate. She knows her stuff.'

Robin thinks he may punch Roland. He is also pleased. He says nothing.

'Well, I'm thrilled you're here, Robin. Very glad. You should come up more.'

'You should come down more. Izzy is running herself ragged.'

'You're entirely right.'

The exchange is infuriating, and Robin goes to find Lucy. She's leaning against a bluestone wall outside, breathing smoke and vapour in the big rapturous movements that come to her at night. He lights one of her cigarettes, and they stand, smoking, shoulders not quite touching, borrowed scarves around their necks.

'You ok?'

'Yup.' Robin exhales. 'Is he what you expected?'

'No. I expected a Victor, a raconteur – anecdotes and swagger. But he's a producer's producer. An introvert. A proper craftsman.'

'A Martin Gore, not a Dave Gahan.'

'Exactly.'

They blow smoke at the moon.

'How did you spring from here,' she says, 'big eyed and sweet voiced, a baby Richard Hell, without demanding an album from Roland?'

'Because one, I don't demand things from anybody, least of all Roland, and two, I'm also an introvert. I only sang that night to impress you. I'd have to drink myself dead to do that with any regularity.'

'It's annoying that you're all talent and no desire, Robin, whereas I'm all desire and no talent.'

'I hope that's not true.'

'Well, it's reductive. I'm fairly good at parsing A++ obsession through modest skill; it gets me by. But I'm still annoyed by your surfeit of raw excellence: mainly that it's underused. You should want things more.'

'It's been a year of wanting things more.'

'Good. What will you do next year, then?'

'You mean when my grandmother's dead?'

'Yes.'

'No idea – I don't want to think about it. What will you do when you finish the book?'

'I've no idea either. Find a better repository for my excess excitements, maybe.' She lights another cigarette. 'Music is butter and blood to me, and listening has never been enough – I need to get inside it, inside the people who made it. A Pentecostal fervour crashed through one of my high schools, girls newly concerned about dying, about the concept of hell. They'd get baptised, going to church in chattering packs, inviolable and smug because they'd identified life's fundamental question AND found the answer before turning 17. Which is not to say I was any better or any different. Most teenagers are struck with a strain of religious impulse: mine just happened to be music, borne out in ecclesiastical frenzies along the cliffs with my Walkman. This was when Richey Manic carved "4 Real" into his arm, so the notion of bloodletting, of sacrifice, wasn't a stretch. The other girls – I only paid attention to the girls – got boyfriends and cars, got over religion soon enough. They got sensible jobs and brown leather handbags. But I'm still chasing the god particle.'

'What you're describing is a universal reaction to music, Lucy, not an affliction. It's a rapture any 12-year-old Britney fan understands. Maybe the girls at your high school were just listening to the wrong stuff.'

'Ha!'

'I haven't grown out of it. Roland hasn't.'

'Yes, but you're both *making* things. I'm unpicking the fixations of others – mostly old and dead men. I want work that has a pulse of its own, a sense of inevitability, even if it's only inevitable because of the millions of trivial actions I've enacted until that point. I'm pitching for total action and no thought: all sensation and no feelings.'

'A state of flow.'

'Heightened flow. That urgent shift when the universe clicks into place. The acid hitting your blood. The orchestra picking up their instruments. The declaration that can't be retracted.'

'A safe going over a cliff, then.'

'A *piano* going over a cliff. The best car crash you've ever had. Anyway,' she says, with a full-body shiver, a theatrical stomp of her feet against the chill. 'Let's never discuss the book again. Let's go and drink heavily.'

They get a taxi home, Roland up front talking with the driver, Lucy and Robin in the back seat. Her leg rests gently against his, every point of contact a flare of complex electrical activity. He has the perverse sense of them being children, being driven home well past their bedtimes after a gala night of spaghetti and ice cream.

Roland goes to the cellar for more wine. Robin builds a fire. Lucy arranges herself on the white sofa, smoothing lace over her knees.

'Can I smoke here?' she asks Roland when he returns, his arms full.

'I don't see why not, my dear. Everyone else does.'

Roland and Robin take charge of the stereo, playing ESG, Junior Boys, Love and Rockets, Cleaner from Venus, Margo Guryan, Barry Adamson, The Teardrop Explodes, Machinations, and the new Pilooski Northern Soul edits. The Bösendorfer at which *Nothing Counts* was composed is opened, and Lucy taps out the bottom notes, Roland the top. She stands often – to light cigarettes, to exclaim over a cover, to ask Roland a question and scribble the answer, to dance alone in taut spirals – but always returns to her perch next to Robin, her body folded in a Nabokovian Z. Hours pass. Roland puts the records in their sleeves: a ritual, a bridge, a segue. He kisses Robin and Lucy on their heads and goes to bed.

'You still love it,' says Robin.

'What?'

'Music. The interrogation, I mean, the work of it.'

'Of course I do. I hope I haven't given the impression of being a tragic waif, that the magazine was all bad. I loved the job. It was everything I'd ever wanted, and I delighted in it most days.'

'What did you love?'

'I loved my writers, especially the baby ones hitting their stride. I loved excavating the right words to describe things, so I could transmute the essential thrust of new music while people waited to hear it themselves. I loved the padded envelopes of CDs that arrived every day, giving the godlike sense of knowing everything within a defined sphere, of missing *nothing*. I loved sitting side-of-stage with bands on the ascent, watching bands we revered, holding hands and having oceanic feelings. I loved getting inside the architecture of songs and cracking their particular genius: that Gary Numan's "Cars" is singular because it doesn't have a chorus; that "Are 'Friends' Electric?" is singular because it doesn't have a verse. I loved being told secrets. I loved being a handmaid, a nursemaid. I loved having songs written for me and getting thank-yous in the liner notes. I loved the jigsaw puzzle of the pagination. But no one goes into music because they're well-adjusted and it's a fun career choice – you go into music because it's a compulsion, because you have to, because you won't consider anything else. And there's a finite period you can live in that way.'

'Anyhow.' She stretches, the cuffs of her jumper wine-dyed. 'I leave for Berlin Monday night: my last dance with the vanguard.'

This is news to Robin.

'I told you,' she says, 'I know I did!'

'You did not.'

She considers this. 'Well, I thought about telling you. In detail.'

'How long will you be gone?'

'Only two weeks. I've got cousins there. I booked cheap flights over a year ago, incited by an Ellen Allien mixtape, but to be honest, I've been dreading it since. I'm a lousy flyer, an anxious traveller. Plus, grey days and dark music might be bad medicine right now.'

The idea of going anywhere, after 10 cloistered months in Abergele, is unfathomable to Robin. Driving here had been enough. Still, he says, he wishes he was going to Berlin on Monday.

'I wish you were coming with me to Berlin on Monday.'

Robin puts on *Diamond Dogs* and opens the last bottle. Lucy fills their glasses, lights a cigarette. 'I misheard "Fashion" until

I was 22,' she says. 'I always thought the bourgeois were coming to town.'

'A rare improvement on Bowie.'

'There's no improving on Bowie. Did you go to the concert last year?'

Robin did not.

'My dad texted in the middle of the show, asking me to call. I hadn't heard from him in ages, so I assumed someone had died. "All the Young Dudes" had just started, and I bolted to the foyer, near hysterical. He answered after five rings, calm as ever. He was visiting the city the next day, and might we have lunch? The twins were fine. My second pill had just hit, so in a rush of jubilant relief, I said we should *totally* have lunch, I love you, we don't hang out enough, lunch sounds *wonderful*, etc. Dad asked where I was, dour suddenly. When I told him David Bowie, he said goodnight, Lucinda, I must go. And he hung up.'

'Did you have lunch?'

'I don't recall. I don't imagine so. The issue wasn't that I was clearly chopped to oblivion; the issue was being so loose, so affectionate, so casual with the word love. And *that's* how we do things in my family, Robin.'

'Oh dear. It's not much different in mine, if that's any consolation. What's your dad's take on Bowie?'

'My dad adores Bowie. He's as obsessive about music as I am. Oh well.'

The speakers are excellent. The bass of 'Sweet Thing' treads the floors, a sure-footed animal on the hunt. The piano vibrates the windows in sprays of quicksilver brilliance. The sax slides around their necks, inquisitive. Robin takes Lucy's hand, drawing a thumb across her knuckle. Six months to work up to that.

'I really like you,' says Lucy. 'Which is inconvenient.'

'It's not so inconvenient,' says Robin. 'I'm crazy about you.'

'Shhhhh,' she says, stubbing out her cigarette. 'Silly rabbit.'

It's not clear who reaches for who, but she's in his lap, all soft hair and sharp elbows, eyes enormous in the almost-dark. The hand at the back of his neck is cool, firm. The lightshade swaying behind Lucy is the final quaver before the piano topples over the cliff; an illusion the descent isn't already underway.

'Are we doing this?' Lucy asks. 'Things will sting later, regardless.'

'We should absolutely do this. Things already sting.'

'Ha!' She bends to kiss him.

Their mouths are smoky, dry. Lucy stops and takes a deep drink from her glass; passes it to Robin. He drains it to the sediment. Lucy, who Robin has watched do everything in a manic thrum these last few months, is languorous, serene, economical with her movements. Slow, slow, slow, slow breaths, her tongue slowly pushing into his mouth, her fingers slowly pushing into his neck, the old house shuddering around them. The slow melt into his lap and lithe unstacking of vertebrae as she moves back onto her shins, all engineered to torture. She takes off her fisherman's jumper and he throws it away with the full power of his arm, having finally defeated it. When he pushes her dress over her thighs, fistfuls of lace disintegrate in his hands.

'It's very old; get rid of it,' Lucy says, but the ancient saw-toothed zipper won't budge. She's in his lap again, saying rip it, just rip it, so he does; pulling the tatters over her head and ensnarling a piece of hair. She yanks it free with an audible snap. Robin takes in the stab of her clavicle, a jagged scar sickling her side, the bruise the length of one arm, the bluishness of her waist in the low light. She removes his T-shirt and in a low delighted voice, says you're so skinny, Robin, it kills me, it wipes me out, and his blood clatters. He wraps his hands around her ribs, six months to work up to that, fingers between the hard pleats, and her breath shifts pitch. He gets his left hand into her tights, two fingers inside her. Utter opioid relief.

'Fuck, fuck, fuck,' she says into his throat. 'Is Roland likely to hear us?'

'I think not. I hope not.'

'Good, because I don't want to go anywhere, I don't want to move. You're not getting away from me, Robin.'

'What did you say?' He repositions his hand, three fingers poised. Her teeth are against his neck.

'I said you're never getting away from me.' They watch each other. It's a high-stakes dare, dangled out in the minor keys, capsizing them in different ways. Lucy crushes one arm around his neck and bends the other across her eyes, turning her head away in silent convulsion. Well, she says at length, as we were. She stands, stumbles, peels away her tights, and pours more wine. She sits back on the couch, watching as he takes off the last of his clothes. He drains his glass and they kiss, heedless ravening life-ruining kissing that runs on and bonelessly on. She shifts, one hand hard at his jaw, the other on his shoulder. The thumb in his clavicle, pulling him in, is strikingly unbearably tender. 'This,' she says, with a prolonged intake of breath, 'is not what I expected, Robin.'

'How does Julian fuck you?' It's out of his mouth before he realises, but not undeliberate.

'As if it's a competition,' she says. 'Or a job he happens to be good at. One tires of it.'

They keep their movements compact, tight against each other, trying to be as quiet as possible. There's a distant creak, and they both freeze. Robin says it's just the house, and they begin again; Lucy says they should probably get a condom and stops to dig through her bag. As they move back into each other, Robin, without thinking, takes her face in his hands, and she stiffens, mute with pain. The cut. She looks as if she might vomit. He apologises over and over, and she whispers it's ok, it's really ok, and turns, angling her back to his chest. He manoeuvres a hand under her hip, and they shift again. 'This is my very favourite thing,' she says, voice blitzed and gauzy, and that completely undoes him. The record ends and jumps in its groove. The fire wheezes, collapses.

They collect their things, tiptoeing with the pantomime stealth of the very drunk along the hall to his room. The sheets are two panes of ice. Robin is even more intoxicated now – lethal accumulation, the ceiling moving – and knocks over the bedside lamp. The crash and resultant shatter sound far away. Oh god, he says, we need water, and Lucy is off and back with two glasses. She holds one to his mouth.

'Thank you,' he says. 'It's like that day.'

'What day?'

'When I had heatstroke and you brought me water. I had a filthy dream on your couch.'

She sets down her glass with a clatter. 'Really?' Her cheeks are two bright spots. 'You should have told me.'

'I couldn't,' he says. 'I had an excruciating hard-on, and a fever, and you were leaning right over me – it was torture.'

They're crushed together again, knotted into a dense constellation without effort, talking in low voices of the other days, the other places, the missed possibilities. You should have told me about your dream, she says, even if you were too sick to do anything, Robin, oh, the things I'd have done to *you*. He pushes her hair back from her face, very careful this time, and gathers it in a tight fist at her nape. More, she implores, and the atmosphere sharpens. They set to work, total obliteration. He bites the inside of his mouth accidentally and loses time, forgetting where he is, the metallic taste on his tongue confusing his senses, and they're much louder than before. She takes one of his hands and holds it against her mouth, biting at the thenar eminence. And so it goes.

Robin wakes late. They didn't close the curtains, and the light through the window is blinding grey.

Lucy is zipping her bag, fully dressed in jumper and boots, hair wet and straight, cheek worse than yesterday. There is blood on the pillows – from his mouth, from her face – and glass mottling the floor.

'Robin,' she says gently. 'We've gotta go. I haven't packed.'

The sentence makes no sense. He takes his glass into the bathroom and closes the door. The capillaries in his right eye have burst. He gargles, vomits feebly, cleans his teeth, and angles his head under the tap so icy tank water sluices his face. He scrabbles around the cupboard for anything that might dull things.

Lucy watches him crawl back into bed.

'Berlin,' she says. 'I'm flying to Berlin tomorrow night.

I haven't packed. I've no clue where my passport is. I need to get back to Abergele.'

He pulls a pillow across his face. 'I beg you, Lucy, lie down for a minute. I may be dying.'

Lucy regards him. She kicks off her boots, turns back the sheet. They lie face to face. He puts a thumb through the belt loop of her skirt, pulling her to him. He is still naked. She runs a hand over the planes of his back, waist, thighs; kisses his forehead, his eyelids, his mouth. 'You're extraordinarily beautiful, Robin; you have no idea. If you did, you wouldn't be so nice.' She bends her head to butt his forehead, gently, faunlike.

It's unbearable. They attack her jacket, her jumper, her skirt, her tights. Robin spans his hand across her lower back, slips an index finger and thumb into the two indents there; the relief of it.

'We've got 10 minutes,' she whispers, pushed up on her arms, holding things in terrifying suspension. 'Ten.'

Robin is very ill as they say their goodbyes, and Roland hugs him for a beat longer than usual. 'Are you alright?' he asks, and Robin nods, completely sapped of the will to perform. 'Just hungover, very hungover,' and Roland nods, clearly understanding, clearly glad nothing is required of him.

In daylight, the landscape is exposed in all its shocking grandeur. Shelterbelts of hoop pine alternate with trembling chorus lines of willow myrtle. The corrosive hand of winter is across everything: clenched fists of fading hydrangeas, skeletal outlines of thistle, broken umbrella heads of wild dill, the sulphuric blaze of European poplars. A felted sweep of grass brushed in one direction suggests strong wind, although the air is utterly still. It's a winter that never touches Abergele: roofs pitched steeply against the threat of snow, sheep in full coats and chocolate socks and mittens, smoke rising from kinked stone chimneys, cattle grids furred with frost. Lucy drives, and Robin rests his forehead against the window, everything painful in its intensity: the patchworked tin sheds, the odd little hills without context. She navigates the pass without expression, edging along the hairpin turns. Massed ferns soften the awful drop to the left.

At the bottom of the mountain, Lucy stops for petrol, and it's Robin's turn to sit inert in the passenger seat. She returns with a Coke for each of them and cigarettes, and they're off again, the Fiat gobbling yellow lines and spitting them out. She keeps a steady 20 kilometres over the speed limit and fields race by: ducks perched on the backs of drowsy cows, occasionally sparrows on the backs of the ducks. She grinds through the gears; powerlines bisect the darkening sky. She asks him to light her a cigarette. He takes this as a cue to start talking.

'So.'

'So,' says Lucy from her shroud of smoke. 'That was fun.'

'Indeed.'

'And clearly, no one can know.'

They drive.

'I'm not sure what you had in mind, but Meg has a vile temper, and I'm on unsteady ground as it is, so please, let's leave it for now.' It isn't evident if this unsteady ground pertains to Meg or things generally.

'You told me to want more, Lucy.'

'That's not exactly what I meant.'

'Right.'

She speeds up, gravel spraying from a rear wheel.

'Luce, could you slow down?' She ignores him, her profile inscrutable.

'I'd love for you to slow down. Or better yet, stop.'

She pulls into a shoulder. The clouds have rendered the sky monochrome. They park next to a field of trees bending crone-like to the ground and climb from the car. More of the blue-green rocks rise with the regularity of tombstones. 'Where's that Leica, Robin? You should be taking photos.'

He retches pointlessly over the grass. 'How are you not puking right now?'

She smiles, her first that day. 'I've had plenty of practice. On nights like that' – the 'that' is vague – 'booze barely makes a dent. Don't worry; it'll get me soon enough.'

They lean against the Fiat, flank to flank.

'Once,' she says, 'when I was much younger, I found myself in a car with friends who were a bit older, and a man who was much older, 30 maybe – a big shot of some description. We took these crazy-strong pills and drove to an amusement park where the attractions hung over the sea. Everything was intense retina-scorching neon, blurred out. We rode on the rollercoaster: tracks roaring like the first seconds of a California earthquake, crushed together, screaming. It felt like I was on the edge of a terrible dream, but my whole body vibrated with excitement. And drugs, I guess. When we got back to the city, the man pulled alongside a square full of statues – Madonnas and peeing cherubs – stroked my face, said I seemed nice, and told me I didn't want to be there. He gave me $50 for a taxi and drove away.'

'And?'

'It was terrifically insulting, but correct: I didn't want to be there.'

'What did you do?'

'I kept the 50 and took the train home. It's obvious now it's because I was underage, but I like to think there was kindness in there, too.'

Robin rubs his eyes, getting the fists right into the sockets. 'I don't understand what you're saying.'

'You have been wary of me this year, correct?'

He hesitates. 'Sometimes, yes.'

'Right, well, number one, that hurts my feelings, and number two, that wariness deserves your attention.'

'So you're handing me a 50, pushing me from your car.'

'Yes. I'm not burning down my life to be another thing that happens to you, Robin. You don't get that after sleeping with someone once.'

He nudges her foot with his. 'More than once, if I remember correctly.'

She kicks him back, jangles the keys. 'Come on, Christopher Robin; I have a flight to catch. Can you hold it together until we get to Abergele?'

Back on the highway, she drives with more care, past llama farms and chestnut farms and the slow rotation of faraway wind farms. It rains. She puts on 'Bela Lugosi's Dead', tapping out the skittering drums on the steering wheel. 'This was recorded in one take,' she says. 'It was Bauhaus's first time in a studio; Peter Murphy's first time singing into a mic.'

'Oh god, stop!' he says, covering his face. 'Lucy, please stop!'

'Stop what?'

'Stop with the Bauhaus talk! I can't do it right now.'

'You stop!' The car veers left, and Lucy jerks it savagely back on course. 'Stop yelling or I'll crash, and it might not be an accident.' And so Robin shuts his eyes, the only available line of flight. He's soon asleep, head bouncing against the glass. He doesn't wake until they're on the outskirts of Abergele, where Sundayness has settled in a fog. The sprawl contracts and the lake unfurls. She slows outside his house, at last exhausted.

'Robin, listen. I'll be back in two weeks, ok?' Her hand is at her face again, the right socket pillowy, inflamed.

'Your poor eye.'

'*Your* poor eye. Jesus, Robin, you look demonic.' They have returned to themselves, and it's an immense relief.

'I feel demonic. The room was full of blood and broken glass when we left.'

'That's my speciality.' She leans and hugs him, arms tight around his neck. Her jumper smells of fireplaces, a humidity that clings to them both. The seats creak, the rain thickens. 'Just don't tell anyone, don't do anything, and we'll talk when I get back.' She pushes him, not without affection, not without force. 'Go.'

A few days later, Robin receives a text from Lucy that reads, 'I just want you to know, when I do it, it's with the thought of you.' Five hours later, he gets another: 'Sorry. I was out, overdoing it. Disregard.'

GAME AND PERFORMANCE

September 2004

Tabitha and Harry invite Robin around for dinner. He arrives with two bottles of the best red he can afford at seven o'clock. It's a house of two academics: plump armchairs and runty cats, broadsheets and periodicals, highlighters and index cards, ashtrays and oil heaters. Tabitha makes lamb shanks with puy salad, and they get drunk to Tom Waits.

He watches her cook in the snug kitchen, jars of lentils winking on the shelves. Tabitha's pixie cut has grown out so locks of hair fall around her face – tawny tortoiseshell chunks of brown and auburn and caramel. Her movements are even, precise, considered; reflective of the care she takes with her citations, her vinyl, her mother's old jewellery, with other people. Tabitha in her autumnal show-jumping wardrobe of cords, tweeds, trenches, wool and buttered leather, most of it second-hand, most of it carefully repaired. Tabitha in heather tights and old riding boots, carefully measuring ingredients, carefully wiping the benches after herself, immune to the wilder flame-outs that engulf the rest of them. Tabitha in control of her winged horses.

She catches him at it. 'Stop it,' she says. 'Get me wine for the sauce.'

They eat at a round table, cats winding about their ankles, discussing things they never discuss on the terrace. He guesses, or hopes, that Tabitha and Harry are his friends, even outside the magnetised points of Lucy's orbit. The marimbas of 'Clap Hands' clatter like wet bones. The windows fog. Harry dances with his plate of poached pears held aloft, pulling Tabitha in for a slow corkscrew twist as she passes. Robin asks her what she's working on.

'I've got an article due next week on the cult of perfect taste. How the Vita Sackville-Wests of the world signal their wealth and cultural authority with mouse-eaten cushions and threadbare jumpers. It's more involved than that, but you get the drift. And then I've got to return to the PhD, unless I get hit by a car, just a bit – which might be a blessing. Those goddamn genius directors and their goddamn genius videos; it's getting to be a real slog.' She posits, through wine-red teeth, that genius is nothing more than neurodivergence, persistence and luck.

'What about Tom?' says Harry. 'You cannot say that Tom Waits isn't a genius.'

'I'm sure he's a lovely guy,' she retorts, motioning for Harry to pour her another drink. 'A lovely, obsessive guy who drives his wife nuts. But he's not a genius. Believing in genius is as lazy as believing in god.'

'As the son of a supposed genius, I'd agree,' says Robin. He files away those three words, neurodivergence, persistence, luck: ammunition in a mute, one-sided battle.

At some point, Tabitha goes to clean her teeth and doesn't come back. Robin and Harry set about murdering a quart of Scotch. 'Genius!' says Harry. 'Tabitha will vanquish your every whimsy.' And Robin asks if Lucy doesn't vanquish his whimsies too, all their sparring over Prince, and Harry laughs and knocks his glass onto the floor where it bounces, a coda of satisfying plinks. 'That's just Lucy having loud feelings. But Tabitha's arguments are made from spider's silk: you will never, ever best her. Believe me.'

They're slurring now. Robin produces his weed, Harry produces his tobacco, and they fashion an immoderate joint. He asks Harry what he's working on and Harry says, 'Life!', motioning around him, and then gives Robin a flyer for an exhibition he's part of next week. And Harry asks Robin what he's working on, and Robin has to say nothing really, music when the house is empty, which isn't often. And photos here and there, but maybe it's time he took it more seriously. And Harry, pushing a sheaf of newspapers from the couch so they can sit, says that Lucy had mentioned as much.

'What exactly did she mention?' says Robin through a lungful of smoke. He is not unsusceptible to this: triangulating the self through the opinions of others.

Harry puts on Ace Frehley's 'New York Groove' at a volume sure to wake Tabitha. 'How good your photographs are, how great you are, the recitation of your many worldly virtues.' He dances with the speakers in triumphal movements; unworried, unhurried. And he tells Robin, in a convoluted way, about a conversation Lucy had with Tabitha back in March, in which Lucy told Tabitha she was in love with Robin, a conversation Tabitha recounted to Harry after the boat trip. How everyone has been waiting, and disappointed nothing has come of it. That Tabitha thinks Meg is having the first truly good sex of her life, which is why she's putting up with this.

'Jesus,' says Robin.

He gets home at threeish, vomits prodigiously, and crawls under the covers without undressing. He doesn't remember the exchange until much later.

The exhibition is a group showing with some artists Harry met on one of his gregarious rambles around Abergele, held in reclaimed water board offices. Robin arrives alone and accepts a glass of cask wine. Harry's photographs are a surprise: blown-out abstractions in blazing pigments of red, orange, sulphur. Those careless clicks on the houseboat decoded – not careless at all. The effect is replicated in hand-painted, hand-sewn cushions along the floor; amorphic and intensely huggable. Robin goes looking for another drink, warm and pleased, pleased that Harry's work is so good, pleased that he knows him. And there, at the entry, is Julian.

It's a technicolour assault: Julian in a jumper of lurid knitted parrots that could only be intentional in its ugliness, his hard fall of hair, his commanding height. It takes a moment for Robin to realise Lucy is tucked into his side; the shock doubly compounded by the recoil.

'Robin!' Julian claps him on the arm, charming as always. He mentions drinks and is swallowed by the room.

Lucy kisses Robin on the cheek without meeting his eyes. Her hair is shorter, lopped to a chin-length bob and ironed scalpel straight. She is noticeably thinner, seemingly taller, tired. Fitted black dress high at her neck; gold cuffs weighing down both wrists.

'How was Berlin?' he asks.

'Cold. I think I arrived 20 years too late, but that's true of every place I visit. Still, I found enough abjection to fill five books, once I broached the stairs and discovered the right clubs.'

'Your cousins know Berlin well, then.'

'Oh. No, I ended up staying with friends, performance-art electro kids I met through the magazine. They live above a bar called Zu Mir Oder Zu Dir – Your Place Or Mine. Clever.'

'I thought you were getting home tomorrow.'

'Nope, yesterday.' Her affect is off, her eyes flat.

They stand at the room's centre. Helen's 'Witch' plays loudly, the gallery now full of people Robin doesn't recognise. He gets the sense he often does with Lucy; that he's in a minor-key '80s movie whose plot machinations are evident to all but him. The serrated cut still blooms under her eye, dulled with make-up.

'Sorry,' he says.

'What for?'

'I'm not sure.'

'It's fine,' says Lucy, looking over his shoulder. 'Although I specifically asked you not to do anything, not to break up with Meg. There are rules and etiquettes around these things, Robin.'

'You can't ask that of someone. It had more than run its course.'

'Especially since she was pregnant.'

Robin steps back a fraction, stung. 'She hasn't been pregnant since July, and I didn't know about it until last week. How do you know?'

'Julian has knocked up three people in my circle – at least. You should compare notes with him.'

Her gaze is still over Robin's shoulder.

'You're being a dick, Lucy.'

'Well, she called today, Robin, and it was like being 14 again when Meg, belle of the ninth grade, ended me overnight. Complete ostracisation; the foulest insults and folded notes and graffiti arrowed from every direction, so I couldn't even walk to the library to eat lunch alone without someone calling me a dumb slut, or – illogically, given this was supposedly over a boy – breaking my nose for being a dumb lesbian. At which point, I just stopped going. My parents made me finish the term at an even worse school, and then we moved to the next place. So yes, you're right – I'm not very nice. I haven't been nice for ages.' She taps a cigarette neatly from its case and looks at him for the first time that night. 'Finally, we're getting to know each other properly.'

On one of those caustic October days, wind whittled to inflict utmost discomfort, Robin sets out for a walk, avoiding the desire lines of the cliffs in favour of the beach. Lucy has beaten him – calf-deep in water, dress plastered to her legs, fisherman's jumper in Muppety animation as she conducts the waves.

Now and then, he hears the Fiat groaning up the hill and hiccupping back down. He's taking out the garbage one morning, and the Trans Am burns past. He braves the walking track and steps over one of Lucy's fuzzy gloves, lolling in a puddle.

Tabitha drops by one afternoon with some of his books. He'd been asleep on the couch.

'Oh dear,' she says when he opens the door.

Robin has the disorientation that comes from sleeping too much at the wrong time, the particular kind that comes from trying to sleep away bad feeling, or in Robin's case, several concurrent bad feelings. The shrill alarm sounding the approach of imminent grief. Acute self-disgust. Generalised nausea of life compounded by too much to drink; not enough to eat. The old cocktail of exhaustion, dislocation and guilt, poured out in toxic new measures. He finds his glasses on the rug. Putting them on improves matters marginally.

Tabitha is in the kitchen opening cupboards, making tea. It's her first visit to his house.

'How's Meg?' she asks, setting a mug beside him. He knows she must know. That, by extension, everyone must know everything.

'We're not talking. She said there's part of me missing, which I suspect is correct.' He doesn't mention the scenes of the last month. His seasick euphoria as he worked up to ending things, the imagined relief, then Meg's hail of invectives as she pulled apart his room. That he'd let her into his life with no real emotion or intention. That he'd let her ferry him to the hospital all year, let her comfort him after these visits – like a vampire. That's he's an alcoholic, a cheat, a sneak, a robot impersonating a person. That she'd quietly had an abortion – the day before Lucy's birthday party, in fact – because it wasn't something he could be trusted with. Everything she accuses him of is, to a greater or lesser extent, true.

He doesn't mention Meg returning to interrogate Isabella, or her call to Lucy. He doesn't mention that he's only just realising how badly he behaved, not just this time, but all the times. That Robin, feeling as insubstantial as he does, skating across the surface of life, never thought he could be the source of such fury. That he's only just perceiving the things that girlfriends conjure around him, filling the irresistible silence of what might be voids. That he lets this happen, passivity becoming the defining narrative flatline of his existence.

'Meg has her parents and her own friends; she'll be ok,' says Tabitha. 'Although she did call me last week, asking how long things had been going on between you and Lucy. I said it had little to do with me, and your account would be the fullest, but I don't think she found that satisfactory.'

He removes his glasses, pushes his fists as deep into the sockets as they'll allow.

Tabitha is gentle. 'Robin, what did you expect to happen? What did you want?'

'I'm not sure.' Isabella has asked the same questions.

'Well, that's something to consider. Lucy is never not thinking, problem solving. She turns things over obsessively, testing every conceivable outcome to every conceivable end, doubling back to check her work. And in the morning she starts anew. Whenever she's smoking or walking, that's what she's doing: ruminating, recalibrating, world-building, world-burning. So if you're going into a situation with her without considering what you truly want, then you're going in unarmed.'

'Unarmed! Ha!' He has picked this up from Lucy. 'What did she say?'

'Babe.' She cocks her head. 'I'm not telling you what she said.'

'How is she?'

'Unbearable. Eating Dexies by the handful to finish these last chapters; subsisting on cold sausages, tomato juice and cigarettes. It's worrying, to be honest. You should talk to her. You're both being ridiculous – 25 is old enough to sleep with someone you like and have a proper conversation about it afterwards.'

'She has emphatically cut me out, Tabitha.'

'Yes, she does that: the editrix and her neat expulsions. But I don't expect this one is final. She threw Julian out of a hotel after a three-day kamikaze sex bender, threw her phone out of a car, junked her job and apartment, and decamped to Abergele. An emphatic The End. And what happened? Julian was on her doorstep two weeks later with a toothbrush in his record bag – Julian, who I can't imagine makes a habit of packing toothbrushes – and they've been building ritualistic chemical fires ever since. The whole thing looks exhausting to me, but some people go to dramatic and complicated lengths to get off.'

Robin drains his tea.

'Go and talk to her. Take bread. Get her out of the house.'

'Ok.'

'Good. Now, do you need anything?'

He hesitates. He wants to crawl into her lap, die there.

'Do you think I could borrow your car tomorrow morning to visit the hospital?'

'Of course.' She squeezes him. 'You can borrow the car anytime. But go to Lucy's, Robin.'

*

He doesn't go to Lucy's. But he finds her on AOL that night.

Heya Lucy.

Oh heya. It's been awhile, etc.

Indeed. How are you?

I just found an insane piece on The Associates. Read this: *The band moved into the Swiss Cottage Holiday Inn in north London. Billy MacKenzie booked an extra room specifically for his pet whippets and began feeding them on smoked salmon from room service. He bought about 16 cashmere jumpers and put them on the bed and rolled around on them. Vast quantities of cocaine were, inevitably, involved.*

The only way to make an album like *Sulk*. It's one of my favourites.

But it keeps going, Robin! *The album's contents were spellbinding and mysterious, swathed in echo and electronic effects: tortured ballads; strange, skittering pop songs; a spellbinding funk version of 'Gloomy Sunday', the 1933 song that at one stage was fancifully alleged to have inspired hundreds of suicides, including that of its composer. 'Party Fears Two' was its centrepiece, offering an oblique melody, puzzling lyrics, an astonishing vocal performance from MacKenzie. It reached No 9 in the singles chart, prompting the first of a series of Associates appearances on Top of the Pops, where the band managed to carry the Sulk sessions' atmosphere of extravagance and rule-breaking audacity into British living rooms.*

Are you pinging?

A touch. Ok, this is the last bit. *During the performance, Alan Rankine sported a fencing suit, samurai make-up and chopsticks in his hair, while MacKenzie sang gazing not at the camera, but at his own image in the TV monitors at the side of the stage. On a subsequent one, Rankine played two guitars made of chocolate, one of which he fed to the audience as the song progressed.* JESUS, Robin. If only I wrote that way; if only we lived that way. Except Billy MacKenzie killed himself in his mother's doghouse just shy of 40, because what can you *do* after scaling those heights?

Move to the country, I guess. Become a gentleman farmer – an Alex James. Or a physicist – a Brian Cox.

Grow old gracefully. Or marry someone much younger and have a second batch of children. Tend to a vegetable garden. Make cheese. Mostly give up smoking – just one Marlboro Light of a Saturday evening. That's the dream, Robin, moderation. Or at least an acceptable synthesis of the sacred and the profane.

You could become a professor. Alan Rankine is a professor now yeah? And John Foxx. And Martha Ladly from Martha and the Muffins. A solid strategy.

That's Tabitha's trajectory. She's always one step ahead of us. You know, it's fun talking this way – like we're exchanging letters.

Kafka called letters 'intercourse with ghosts', a visual I've always enjoyed. The addressee is a ghost, but so is the shadow-self conjured through writing the letter.

Good old Kafka.

So how are you really, Lucy?

I have bronchitis again, and the steroids I'm taking are keeping me awake, so I'm strung out. Plus, the wind is driving me nuts, Robin. IS THE WIND DRIVING YOU NUTS?

It is unsettling.

Right? It always gets wild come late winter but sounds particularly aggrieved this year. I'm at the point in the draft where all human endeavour feels pointless, because all human endeavour IS pointless. Everyone is losing patience with me. Tabitha keeps giving me that withering look.

She's excellent at that look.

Yes, and she –

Ok, one thing at a time. I wanted to make sure we're still friends.

Of course we are. I'm about nuclear-bomb-shelter friends; end-of-the-world friends. Everyone needs 10 people they could call on in a crisis – for a loan of $500, or codeine for a migraine, or a place to sleep for a week, or help finding their shoes on the beach after too much acid – and 10 people for whom they'd do the same, in a heartbeat. For my manifold faults, I have those 10 people, and I'm that person for 10. You included.

That's unusual, Lucy. I don't have 10 nuclear-bomb-shelter friends.

Well, friendships are the only healthy thing in my life. Unfortunately, men are the source of my worst behaviour, which puts us in a bind. It seems I can't be friends with men – straight men, that is – because I suspect I inherently mislike them. Which might be somewhat justified after the last few years.

What about Harry?

Obviously, I love Harry, but he's a rare good egg and belongs to Tabitha, so he doesn't count. Anika thinks I don't see men as real people unless I'm enamoured, and once I'm enamoured, things go awry. What starts as hot dialectical positioning becomes a battle of control – both of us using the other to cure some lack, while trying to prove no lack exists. Inevitably it ends badly, because why else would something end? You understand my problem.

I do.

But yes, we're still friends. Absolutely. Fuck, how is your grandmother, Robin? That should have been my first question.

It must be close. Roland's coming tomorrow.

I'm sorry.

She's 72. You'd think this would be of comfort, but 72 feels too young.

I'm sorry. And I'm sorry I've got nothing useful to say. Is Meg still going with you to visit her?

No. Are you still walking?

Nope. No time for that. Tell me a story about your grandmother, a funny one.

You can't put me on the spot that way!

Go on – a story from when you were a kid.

Funny isn't her thing. But she found me and Izzy amusing as kids, especially Izzy, because Izzy was quite kooky.

You can tell. She's still kooky.

Yep. Izzy was always creating dance routines to Madonna that verged on inappropriate. Cracking surreal little-kid jokes that had my grandmother in stitches. And forever dressing up for involved imaginary games – bedsheets as ballgowns because our bunk beds were the *Titanic*, or putting on every skirt she owned to be an 18th-century chilli farmer. We spent a whole day harvesting chillies from the garden and came up in ferocious welts. God, they were painful.

Ha!

Ok, I have one. Once the three of us were watching *Countdown* reruns, and 'Wuthering Heights' came on. And my grandmother, who'd never said a bad word about anyone, lost it. A full castigation of Kate Bush: that her dancing was sorcery, that it was show-offy and wicked; in fact, not even *good* dancing, but she'd cast a spell over every man in the world so they'd love it.

Goodness!

She kept going and going, Izzy crying with laughter because we'd never seen my grandmother so animated. And Izzy protested she wasn't a man, and she LOVED Kate's dancing. And Gran said, Well, Isabella Ellis, we'll have to keep a close eye on YOU.

That's fascinating – and weird as hell.

Yes. Both my grandmother and Kate Bush are from Kent, so who knows? There could be all kinds of slights and scandals at play.

Izzy's moonlight serenades on the terrace make sense now. That's hysterical, Robin.

I'm glad you reminded me of it. You'd like Gran – I should have taken you to visit her.

Well, that was always Meg's domain. And hospitals make me anxious – I'd be an unhelpful presence.

Maybe.

Heya, I'm happy you messaged, but I should go. I've still got mountains to write tonight, and it'd be a shame to waste this Dexie.

Do they help?

For sure – it's real *Flowers for Algernon* shit, especially if you have trouble sitting still like me. Chemistry is an astonishing thing. But I reckon I've got 50 to 70 minutes before I turn dense again, so I must go as fast as possible.

Ok.

I'm going to have a party when I've finished this draft – a good one.

I look forward to that party.

Onwards, yes? I hope everything goes as well as it can, Robin. I hope you're ok.

Onwards is the only word for it. Goodnight, Lucy.

He logs off. And as it feels reasonably safe to leave things, Robin does.

Two weeks later, he finds an envelope pushed under his front door, addressed in Lucy's loping hand. He rips it open to find one of her index cards.

Dear Robin,
The book is done. Henceforth, I shall only listen to guitar music, starting with The Kinks. I'm having a few people over this Saturday by way of celebration – and apology for being such a bore of late. If you're free, I'd love for you and Isabella to come. 8ish. Bring nothing.
All my ghostly soft returns,
Lucy

Robin goes alone. It's the first sultry day of the spring, and Lucy's few people, typically, is significant: bodies on the terrace, bodies by the swimming pool, bodies splayed across the living room. The furniture has been pushed to the walls, and the just-leaked LCD Soundsystem album rattles the windows. Everyone has dressed for the yacht club again, but it's a 1992 yacht club this time. By habit, Robin makes for the kitchen, taking everything in.

Lucy's sitting on the bench, ashing into the sink. Robin had put it all aside as things at the hospital accelerated, but the sight of her strikes him with acute, unexpected pain. Her eyes are ringed in liner. Short lavender polka-dot dress, tiered skirt, black suede heels. She's swinging her legs, shins badly bruised. Someone Robin doesn't recognise sits next to her, their calves brushing as he swings his legs too.

'Robin!' she exclaims, stubbing out the cigarette. She's off the bench in one graceless movement, coughing into her shoulder. 'Let me get you a beer.' She pulls him by the sleeve past the ice bucket, collects a bottle, and walks them to the powder room next to the study. Robin watches her flick the lock, pat the windowsill, and produce a baggie.

'Have a line with me.' Robin doesn't want a line, but nods.

'Congratulations,' he says feebly as she rakes out grains on a mirrored clutch, bisecting and bisecting again. 'On finishing the book.' She ignores him and does a neat line, then passes him a puckered 20-dollar note, motioning he should have the other three. Robin obliges, then stands to face her. She is taller than him tonight, owing to the heels. There's still faint spidering under one eye from The Terrible Lakes, and a spray of something itchy-looking across her forehead and jaw. She motions for his beer and drinks, her eyes telescopes.

'What did we just snort?' says Robin. His synapses are savagely alight. 'Was that meth?'

'There's no coke in Abergele.'

'Fuck, Lucy.' He sniffs. 'You might have warned me.'

'You might have asked what it was before sticking three lines up your nose.'

'Noted. How did the book go?'

'Good, maybe. Wobbly at the beginning, best in the middle. I bet you know it better than me now. But I killed it.'

'What do you mean, you killed it? You said it was finished.'

'I didn't say it was finished; I said it was done. I cashed out my credit card and paid back the advance.'

'Jesus Christ, why?'

'Well, it depressed the hell out of me. Once it turned cold, that crush of abjection made me want to kill myself. And I realised – late – that I was writing on genres that structurally exclude women, structurally exclude anyone who isn't white and straight, in fact, and that depressed the hell out of me too. Otherness is tolerated, in trivial quantities, but it's not invited – it's not core, not canon.'

'Surely you knew that when you started.'

'Maybe. The real end was realising, or letting myself finally understand – a slow understanding that eats through your organs – that I'm a tourist. I'm a stupid, spoilt girl living in her grandfather's beach house. I've never been in a band. I've never programmed an 808 or an ARP or done heroin. I have no authority – I peek into the abyss periodically, then take two frantic steps back. They'd eviscerate me: Julian, Victor, Pink Fist, everyone I wrote about. It's happened before. So it's done, and I'm done – I'm retiring.'

'From what?'

'Everything that ever meant anything. Ha!'

She leans against the door, and Robin leans into her. They reconfigure their limbs instinctively. Slow release. He can hear breath catching her chest in a rusty serration. Her hand is on the ridge of his hip, and Robin shuts his eyes. She closes her cool fingers around his wrist, and his pulse jangles. She tips back her head, and they liquefy into a blister-chilled narcotised kiss as 'Losing My Edge' vibrates along the door.

'We've never made out on drugs,' she says.

'It's very nice,' he whispers, wondering how to get her out of here, away from this party, these people.

'I am not a good egg, Robin. It would be generous to call me a curate's egg.' She has stepped out from behind him and is lighting a cigarette.

'I'm not a good egg, either. But then I don't understand what impossible standard you're holding us to.'

'Impossible is a good word. Everyone is tired of me, and I'm very, very tired of myself. I've recreated my old life here in hermetic miniature, on the same unstable scaffolding of obsession, and I can't find a way out.' She coughs into her shoulder again, stubs out the cigarette. 'We might be best to end things here, Robin.'

Meth shrapnels the backs of his eyes, its buckshots urging him forward.

'Did you tell Harry you were in love with me?'

'No, I told Tabitha, who told Harry.'

'Since when?'

'The day you came for tomato juice. Your Einstürzende Neubauten T-shirt, your big tragic eyes.'

Robin breathes, a cramped roar. 'That whole time.'

'Yes.'

'But then you pushed me from your car; iced me out.'

'Yes. I was trying to take more care with my life this time. Between your indifference to Meg and wariness of me, it didn't seem an intelligent bet.'

'That makes no sense. I was at your house every day, Lucy.'

Lucy shrugs. 'So what?'

'I was clearly nuts about you.'

'That wasn't clear. It was clear you enjoyed the walks and the dinners and the parties and the drugs and my friends and the full, incandescent beam of my attention. It's clear you enjoy being adored without having to do too much work – and not just by me: by Gudrun, by Tabitha, by Julian, by Meg, by James. By Isabella! By all of us! *Stay passive, stay adored, make no sudden movements* might be your life manifesto, Robin, if you had a life manifesto.'

He takes a step back.

'I wanted to know what would happen if I took it away,' she says, 'if you'd make a gesture of want, of forceful reciprocation, and you did not.'

'I broke up with Meg.'

'You've been trying to break up with Meg since you got together. That was for you, not for me.'

'A game, then.'

'Not a game – that's horrible. A test, for my understanding alone.'

'Fucking hell, Lucy. I have needed you, like desperately needed you, these last few weeks.'

'Well, you might have told me. That would have been gesture enough.'

He rubs his eyes, a blur of explosions. 'We're both idiots.'

She is impassive. 'No. We both have good reasons for behaving as we do. We have strong self-preservation instincts, even if we're trying to preserve things in ourselves and our lives that are ultimately unhelpful.'

She unlocks the door. 'I'll be back in a minute, ok? I'll come and find you.' She slips beneath his arm with oiled ease. She is gone.

Robin is high, unpleasantly so, and downs two beers in an attempt to blunt the edges. He finds Harry at the kitchen sink, and they talk of things promptly consigned to oblivion, and Robin drinks a third. He spots Lucy on the other side of the swimming pool, head in Gudrun's lap, stabbing at the moon with her cigarette, but by the time he makes it across, she's not there. He drinks a glass of abandoned rum. The polka-dot twitch of Lucy's skirt vanishes into the powder room, but he misses its reappearance. And so he goes back onto the terrace, drinks another beer, accidentally knocks the bottle off the railing, and follows the slapstick sound of ineluctable smash to see it has missed a pair of peach-clad girls by a dangerously slim margin.

Robin is hot, every atom, electron and orbital of his body announcing agitation. He turns, and there, blowing smoke at the sea with imperial poise, is Julian. Close up, he's The Unspoiled Monster amplified: grey linen suit, thin T-shirt, impeccable cast of stubble, a crate of records at his ankles.

'Hullo, Robin,' he says. 'Having fun?'

'No.'

'Interesting.' Julian's jaw tenses. 'Me neither.'

'I can't find Lucy.'

Julian fixes Robin with his hard, green gaze. 'Oh, really.'

'I need to find her.'

'Let me guess: she stalked you like a teenage girl stalking her favourite member of Duran Duran, your unavailability – emotional, physical, whatever – being irresistible. She projected all her obsessions and desires onto you, making you feel terribly interesting, and this drove you both into an erotic frenzy. You eventually fucked, and she moved on to her neurotic performance of advance and retreat, advance and retreat. Now it's very tragic. You've been shipwrecked on that chunk of ice in her veins.'

It's an impressive monologue. Julian has been into the meth too.

'You're a smart guy, Robin,' he continues. 'You must know she has a whole anthology of people she does this with. But only people who are unviable in some fatal way. I always thought dopamine was the pleasure chemical, but it's not. It's the chemical that makes you *chase* pleasure, and that's 100 per cent Lucy's drug. It's all obsession, sustaining obsession, and taking obsession to its most illogical conclusions, no matter how sick or miserable it makes her.'

'Who told you that?'

'Which bit?'

'The dopamine bit.'

'Anika.'

Arcane medical facts, landing as punchlines.

'Well, it seems reductive,' says Robin. He remembers Lucy's insistence that Julian was pure instinct, never wrong.

Julian shrugs. 'Maybe she's just a pain in the ass. But you don't care about anything I just said, do you?'

'Not particularly.'

'Ha! Well, I don't care either. I'm going home. Give me pure pleasure any day – the rest is a headfuck.' He hoists the crate onto his shoulder.

'Goodbye then, Julian.'

'She'll completely subsume you, Robin. But perhaps that's what you want.' And with that, as much as anyone ever has, Julian disappears into the night.

*

Robin returns to the kitchen to find the entire party huddled in dense cigarette smog, smoke alarm decapitated and hanging from the ceiling. Tabitha is at the sink, riffling around cupboards.

'You're here,' she says. 'Good. Lucy has taken herself to the hospital.'

'What?'

She is weary, blood at her nose. 'Lucy has taken herself to hospital, but instead of telling me, she told some random on her way out, who relayed this through another random, so I don't know which hospital, or why. Now I have to find her.' Tabitha locates her bag and wrenches it from the cupboard, dislodging a jar of mayonnaise that shatters on the slate. 'Oh, Jesus Cunting Christ.'

'Want me to go with you?'

'No, I'll take Gudrun. Harry, annoyingly, left a while ago with the gallery crew. I need you to get rid of everyone, whoever the hell they are, and lock the house. Watch the records, yeah?'

'Has this happened before?'

'Twice. The old party-dehydration-taxi-emergency-room routine. It'll be fine – she's probably hooked to a lovely saline drip right now.'

'In that case, try the Sisters of Charity first.'

'Thank you.'

'How will you get there?'

'I'll take my car – I think I'm ok to drive. I'll call you soon, yeah? Remember to watch the records.'

It is remarkably easy to make people leave, although there's a crowd outside for an hour as Abergele's four taxis work in relay to disperse it. Under Tabitha's instruction, Robin checks the powder room's windowsill: meth dregs, half a pill in a Hello Kitty baggie. He checks the drawer of her bedside table. Bobby pins. At least 10 lighters of varying colour and size. A half-empty sheet of paracetamol and codeine. A half-empty sheet of contraceptive pills. An empty sheet of throat lozenges and another of steroids. A bottle of Xanax, near full, the top pills bitten in half. Antibiotics. Nasal spray. A zippered purse of woven elephants stuffed with more blister packs: Somac, Zyrtec, Mersyndol, Temazepam, loose pills stamped with the number 5, the same as their Easter Dexies. He pats the table's dusty wooden surface, ringed by careless mugs. Tucked under the lamp are two dog-eared business cards from the magazine, lists inscribed on their backs.

Black Strobe. Black Devil Disco Club. Black Rebel Motorcycle Club. Black Dice. Big Black. Black Milk. Black Moth Super Rainbow. Black Meteoric Star. Addis Black Widow. Black Box. Black Lace.

Chimera. Facinorous. Lupine. Ephetic. Epicene. Exigent. Nikhedonia. Kismet. Seratonic. Unicellular. Limerence. Transitive intimacy. Dimensional slippage. Inflection point. Vim.

He shakes out the blanket on her bed and finds loose tissues, a volume of Nabokov stories, three mismatched socks. He goes into the bathroom. A cup with three fingers of tea curdling at the bottom. Eyeliner. Perfume. Shells. Pigface in Limonata bottles. A tangle of slinky gold chains. An old porcelain dish to catch drips. He lies down, head on the apple-y cotton of her pillow, and texts the list of consumables to Tabitha. 'Found her,' she texts back. 'Pneumonia, apparently. More soon.'

Robin rinses cigarette butts from bottles and scoops the fetid remains from the sink. He washes glasses, empties ashtrays, picks the broken glass from the floor, and mops the mayonnaise. He puts the ashtrays outside and returns to blast them with the hose. He piles forgotten jackets under the window and sweeps the slate. He unplugs the stereo and moves the couches back. He tidies the study and shuffles her index cards into a squared pile, sitting at the desk to read them.

'It is not enough to conquer; one must know how to seduce.' VOLTAIRE, 1743

'Attention is the rarest and purest form of generosity.' SIMONE WEIL, 1942

'The common assumption is that there are "real" people and there are others who are pretending to be something they're not. There is also an assumption that there's something morally wrong with pretending. My assumptions about culture as a place where you can take psychological risks without incurring physical penalties makes me think that pretending is the most important thing we do.' BRIAN ENO, 1996

'Everything's gone bad in this world. So we're going bad as well.' DAISIES, 1966

He fishes leaves from the pool. He hangs up the dresses that have been draped on the wingback chair since summer. He re-sleeves records and tucks them back in the shelves, adhering to Lucy's abstruse systems of genre. He turns out the lights and closes the front door, walking home with midday sun searing his neck.

Three weeks pass, and Lucy doesn't reply to his messages. One morning, a morning with nothing to do and nothing else to be done, he decides he'll go to the house. He finds two half-joints on his windowsill, smoking them both before setting out.

There's a sedan parked in the driveway. Two blondes, neither of them quite Lucy, lean against the car, their arms crossed and a single pair of headphones threaded between them. The twins. One of them, Clara from Lucy's descriptions, is pale and wistful, vaguely anaemic; the roller-skate skinny of 13-year-olds. In the other, Rosemary, the crooked bits of Lucy have resolved into dangerous adult symmetry. Her blonde hair has a burnt toffeed quality, her large eyes a surly cast. A slight woman with a red-white-blue bag on her shoulder comes through a gate, one Robin has never seen used, and she locks it with care, calling to the girls anxiously that they need to hurry, that they're running very late. Rosemary spots Robin and narrows her eyes – he steps back. Doors slam and the sedan reverses hesitantly into the street, then drives away.

He goes home and does the dishes. Just as he's drying the last plate, Lucy calls.

*

The afternoon has turned cold, polar blasts blowing from the coast. Robin cuts across the cliffs through the cemetery, chalk and carbon and salt and stone crumbling into the sea. The fake flowers are in full bloom, the cut arrangements in slow rot, the crosses choked in ivy. He is lightheaded. The dominant feeling of the past month – of having misplaced himself – intensifies, and his chest hurts. The air is redolent with new freesias; the headstones drip blue-green verdigris. He follows Tabitha's hand-drawn map past the crumbled pier and the string of piers beyond, all bleached with sea spray. He starts up a hill, an ascent that mimics the mystifying oddness of climbing a stationary escalator. The houses are smaller here, the air thinner and colder, the sea muffled.

Number nine is a neat wooden cottage. Lucy sits on the porch, a cobalt shawl gathered in voluminous folds at her shoulders and neck. There's a girl beside her in a shawl of rust. Their knees are drawn identically to their chests in a sanatorium air of convalescence, as if taking their prescribed dose of fresh air for the day.

'You found me,' says Lucy.

'Not easily.'

'No.' She coughs. 'This is Nicole.'

The girl stands, scowls, goes inside.

'Whose house is this again?' he asks.

'My godmother. My parents were insistent I fly back with my mother and the twins today, so staying here was the compromise. I guess they decided it was time for an intervention.'

'Who's the girl?' He is confounded, again, by the people Lucy has tucked away.

'Nicole is my godmother's youngest. The poor kid is 16 and lavish with angst.' Lucy turns her head, her sly mode of punctuation, of closing things off. And so he sits beside her, their shoulders and knees just touching. Robin is exhausted, a hangover gathering force as icy wind whips off the ocean and bites at his face, but his guts are warm, the flank of his leg against hers hot.

'You reek of Nag Champa.'

'That's Nicole. Didn't you burn Nag Champa endlessly at 16?'

'When did you get out of hospital?'

'Yesterday.'

'It must have been bad for them to keep you so long.'

'Apparently. I caught up on sleep, at least.'

'You look frightful.' It lands lightly, but Robin finds her appearance disquieting, void of all salt and marrow.

'Ha!' she says reflexively. 'So do you.'

'Well, after that meth at your party, I was awake for three days. Then my grandmother died. You vanished for weeks, and I did wonder if you might die too. So, things have been unbearable, and I've been wasted most of the time.'

'That's very goth, Robin.' The wind trips across the cliffs. Lucy takes one of his hands, holding it like one might a small bird. Her elbows are sharp at his waist, her temple bloodlessly cool against his lips. 'I'm sorry. It's inadequate verging on ludicrous saying it now, but I am very, very, sorry. About your grandmother. About taking so long to call. About everything.'

'I am too.' He pauses. 'I slept with Meg after the funeral.'

'Goodness. That's to be expected, given the circumstances. I bet she's pleased with herself.'

'I don't think so.' He gathers what he has left. 'You must understand that when I don't talk about things, when I don't announce things as you do, it's not because I don't want to, it's because I can't. It's crushingly, asphyxiatingly impossible – as if someone's standing on my throat.' He stops, starts again. 'Maybe we're terrible people, Lucy, but I think we'd be less terrible together. I'd cut out my organs for you.'

'Is that a declaration of love?'

'Yes.'

A few beats pass. 'If you're game. I have approximately 52 weeks of psychotherapy ahead of me, old-school expensive therapy. My lungs are shot. I've got to nix the fun drugs and take boring ones instead. You might feel differently about me then.'

'I have a drinking problem. A passivity problem. We'll figure it out.'

She pats the ground next to her uselessly for cigarettes. 'Christ, I miss smoking.'

'Lucy. Please.' He closes his eyes. When he opens them, she's looking fixedly at the horizon in a chain of rapid calculations. 'Ok,' she says finally. 'But you'll have to bust me out of here. And then we'll probably have to leave town.'

Without Lucy and Robin's ministrations, the house has capitulated to the sea. The front path is crunchy with salt, the windows opaque with it.

'I can't get the door open,' says Lucy.

'Your mother left through the side gate.'

'I don't have a key to that gate. Here, help me.'

They lean their full weights against the door, the swollen frame groaning, then inchmeal yielding. The forgotten party jackets are still under the window. The plants are limp with thirst, the new lettuces at the back step dead in their beds.

While Lucy fills a watering can, Robin heaves the door closed, and it will stay closed for days.

They box Lucy's records, stopping to play Gwen Guthrie, and Deerhunter, and Eddie Cochran, and Jimmy Cliff, and Neil Diamond, and Rotary Connection, and Bat for Lashes, and Fela Kuti, and Arthur Russell, and Broadcast, and Ulrich Schnauss, and Neneh Cherry, and Clinic, and The Marvelettes, and The Boomtown Rats, and The Flirtations, and The Chills, and The Church, and The La's, and The Stems, and The The, but none of the other stuff, the abject stuff, which won't be unpacked for years.

While Lucy sleeps fitfully on the couch, coughing in a bass-note way, collarbones purplish, arm thrown over her eyes, Robin bundles old copies of her magazine for recycling. There are storms every afternoon, and they nap side-by-side beneath the narcotic crisp of the sheets, curtains blowing wetly across the slate. They pick the first tomatoes, resplendent with neglect, the morning sun a balm on their backs.

At night, they crawl into bed – cautious, pyjama-fresh, teeth squeaky with brushing – and smooth the blankets against their sides. They don't have sex, because Lucy assures Robin her lungs will give out if they do, but more so because they're shy of each other, each word and gesture now freighted with import. They sleep flank to flank, their fingers laced as at Roland's. There are sighing turns in the night to curl into one another, Lucy's hand at his neck, but that's it.

On the third night, Robin wakes from a nightmare. What's wrong, she says, but he can't answer. He lies stricken, breathing hard, trying to piece the unfamiliar room together. The world has been redrawn; he is motherless all over again. Lucy flicks the lamp and finds Tramadol, snapping out one for each of them and holding a glass to Robin's mouth while he swallows. She folds him into her, pushing his hair back in repeated, tranquillising gestures. They turn so they're shoulder to shoulder, faces damp, and the room regathers shape.

'Thank you,' says Robin, 'you can turn out the light,' and she does, lying with her back abutting his chest. They shift in the chain of instinctive acts they're so good at already. He rests his head at the base of her skull, breathing in her hair; his arm around her waist, her fingers braided into his. She curves her spine hard against him, vertebrae stacked against his stomach and scapula spurring his chest.

'You probably shouldn't do that,' he says.

'Why not?'

'Because it will end quickly, and messily.'

'That's for the best, given my consumption. Please, let's keep going.' They wrestle out of their pyjamas, and Lucy pushes the small of her back against his cock in firm, methodical movements. He swears beneath his breath, quietly, arms anchored around her chest, the impossibility of being here again, complete capitulation. He comes almost immediately.

'You were dying,' she says with a laugh, a low sound of protest from her chest.

'A little.'

She throws him his pyjamas.

They lay again, resettling the floral coverlet. As they're falling into a drugged, dreamless sleep, Lucy whispers, 'I love you, and I will kill anyone who hurts you. I will push them down the stairs, I will poison them slowly,' and that, really, is everything Robin has ever needed.

They wake ravenous. They eat the tomatoes and runner beans from the garden, covered in olive oil and the black volcanic salt Lucy's so fond of. They forage steaks from the iced caverns of the freezer. They thaw crumpets and eat them with crystallised honey, hard as amber. They crumble parmesan heels into omelettes, green with chervil, tarragon and cress from the kitchen sill's overgrown pots. They make risotto with dried shitake mushrooms and the last shake of vermouth. They steep weedy valerian in boiling water and take the mugs to bed, nibbling on digestives. They scrape the last dregs from the peanut butter jar, the marmalade jar, the glacé ginger jar, and lick their fingers clean. They eat tins of tuna, baked beans and tomato soup from the depths of the larder, and an ancient can of water chestnuts, until there's nothing more.

They can't stay; they know that. It's scorched earth, at least right now. Besides, there are no jobs in Abergele.

'And my grandfather will be back for his house soon,' says Lucy, counting her 10s and 20s. 'I want you to meet him, but not yet.'

Izzy invites them to lunch. The door opens without protest this time, a spell having done its work, some magic in retreat.

Food has been set out in Izzy's haphazard way – half a bagged roast chicken, crisps, leftover takeaway curry. They eat while Teddy sleeps in his stroller. She tells them she's spending two weeks at Roland's over Christmas, and this tips their decision.

'I wasn't very nice to him at the funeral,' says Robin. 'The thought of crawling back is terrifying.'

'I'm sure he's equally terrified,' says Izzy. 'I'm not saying you have to stop being angry, Robin, but given there's only three of us left, an amnesty might be in order. It'd make my life easier. And it would make your life easier, if only on practical terms. Hide out there for a while. Make him take care of you – both of you. I know it's nicer to be given what you need, but in Roland's case, you have to take it; otherwise he doesn't register any need exists. You've been invited. At this point, you're equally culpable and stubborn and stupid if you don't accept.'

'You're kicking me from the nest again.'

'Yes.' Isabella gives a half-smile, chin resting in cupped hands. 'This time, you can't come back.'

Robin pushes away his plate, nodding to himself. 'I better get my stuff together, then.'

Throughout this conversation, Lucy has been quiet, watching Izzy's perilous scaffolding of chin, hands and elbows sink deeper into the table. 'Are you alright, Izzy? What do you need?'

'The month is catching up with me. Perhaps you could watch Teddy while I nap.'

'Of course.'

'Thank you. If he wakes, there's fruit in the fridge, although it'll need cutting.'

'Grapes halved; watermelon cubed – always.'

The siblings stand for a moment, uncertain, dejected, and start for their rooms. They are children again, exiled separately after a dinner-table scrap over juice boxes.

Lucy's uncle Bruce accepts the crumpled sum of $500 for the Fiat. 'Tell your dad I made you give me $1000,' he says, thumping the car's cracked soft top affectionately. They're parked outside her cousin's house, the same cousins of the lawnmower.

'I tried to give you $1000!' says Lucy. 'I'll tell him it was $2000.'

'Good. And you!' Bruce booms, leaning through the window. 'What do they call you?'

'Robin.'

'Christopher Robin, hey? Well, make sure Lucy doesn't crash the car. This is an original Spider.'

'I'll keep one hand on the wheel, whether driving or not.'

'Good man.'

Lucy shakes her head and reverses cautiously. 'It begins,' she says. 'Each of my painstakingly constructed walls collapsing inwards.'

Errands. Farewells. All that remains is to pack the car. Most of their possessions will stay stacked in the study, a worry for an unspecified hereafter.

Robin asks how she got her things to Abergele to begin with. Lucy had spoken lyrically of her last flee – the single suitcase stuffed with money, the taxi to the airport, acid still pinpricking her vision, sideways rain on the window mercifully softening the world outside; of standing between terminals pretending she still might fly to New York – but had glossed over the actual mechanics.

'Gudrun packed my apartment and used her magic Rolodex to get it backloaded. I gave her my mirrored coffee table and a lovely old '60s dresser for her trouble. The looking-glass was ringed with pearlescent lights and ludicrously flattering – everyone used to crowd in to get ready, admiring the best versions of themselves. I'll never find another like it.'

She writes 'I Abject' on a box of papers, the pen giving out mid-underline. 'Oh well. At least I'm slightly more organised this time.'

They leave mid-afternoon, Robin behind the wheel. The concrete of the Old Pacific Highway roars beneath them, a noise they only notice when it drops away. They're on the new tar Pacific now, needle creeping towards 120. They're silent until an hour out of Abergele.

'I feel better,' says Lucy, sitting up abruptly. The trees are denser, no salt in the air. She's magically tall in her seat, tendons in her neck thrumming. That mad desire to keep driving, the one that propels her through life, has transfigured her face. Robin thinks of his first time in the Fiat, that sensation of controlled burnout, of drift. He yields to it, hands loosening on the wheel, foot nudging the accelerator, hot wind skittering across their shoulders.

'Me too,' he says.

CONSTRUCTION TIME AGAIN

December 2004

Roland meets them on the driveway. The mountain hums with insects, netted fruit trees tremble like brides. He has brought on a housekeeper for the summer, he tells them, and dinner isn't far. He asks Lucy to choose wine, wine they won't drink.

And so Robin leads her along the old passageways to the cellar, tunnelling darker and damper, more and more potent with old earth. He closes the door. There's a long table where bottles are sorted and decanted, and Lucy hoists herself up with an alto clatter of glass on glass. They are quick, very quick, pushing aside their clothes, a streak of compacted shocks amounting to exorcism. The utter relief of being bone-on-bone, the hoarse incantation of each other's names. 'You've got a magnificent grey thatch,' she says, pushing Robin's hair back from his forehead. 'I love it.'

Summer unfurls across the mountain in a tremendous pastoral pageant. The wattle heaves; the gums rustle in hallucinatory detail, each leaf brushing audibly against the next. Robin rebuilds a fallen portico on the east corner of the house and accompanies Roland to check on the new lambs. Lucy descends on Robin's mother's old garden, pruning the tips of the rosemary and lavender so tender new tops appear, hacking back the sage and the lemon verbena, scattering fennel and poppy seed, medicating the arthritic heirloom roses, digging out the leggy cosmos that have gone to seed and planting new ones, coming to bed reeking of sticky oils, covered in scratches, shins lashed with nettle stings, nose flaking with sunburn.

She hauls bags of manure from the sheds and thins the overgrown mass of what Roland calls the tea garden, where bands take breaks and smoke. Everything bursts back in flaming scent: pineapple sage, borage, mallow, chamomile, burdock, yarrow, sorrel, nigella. She's in the throes of her glittery near-mania again, but this time it's directed at the garden, this time it's directed at Robin. They set upon each other in fields, by the creek, in the cubicles of the Hungry Hunter. Lucy flings herself across surfaces with scant regard for inconvenience or danger. Her hair splays on the ground, exposing the pale arc of her neck. She writhes as if drugged, brushing pebbles from her stomach and hips afterwards, rocks she didn't realise were there. He's horrified to see her waist ringed with bruises, afterburns of his fingers, but Lucy is unconcerned. 'Oh that,' she says. 'That happens all the time.' They finish dinner hurriedly to get to bed; at 8pm, they've closed the door, smug and drunk on each other. Roland watches them – with curiosity, maybe alarm – and this makes Robin possessive, filthy, loud. On a night Roland is away, they sneak into the studio, emerging with the dials imprinted on their flesh. They're hardy and hale, browny-pink from the hours outdoors, Lucy's rattle gone.

She assembles old music as new, indexed broadly as Bucolicnalia. Talk Talk's 'Life's What You Make It', Beat Happening's 'Indian Summer', The Wake's 'Here Comes Everybody', The Cocteau Twins' 'Blue Bell Knoll', Tindersticks' 'Another Night In'; Nico's 'Wrap Your Troubles in Dreams', Psychonauts' 'Hips for Scotland', Kate Bush's 'The Sensual World', Cranes' 'Come This Far', Julian Cope's 'Charlotte Anne' and 'Sunspots'.

They play 'Sunspots' over and over, so much that landscape and soundscape cleave in mystical symmetry. Chiming guitars peal over the sighing grasses, the wind-bleached Anglican church, the dip and weave of wedding-veil moss, the pom-pom heads of spring onion and shallot, the wisteria frothing over the house, the starched snap of washing on lines. Robin cycles into town to buy bread most mornings, camera at his shoulder, humming the refrain of being in love with your very best friend. The choreography fans out endlessly: woodwind snaking with pied-piper intent along the steel bridge buried in wattle fuzz at both ends, past the controlled fires being alternately lit and snuffed out in every field, through the fullness of the jaunty old pub and the emptiness of the sandstone school of arts; charting places unknowable.

Those four chords, doubled and redoubled, jangle the grain silos and water tanks, set the foxgloves in front gardens dancing. They desiccate petals and salt them over the mountain. He thinks of Julian Cope – slashing open his chest with a microphone stand, dancing in white stockinged feet on a piano, living on Mars Bars and speed pills – and then retreating to the country. Retreating to fables and folk tunes, retreating to his collection of toy trucks, retreating beneath his antique turtle shell, retreating to drop acid straight onto his eyeballs and attend to his self-mythology – and impossibly emerging with *this*. He thinks of Cope holding two narrative arcs in perfect tension: things happening to you, you happening to things. Immanence and transcendence.

A band called Glass Casket are recording on the farm, one of the many Glass bands of that year. They're a four-piece: two keyboards, three men, one woman, ambiguous sleeping arrangements. Good eggs, it would seem, but Robin and Lucy hold them lightly, keep their distance.

The band have finished five tracks and are rewarding themselves with a celebratory lunch on the patio. Robin and Lucy make sandwiches and set off for a walk; celebratory lunches a thing to be avoided right now. They walk for hours, to the dam, to the glade of gnarled Norfolk pines, swimming in the cold creek full of catfish on the way home, but lunch is still going. They sneak past the band to Robin's bedroom, Lucy's bedroom, their bedroom. He pushes away her dress, rests his head in her lap. She stretches extravagantly as Robin obliterates himself in her. And so it goes, as with most afternoons here, a state of mindless grace. The sounds of lunch echo from outside, glass tinkling and smashing, laughter and smoke wafting through the window. 'Come up here, please, come here now,' she says, and Robin moves so they're length to length, her arms crushed around his neck. He knows he won't do life without Lucy; they've said as much to each other. It's muggy in the room. She is at the windows, adjusting the shutters. 'That was us not so long ago,' she says, watching the patio's fading tableau. 'They have exactly 10 minutes until things start getting ugly at the edges.'

Christmas Day. Isabella, Teddy and the Invisible Anaesthesiologist have arrived. Christian, a farmer from one town over, an old friend of Roland's, has joined them for the day.

Isabella is pregnant and wretched with it. Throughout the week, she curls involuntarily into sleep on whatever couch is closest. Robin can't bear it – the infirmity, the way she pulls cushions over her face; it's too soon after the last year of illnesses – whereas Lucy is practical. She takes Teddy to the kitchen and lets him paw through cupboards, pulling out measuring cups and saucepans to fill with water. She brings Isabella snacks: crackers, fruit and juice, the salts and sugars of convalescence.

'It's very Cronenbergian,' says Lucy, setting down a plate for her.

'Yep.' Isabella sits to make room for them. 'A nine-month battle between parasite and host, and an asymmetrical battle at that. The invader mainlines nutrients. The invader issues directives straight into your bloodstream. You just have to wait them out.'

'I knew it was bad. My mother had three miscarriages between me and the twins, nasty ones. But you've just made it sound even worse.'

Isabella stretches. 'I've seen the full gruesome parade at work. And it killed my mother. But I got through it once unscathed, so hopefully, I can do it again.'

She is well enough to join them by lunch, and they eat on the patio. Lobsters in aspic. Chilled green gazpacho. A plate of tomatoes from the garden and a bowl of just-picked raspberries. Glassy terrine, cheeses and bread. Pasta and fruit for Isabella and Teddy. Lucy is in her element, digging brown speckled pottery, cabbage-shaped tureens and lettuce-shaped dishes from the pantry, plating the containers labelled by the housekeeper. She loves the orphaned glasses, the oddly shaped forks, the frayed-edge linen napkins. She loves it all.

'Do you think they're together?' she asks Robin as they conference at the kitchen bench.

It takes a beat to understand she means Roland and Christian. He has not even considered this.

She prods a lobster antenna into place. 'I think they're together.'

So Robin watches them. Those drinking have gravitated to one side of the table, the abstinent to the opposite; each side very silly to the other. Robin watches the loosening of inhibitions, the slow melt. They are together – of course they're together. Roland's hair is longer, shirt rolled carelessly to his elbows. He's wearing sunglasses, relaxed, still young; in the great middle thrust of his life, in fact. Christian is deeply tanned, strong where Roland isn't. There's been no one as far as Robin knows, but that means nothing. Roland and Robin have concealed most things from each other, or never found an inclination to reveal things.

The table has been cleared except for the bread and salt and a sweating jug of water. The landscape thrums in psychedelic detail: the ripple on the surface of the cattle dams, the encroachment of invasive pussy willow, the stop-motion spread of wild ginger, the moss-eaten stumps turning from grey to heather, the acidic gums that grow so near to one another without touching. Lucy is to Robin's left in the habit of a lifetime. She keeps her hand on his knee; her fingers cool even though the afternoon is warm. It's a protective film between him and the world, a film that enables him to watch Roland holding Teddy without the unfocused stab of anger this usually provokes.

'I'm so happy, Robin,' Isabella whispers. She has tucked her chin into his shoulder. 'I'm so happy that you're happy.' Lucy, hearing this, moves closer, and the three sit in silent communion. The feeling of the Abergele dinners has returned: love dispersed liberally in the terrace breeze; its targets now clearly defined.

Eventually, everyone peels away to their private corners of the afternoon, footsteps echoing along the sandstone floors. Robin and Lucy undress as soon as the door is closed. 'I am demented on the specificity of you,' she says and takes time recounting the details. His narrow shoulders and ankles; the lean muscles of his arms, absolutely no bigger than necessary. His crooked bottom teeth, the crisscrossed ribbons on his thighs where he ran into a barbed-wire fence as a child, his corded inclines, his bony fingers, his scrupulously cut-down nails, his chromatic eyes. The room is brined in thin gold light, and they lie on their sides, her shoulders knitted into his chest. Her hair carries bergamot and rosemary from the plants on the patio. That drugged motorik repetition, an absence of thought, quiet, quiet, quiet. Robin stops, pulls out, waits, and they begin again, this time at a steeper pitch. He stops again, pulls out. Lucy issues a snarl of protest and twists to look at him. Perspiration grains his forehead.

'What do you want, Robin? Tell me clearly.'

'I want to put my cock in your ass.'

'Is that a thing you've done to anyone?'

'No.'

'Well, I'd like that rather a lot. Get a condom; it will be easier.'

They reorganise themselves. Robin takes in the hard glance of her shoulders, the uncanny softness of her back, the two indents at the base of her spine.

'Is that ok?'

'Yes. You can keep going.'

And so he moves as slowly as he can, angling her waist for one fluid movement.

'Stay for a second.' Her voice is low, forceful. 'See, this is almost the best bit.'

Time stops, arches like a cat. The clock on the shelf, the dust hanging in the air like spent fireworks, the quiver of the fields outside, the murmurs along the hallways: it stops. Lucy, he says, but what he wants to say is I'm drowning.

'Ok, keep going,' she says, a command.

Slowly, slowly, slowly. Her chest emptying of breath, catching in her throat. Total abandon.

'Oh, fuck,' she says. 'I'm going to come, sorry, go faster.'

And Robin obeys, catching his reflection in the dresser opposite. He is ropy, dangerous, his shoulders dark from the sun; an anvil. Lucy's hands are stretched towards the bed's edge, each finger curved upwards in that plastic articulation of hers. He comes immediately and buries his forehead in her neck.

'Well,' says Lucy. They lie still, Robin thinking of fasciculation, paralysis, the sheer relief of surrender. He pulls out, as slowly as he began, his hands on her ass cheeks, pushing them together. 'That's very considerate, Robin.' She rolls over, sits. Her crooked smile, her liquid eyes. 'Merry Christmas, darling. Was it nice?'

He inclines his head, and with the solemnity of a school prefect, recites:

And the angels kiss
Our souls in bliss
Measure the extent
Of a dizzying descent

'Oh, clever Robin,' she laughs. She pushes damp hair from his eyes. 'You're looking all emotional.' He turns away, her scrutiny unbearable.

'Well, that, my love, is why it's worth asking for what you want.'

January. They take inventory of things they won't allow in their lives. The tunnel-visioned accumulation of property and offspring. The canned laughter of Tuesday-night television. The gloomy fluorescence of shopping-mall Sundays. Perfunctory once-a-year gatherings of old friends. Inked-ahead date nights breaking sexless cohabitation. Silent protest. The mediocre horrors that corrode happiness, sly as rust. They stock a menagerie of potential pleasures instead.

Robin thinks often of what Julian said, that Lucy would subsume him. He wonders if this has happened. Or if Lucy, with her cosmic force of will, has sandblasted a chamber of quiet around him, an airlock where, for once, he feels like himself. She inhabits the house freely, and Robin – for the first time – inhabits it freely too. They let themselves be taken care of. They sit at the kitchen table each morning, children waiting for their breakfast. They do the dishes together and, Roland safely in the studio, they lift the keys from the third drawer and burrow through the passageways.

There's a whole wing Robin has never visited: rooms of life interrupted, of covered pianos, broken chairs, arenose glasses, faded gold cushions, of books shut in a hurry. His mother's domain, he guesses. The light reveals the dust (who sang that?) that plays around her face. They open drawers and cabinets – pen knives, letters, photographs, one- and two-cent pieces – but it's a pretence, a precursor. His wrist is between her legs, a drawn-out vivisection, and they pull off their clothes in the deranged trance that's their days now. Gossamer cobwebs garland the ceiling; an amber-like substance stretched stickily between the threads. He has balled a brocade throw under Lucy's lower back, the cloth unspooling at the edges. Slow, slow, slow, slow breaths. Robin thinks of the 78 organs Isabella memorised in her first term of medicine: lungs, heart, brain, bronchi, cerebellum, diaphragm, epithelium, ligaments, liver, mesentery, the marrow of the bones, nerves, tendons, thymus, tongue. And interstitium, the fluid-filled space in between, the spaces they're clawing their way through now. Robin loops her hair around his hand and says, 'I want the sinews that hold you together,' and she says, 'I want nothing, Robin, nothing.' Limbs, teeth, nails dissolve.

They lie with the throw pulled over their chests. Night begins its distant approach: sheep bleating as they're herded home, the theremin hum of cicadas, the smokes of summer threshing the sky, the thunk of racquet-on-ball as Roland begins his end-of-day duel with the machine.

'How do you make this last forever?' asks Robin.

'Constant vigilance, I suppose.'

'We'll get nothing done if we keep fucking like this.'

'No. That's why I love sex: it's anti-work, anti-productivity.' She shifts, falls back into languor. 'It's also why people distrust sex – because it demolishes everything else. Who could be bothered invading a country or razing a rainforest or digging a mine or building a resort or sweating over the stockmarket when you feel this way? Sex doesn't make people behave badly; the absence of its delirium does.'

They stay on the mountain till late summer, when the seeds dry on their stems and pods crumble, dispersing their spoils into the wind and the beds below. 'It's like snow,' says Robin. Lucy rests her head in his lap, and they pass one of the orchard's speckled apples between them. 'I know,' she says. 'Look at those seeds; how many thousands it takes to make next year's flowers. It does make you wonder how monogamy persists.' And they both defer this, another worry for an unspecified hereafter.

It rains for their last five days, thrumming insistent rain that fills the water tanks; needles their shoulders as they dash out for the washing. A steady vibrato on the roof, smashing at the plants, turning every smell in the garden up to 11. It functions as expedited nostalgia, an elegy for the summer not yet ended. They pack, saturated in it, packing much more than they'd arrived with. Roland has filled a leather overnight bag, a relic of a long-dead relative, with books and smaller pieces of gear for Robin. He collects and boxes Robin records: Scott Walker's *Tilt*,

Tangerine Dream, Morphine; the darker, dirgier outings from his collection. He gives Lucy plates, vases and glasses, the ones she favoured over the summer, the forgotten vessels once more shiny with use.

They're dressing for dinner on the very last night while Roland cooks. The windows are open, letting in the tremulous sounds of rain on its departure. Philip Glass's *Metamorphosis* steals under the door in a series of sighing advances; the creak of the piano keys, the pockets of ceremonial hush. It all strikes Robin in a volley of arrows: Lucy flicking her drying hair around her shoulders as she puts in earrings, the intimate tangle of their individual and shared possessions on the bed. The castanet snap of her pill bottles. The old leather smell from the overnight bag. The soapy incense rising from their just-washed skin. The end of their retreat from the world, their retreat into each other. The sense of disparate threads drawing together, an impossibly fragile arrangement. None of this is communicable. None of it should be.

'Roland adores you,' Robin says to Lucy, gesturing at the plates. 'Of course.'

'Of course.' Lucy is shuffling the last of the 10s and 20s, less than 800 dollars now. 'It doesn't hurt that I appeared when I did.' She shrugs. 'Let it be known that I've never overstated my importance to anyone.'

'A transference of responsibility,' says Robin, because he'd thought this too; a transference from one guardian to another, leaving Roland, as always, untethered.

'Yes. My parents will love you for the same reason.' She touches his arm briefly and returns to her packing.

*

Christian is at dinner, his presence mostly discouraging any difficult lines of conversation.

'Will you stay with your family when you arrive, Lucy?' asks Roland.

She crosses her arms. 'We'll see them, but no, we won't stay with them. They have a full house. We're staying with friends.'

'Really?' He looks surprised.

'Really.'

After the meal, Roland leads everyone to the studio to play a Glass Casket track, the grown-ups holding goblets of brandy. It's good, as much of the last year's music is good, but Robin is unmoved. Lucy says the right things and then runs her hands over the mixing desk, asking if they can listen to something older.

Roland's already in the habit of indulging her, this being a cheerful and uncomplicated duty to fulfil. He extracts the eight-minute version of Visage's 'Fade to Grey', attending to the levers. The studio swells to accommodate its keening, terrible want.

How extraordinary, Lucy says to no one, a metallic sheen across her face, to be born in the epoch you were meant for, circumstances aligning like vertebrae and pulled taut. How extraordinary to turn your loneliness outwards and find it's a magnetic cloud for loneliness everywhere; droplets attracting droplets attracting droplets. To be hitched to both the monumental spirit of Bowie and the physical presence of Bowie, the right machines invented *just* in time to express every shade and pitch of your yearning. To find people who experience the same intense longing as you, in the thrall of the same machines; to collectively furnish a new universe. And how devastating: to reach the truest most full expression of yourself so young, so perfectly in step with your time that you'll be out of step for the balance of your life.

Her fingers flicker around a cigarette that's not there. 'But Steve Strange presided over one masterpiece. How many of us even get that?'

The track ends. She turns a catechising look upon Roland. 'You must know. You were there.'

'I was there,' he says, 'but not in the way you describe. I was just a soundboard. For me, it was always work.'

It takes several attempts to load the Fiat. Robin approaches it like Tetris, like chess. Lucy brings him coffee and toast. She watches.

'Why are you doing that?' he asks, pleased.

'Watching people do things well is my second-favourite thing.'

Now they've decided, they want it to be done. Lucy drives faster than she should, and Robin doesn't complain; their ascent played out in rapid reverse. They speed past canola pastures washed in solsticey light, past sage-green fields with tufts of spiky grass curled like hedgehogs into the ground. They navigate the viridian slabs of stone edging the pass, unalarmed this time by the vertical drop. The mountain is soon a smoky-blue blur in the distance. They sideswipe the gargantuan lake, less than half full, and wind through hours of rocky cuttings exposing the very bowels of the earth.

They hit the city's fringes at sunset, a sudden shift from minor to major key. A synthwave vista opens around them: roads laid over roads laid over roads, the sun a cardinal orb, the smog a vast peachy sigh softening everything. It's a life-sized game of *OutRun*. Trucks roar past, automaton dinosaurs asserting their power, as freeway high-masts strobe the car. Helicopters. Billboards, seven metres wide and luminiferous. The city rises in all its danger and promise: skyscrapers pulsing with cubes of silver, the bridge casting slick rainbows on the river, the broken-glass glint of distant streetlights. Then they're inside it: vacant lots and pylons, white lines and yellow lines, the vertical flicker of fences, the plane trees still hobbled in Christmas lights. The car only just makes the trip, giving a resigned shudder as Lucy turns off the ignition for the last time.

Robin's blood has been right against his skin the entire journey, a barely contained euphoria. 'We wasted a whole year,' he says.

'Oh no,' says Lucy, cheeks hot. 'I was playing the long game, Robin. That whole year, with you just out of reach, was the most exquisite torture of my life.'

A NEW CAREER IN A NEW TOWN

February 2005

Robin and Lucy rent the top floor of an old warehouse, generously advertised as a loft. They choose the neighbourhood for its Victorian-era produce markets, its smells of frying dough and cut leaves. That it feels like a hamlet – a maze of tracks and traffic between them and Lucy's old haunts – is unspoken.

Their building is an outlier, defiantly unrenovated in a sprawl of conversions. There are no internal walls, just a cardboard box of a partition around the toilet and the exposed-pipe approximation of a shower. It's punishing to heat, extortionate to cool. But there's a claw-foot bath in the makeshift kitchen, superlunary light through full-height windows, and a rooftop they can reach by ladder. It's cheap, if you factor the rent alone. Roland pays to have their boxes sent from Abergele, along with a load of things Robin inherited from his grandmother: a sideboard with an illuminated liquor cabinet, a squat lamp of oak and mother-of-pearl, an umber Scheurich vase. Lucy finds a second-hand set of Mikasa dinnerware mimicking the slate floor of Abergele, and trains devil's ivy up the windows. They drag wooden pallets to the rooftop and build garden beds. Robin arranges his gear in one corner, drunk with the luxury of space. When the downstairs tenants move out, Lucy and Robin buy their massive old sectional couch: rust-coloured and wantonly deep buttoned.

A layer of soot from the nearby freeway soon covers everything. Snails eat through the contents of the letterbox. Robin exterminates a nest of mice without telling Lucy. There's a gym called Kratos on the ground floor, frequented from late afternoon to early morning by oil-slicked men flexing glorious, weaponised muscles. Robin and Lucy love it here, developing a shared repertoire of things to cook, things to do.

Lucy gets a job writing copy at the Costume Institute, which evolves into leading the marketing arm. It's a right-time-right-place stroke of luck, she tells Robin, throwing her whole being into the new role with a ferocity that awes and disconcerts him. Once more, she has a team of bright young things in her care: smart, driven, intense young women who call Lucy nights and weekends because she tells them they can. Her aural obsessions make space for new visual ones: Bakst's illustrations for the Ballets Russes; the icy heroines of Jeanloup Sieff wearing now-forgotten designers; the melt-into-skin draping of Madeleine Vionnet; the kingfisher and absinthe leathers of Claude Montana. She talks of Schiaparelli constantly. Schiaparelli, broke and jilted with a newborn in New York, living off room-service oysters and chocolate cake because they were the cheapest things on the menu. Schiap, happiest on small boats amongst old friends. Lucy adopts the Institute's uniform, dressing for the office as one might the funeral of a great society figure, every crimped and complicated layer a variation of ink.

She mostly avoids her old music milieu, but makes gentle introductions for Robin. He photographs parties and shows, and the photos are well received. His lack of ego, his ability to melt away, are, for the first time in his life, an asset. He begins doing studio shoots, where his forensic watchfulness comes into its own. The work becomes The Thing That He Does, if not The Thing That He Is. When he can, he makes music. Tabitha and Harry return to the city too: Tabitha teaching at the university while she ploughs through her PhD; Harry finally dropping out to try his hand at graphic design. Lucy delivers other people to Robin – good people, the right people – recreating Abergele's humid affinities with a lighter touch. She makes sure he calls Isabella and Roland. But they are, on the whole, quiet; still smug in their togetherness, still astonished at their good fortune.

And if they continue to be pecked at by self-loathing, tending to private anxieties like demanding pets, it's not the dominant feeling of this time. If they keep their parents at a cordial distance, and wonder how they'll move forward without the things that propelled them this far – because this closed sphere of happiness is just that, a closed sphere – and if they both tether themselves too closely to shifting objects, hoping to stay upright (Robin to Lucy, Lucy to work), and begin developing new cures to replace the old ones, odd rituals and tinctures, that's not what they'll remember from this period. Robin will remember the evenings in the nosebleed seats at the orchestra, suspended right over the pit, of being sucker-punched by Dvořák and Arvo Pärt as Lucy's hand steals into his pocket. Watching the musicians tune their instruments for *Swan Lake* and Lucy pointing out her favourite dancer, the principal who can only pirouette in one direction due to the pronounced sideways curvature of her spine. 'This makes her better in *every other way*,' says Lucy. 'You can see it – the total immersion in her role, the intelligence radiating from her pinkies. It's just like Andrew Eldritch poured all his charisma and force into The Sisters of Mercy, compensating – in his words – for being a very bad fuck.' It's there again: a life where limitations are advantages by necessity.

He'll remember the weeknights in the kitchen, Lucy reading in the bath while Robin cooks, or the other way around, their individual pleasures conducted alone but in easy reach of the other. The way he can't help zooming out when they're in bed to regard its plush spectacle, especially when Lucy relinquishes any veneer of control, becoming pliant, languorous, narcotised, entirely present. The story of their togetherness – of being with other people and running away together, of speeding down the freeway, the Fiat gobbling yellow lines – becomes more densely embroidered in their minds. The wonder that he stole her from Julian, assisted by the Victorian plot hinge of pneumonia, never departs Robin: the consumptive, pale-skinned girl, the cad, the near-death experience, the liberation from vice. This story is heavily redacted, in parts technically untrue, but it prevails, nonetheless.

It has been two years since they left Abergele when Gudrun visits, a brief stop on the way to see her parents. She's been in London for a year, working as an entertainment lawyer and conducting life on a larger scale.

'Your hair!' says Lucy, in the clasp of bone-crushing embraces. It's a short bob, sharp above her jaw.

'*Your* hair!' says Gudrun, because Lucy's has grown into loose waves at her back. They have swapped.

Gudrun adores their warehouse. She adores the light. She gets changed, talking all the while. The jade silk of her jumpsuit is by turns voluminous and scant; the straps at her shoulders no thicker than fishing wire. They walk to dinner, a place Gudrun made reservations for them months ago.

The restaurant is unsigned, sharing a building with a Japanese bathhouse. Shallow pools in the foyer, the holy sound of water on rocks, stairs alighting pink under their footfall. There are private rooms, diners reduced to tracery by rice paper and candlelight, but Gudrun chose the bar. The service is always best at bars, she says, the ambience most potent. She insists she's paying; she wants to try everything; she wants endless savoury plates of colour. She proposes sake then riesling, dry of course, so dry your mouth puckers anticipatorily. Neither Lucy nor Robin mention they're not drinking anymore, because by unspoken conference they will tonight. It's a special occasion, after all.

The procession of plates begins. Lucy makes Gudrun tell them of her Tuesday nights at Trash and Nag Nag Nag and Dalston Superstore, of being destroyed by M.I.A. and Glass Candy and Ricardo Villalobos and John Maus, of the midnight picnic she threw at All Tomorrow's Parties attended by the Yeah Yeah Yeahs, of sharing a bottle of vodka with Johnny Marr backstage without grasping his importance. They're sickled around the bar, Gudrun in the middle, legs occasionally brushing. Robin is acquainted anew with the subtle art of her movements. Her jumpsuit breathes as she does, exposing pockets of gleaming skin. Lucy, chin in her hands, watches Gudrun too with an expression of near reverence. 'I wish I was there,' she says. 'I wish I wanted to be there. But that world exists in headphones now; a sealed vault – it's private.'

'It's always been private for you,' says Gudrun. 'A private rapture, occasionally performed in public.'

More plates arrive, and Gudrun makes Robin tell her about his work. He does, unaccustomed to speaking of it to anybody but Lucy, surprised at his willingness to do so. That photographing music has vaulted him back to the first shows he attended, his first lucid experiences of chromesthesia. Of being 14 and 15 in festival fields, blitzed on mushrooms and weed. Of sound assuming the wavelengths of light. While Lucy catalogued every detail of that Nine Inch Nails show in a wunderkammer of feelings, he only recalls sheets of hypnotic blue, a cast that still dominates his dreams. The ultramarine throb of murdered keyboards. Banks of equipment outlined in amethyst. The wet glaze across the crowd, its silvered sheen of delirium. How he's been trying to get back there ever since, how photography – with its occult powers of selected visibility and revelation of light – has brought him closest. A halo of hair extinguishing a face. The phosphorescent pulse of blood against skin. Gelled borderlights and cycloramas dissolving the borders between body and machine to irradiate them as one.

He doesn't say, doesn't know, that the gradual circulation of these photos has functioned as a passport. He'd been used to shooting three songs from the pit with the other photographers, but now finds himself ushered side of stage to keep going. Because he understands performance is ephemeral, existing only in the now. To capture it verbatim is to snuff out its essence, leaving you with a powdering of moth scales and not much else.

'Brilliant, Robin,' says Gudrun, chin in her hands, mirroring Lucy. 'Big eyes, always watching things.'

And then she asks Lucy about the Costume Institute. And Lucy says she loves it, is consumed with it, natch. But the pay is lousy, and she's fetishising the old and dead again. And if she isn't creating things for herself, or doing a measure of good, then perhaps it's worth trying to make money.

'That's what I'm doing,' says Gudrun, swirling her glass.

'And?'

'Well, it's grubby work and sticks to your fingers. I can't see myself tolerating it for more than five years. But the money is helpful, and it's nice to travel. We all want to do worthwhile jobs, but it's a slippery conceit. Some mistake doing good work for being a good person, but they're not the same. One doesn't absolve you of the other.'

And Lucy presses Gudrun on who she's dating, and Gudrun says who hasn't she been dating. 'They blaze in and out like comets. I end it, or they end it – and strangely, I don't care much either way.'

'You've never cared. That's what drives people so wholly, frantically wild for you. How many times have you been proposed to mid-thrust?'

'When it hits double digits, I'll let you know.' Gudrun empties the bottle. 'Tell me what I'm missing – explain the love thing.'

'It's the violent progression from worrying someone will leave you to worrying they'll die,' says Robin, voluble with the drink and the company and the night. 'There's no cure for this 3am thought. The only comfort is you might die first.'

Lucy is delighted. 'New anxieties at a steeper pitch.'

'You lit grads and your devotion to the Romantics,' says Gudrun. 'It's goth as fuck and I love it.'

It's the perfect temperature outside, an absence of temperature, nothing to separate air and skin. A pale breeze thrills off the water, the night's particles fat with promise. Lucy, tall in her suede heels, holds Robin's arm as she navigates the cobblestones; drunk on Mandrax and dew and crushed moonbeams.

'I do love your hair, Gudrun,' she says. 'It's as if Dorothy Parker assumed the form of Louise Brooks.'

They move on to a nearby bar, one of taxidermied animals, reptiles in formaldehyde. Gudrun produces a baggie of MDMA and they wash down a pill each with highballs of bison-grass vodka and cloudy apple juice. Lucy cadges a cigarette, and another, then buys a packet, smoking in wolfish drags. 'We never said a proper goodbye,' she says, gazing at the ember, and lights a new one from the tip. They're pushed into a velvet booth meant for two; Robin in the middle now, mute and dizzy. The evening gathers the pace of inevitability. He's back in the litter, with something to contribute this time. They melt into one another.

Gudrun asks if they want kids.

'That's complicated,' says Lucy.

'We don't know,' says Robin, reaching for one of Lucy's cigarettes. 'Although we did, in a flush of love, hatch names for four.'

'We did,' says Lucy. 'Although that's two, if not three or four, too many. I get flashes of want. A memory of my parents putting fresh sheets on my bed, which they did every Sunday night in a rare easy collaboration of tucking and folding – a memory you spend a lifetime chasing. Or watching a bunch of tiny kids at the gallery playing with robotic kittens, which burned a hole right through me. But I grew up crooked, Gudrun. It's not fair to inflict that on anybody else.'

'We both grew up crooked,' says Robin. They smoke in silence, massaging each other's hands.

Lucy suddenly stands as if smelling fire. 'It's Metro Area! I haven't heard this in forever!' She cocks her head towards the speakers, eyes closed. 'Do you know they recorded this downstairs from Sonic Youth's studio? That Sonic Youth were so loud it was like God vacuuming from above? And you can't hear that, but oh, you can *feel it*.' She sits. And they can feel it: the thundering bass casting seismic mainshocks, the searchlight synths, the spiritual presence of Sonic Youth's blizzard of noise. When it's almost over, strings emerge – a transient ecclesiastical flourish, what Lucy would call a small shrine.

'I loved this music,' says Gudrun, 'and the sexy chaos it summoned. Burn bright, burn fast, burn sleazy, I say – and leave a beautiful, vainglorious corpse. Life is too grim for grim music.'

'I wouldn't go that far,' says Lucy. 'But yes, as someone much smarter than me once said, "Glamour is resistance."'

'Miserabilists like me didn't get it.' Robin turns to Lucy. 'Remind me of electroclash's central planks?'

She stands again, a roseate spangle across her face.

Leatherette / epaulette / epithet / car cassette
Magazine / limousine / nicotine / strict machine

Telephone / microphone / monotone / overthrown
White cocaine / pink champagne / black blood stain /
hot migraine

Gudrun laughs with a magnificent roll of her shoulders.
'How do you do that?' says Lucy.
'What?'
'That thing, that ripple. You're so effortlessly sexy. I can only
manage consumptive cute.'

'Silly rabbit,' says Gudrun. 'You are pure devastation, and
you know it.' She bends in to kiss Lucy, her hand on Robin's
thigh, his whole body is a pulse. 'Pure devastation, both of you.'
She shifts again to kiss him, her hair falling into his face. Robin
opens his mouth, pushes his tongue into hers, runs his hand
along the gap of her jumpsuit. Her teeth are charged with the
ice-picked chill of her drink. 'Reprise, reprise, reprise,' chants
Lucy into his ear. 'I have missed this terribly. This is the punctum
of who I am.' She's tinsel and static, the Lucy of the foot-high
pavlovas on the terrace once again.

They fall up the stairs to the warehouse at two-ish, second pills
splashing in their intracellular fluids, a psychedelic edge taking
hold. Lucy fiddles with the stereo. Gudrun shrugs away her
jumpsuit in one liquid movement, lying on the bed in exquisite
disarray. She is voluptuous where Lucy is slight, imprints on her
shoulders and waist, her skin browner in delicious tracts from a
recent week in Spain.

'Well, that's adorable,' says Lucy. 'Now help me get out of
mine.' Her dress, midnight satin, has many fabric-covered

buttons down the back. 'Clearly, I didn't think ahead.' In the time it takes to undo them, whole icebergs shift and crash into the sea, the three of them in hysterics. And then a scrim drops away: Lucy pins Gudrun's leg between hers, takes Gudrun's bottom lip in her teeth. The piano goes over the cliff.

The drugs, as drugs do, give the sense of work being achieved superlatively, creatively, with little effort. An Italo mix plays, vibrating synths and shimmering snares hand-in-glove with the pill's acid kick. This is Lucy's hallowed state: all sensation and no feelings. It's unclear whose mouth and fingers are where; vague which undulations are music, which are breath. At length, Robin determines that Lucy's nails are garden-short, that Gudrun's are manicure-sharp. At length it occurs to Robin that they've done this before – with Julian, of course with Julian. His spectre appears, jangling Robin's blood. They listen to 'Call Me Mr Telephone' and 'Dirty Talk' and '(I Like to Do It in) Fast Cars' and 'Sharevari' and 'Hey Hey Guy' and 'Plastic Doll' and 'Satan in Love'. They listen to Clio's 'Faces', its vast luminous chorus breaking over them.

'I think you should fuck me now,' says Gudrun to Robin, and Lucy claps her hands because it's a fête, a gala. 'You should absolutely fuck her,' says Lucy, and Robin holds Gudrun's hips, urging her towards him. There is a scramble for condoms, a repositioning of limbs; Lucy lights a cigarette and declares she wants to watch for a while. Gudrun tips her head to one side, observing Robin intently as he pushes inside her. Total immolation. He knows, because of the drugs, that he'll never come, that he might keep going forever, so he abandons any pretence of it. Pure repetition, all bass and no treble, pushed up on his arms, empty of want. Lucy stubs out her cigarette, her hand stealing across Gudrun. Her knuckles are rigid against his cock as Gudrun comes, neither of them stopping, drawing it out.

Gudrun turns over, ribs heaving, bob quavering at her neck, trying to get a purchase on her breath. They watch her, riveted.

'What's the thing you said you liked, Lucy,' she says, her voice muffled in the pillow, 'that thing where someone spits on your asshole, but helpfully?'

'Oh, that thing,' says Lucy, 'Robin, show her.'

Slick. Flick. Sick. Kick. 'Are you sure?' he asks Gudrun.

'I might die if you don't.'

He takes her hips again and pulls, unhurried this time, Gudrun on her knees in one lissom fold. He does as he's directed, a staccato gunshot. It sends them nuts. Lucy is crushed against Gudrun, tipping her so they're face to face. Please, please, please keep going, says Gudrun, and he slides into her asshole, inch by excruciating inch. Jesus Fuck, she says; low, deranged. She takes Lucy's hand, smashes it to her mouth, biting at Lucy's fingers. They fall into thudding, amphetamine rhythm, Robin fucking Gudrun, Gudrun fucking Lucy with her hand, all drenched in sweat, much louder than usual. They instinctively slow down every so often, threatening but never quite dropping out of time. Gino Soccio's 'Remember' ripples out from the mix, those walloping synth pads, the whispered French of a girl affecting disinterest – Robin knows this is what undoes Lucy, a sustained paroxysm that sets off a chain. Robin, it seems, can come after all.

'Goodness,' says Gudrun.

They lie in the softest small movements now, Robin's head bent into Gudrun's neck, Gudrun's hands around Lucy's face, stroking her jaw, Lucy's arms around both of them, ministering to Robin's ribs. Eventually, they peel away, taking showers, disposing of condoms, remaking the bed. The music has sputtered and died. They lie flat on their backs, trying to sleep.

'It's impossible,' says Lucy. They never figured out how to cover the windows, the sun merciless in its morning rise. 'I'll never sleep again.'

'What do you have to drink?' asks Gudrun.

'Nothing!' says Lucy. 'We gave up.'

Gudrun rummages around her bag, pulls out a litre of whisky. 'Duty-free.' She swigs, passing the bottle to Lucy. Lucy drinks, passes it to Robin. She lights a cigarette, takes a drag, and passes it to Gudrun.

'God, all those dinners in Abergele,' says Gudrun. 'Pastel days and halcyon nights.'

'But it was so brief. You can hardly call it halcyon.'

'The best things are brief,' says Gudrun. 'Edie Sedgwick and Andy Warhol were only friends for a few months – a blip – but it had the intensity of years. Anyway, I loved tearing down the highway in a Trans Am every weekend to your Pacific West Egg, your folly of smoke and aspic.'

Lucy and Gudrun keep talking of the people they know, the principals, the minor players, the cameos. How the act of knowing people, with just enough frequency, for just enough time, becomes the substance of life itself. Lucy asks for the etymology of Gudrun, and Gudrun says, 'God's secret lore'. Lucy proclaims this counter-instinctual to everything that makes her Gudrun, yet still perfect and correct. Gudrun puts the question to Lucy, who says 'Lux, meaning light, meaning flighty, probably'. The whisky is hot in Robin's veins.

Gudrun shifts, a simmering movement. 'I have coke, you know.'

'I do declare!' and Lucy is up, clear-eyed and morning-fresh, gathering implements, putting on *Love and Dancing*. Gudrun rakes out lines, and Robin declines: for him, the drugs are in woozy retreat, potions evaporating to leave the pure impetus of sex. He waits.

Lucy skips ahead to 'The Things That Dreams Are Made Of', the mostly-instrumental version.

'Fuck, this song is good,' says Gudrun, gulping whisky, passing it to Robin.

'Isn't it?' says Lucy. She's on her shins, hair flicking out in maypole ribbons, each stab of her shoulder an exclamation, the dancer becoming the dance. Bruises blossom on her skin. Hollowed thudding tunnelling fills the room, the result of tape hand-cut and restitched in obsessive frenzy, over 2000 times, to the point of disintegration. 'Martin Rushent wanted to quit producing after this because – like an astronaut who'd gone to the moon – he had nothing left to conquer, nothing left to *do*. And Philip Oakey said the day "Don't You Want Me" went to number one amounted to the worst day of his life. He smashed a phone. He realised it could only be descent from there. But oh, Gudrun, we have *this*.'

The things dreams are made of echo through the warehouse, excavating new caverns and spiralling into oblivion. The bed is a mess again, ash everywhere, what Julian would call a sex nest. Gudrun is lost in a haze of smoke, Lucy far, far away.

Robin rolls over to hold Lucy's ribcage, resting his forehead against her hip. A murmur, a hiss.

Gudrun puts out her cigarette. The sun hits her face, and her cheeks are blotchy, rubescent.

'Let's do something for Lucy.'

'What?' says Robin.

Gudrun regards him, considering. 'Something you want someone else to see.'

Robin finds the sash to Lucy's dress, passes it to Gudrun, and Lucy, eyes glassy, says do whatever you want, just set yourselves upon me, and so they do, at the outposts of mania now. Gudrun gathers handfuls of Lucy's hair in strict fists, and Lucy says more like that, please more like that. There's a cascade of wet slaps, total dissolution, total rapture, full blaze of morning across their soaked skin. Lucy – who is so often concocting labyrinth mixtapes in her head, making eternal lists, furnishing the rooms of her imagined universes – is totally present, pale and crooked, the things she has engineered to this point falling into oracular inevitability, Robin's fingers in her mouth while she says fuck, more, more.

And so it goes.

They sleep in a clean soapy pile. Just past 11, Lucy unhooks herself. Robin watches her hunt for painkillers; slice bread as a precaution against stomach ulcers. He has been awake, feigning sleep, for over an hour. He hears Lucy showering again.

Gudrun wakes prettily; expansive stretches, hair switching the air. 'Good morning, Christopher Robin.' She turns towards him, wraps her fingers around his cock.

'That might be against the rules,' he says, but doesn't move her hand.

'Lucy, darling,' says Gudrun, her voice chiming like a spoon on a glass, 'come back to bed. Look how dreamy he is.'

Lucy returns, pulling on tights, looking remarkably well-rested. 'I'm going on a supply run for us. I'll be back in a couple of hours.' She kisses them both on the forehead. 'Have fun, but don't fall in love.'

For years afterwards, he wonders why Lucy does this – whether it's a gift, a bargaining chip, or a stratagem for sustaining intrigue.

She returns with bread, sherry, tins of smoked mussels, German riesling, more cigarettes. They drag cushions up the ladder to picnic in the treacly autumn sun, lulled by Sunday noises of distant traffic and a big football game climaxing before its crowd scatters.

Lucy keeps unpacking things: a chocolate orange, a hunk of manchego, two kielbasa sausages which she slices at acute angles, a jar of the hard Sicilian olives they like, a pot of smoked trout terrine, miniature cucumbers that snap pleasingly in half. They finish the coke. Lucy and Gudrun talk with their characteristic ease, passing each other lighters and bread and blankets and cardigans. Robin is mostly quiet.

After Gudrun leaves for the airport, and they've put the warehouse back together, and changed the sheets, and Lucy has scrubbed the nicotine from her fingers and thrown away the cigarettes and ordered in dinner, after she's found them both a Valium from her old stash, they curl in bed, moving instinctively into each other, exactly the same height. And Lucy says into his hair, 'Enjoy it, Robin, but don't pick at it too much. That way insanity lies.'

He walks around with a low throb in his guts for a week, the thought of all things Gudrun, but it passes.

*

It is Lucy who comes home drunk on Friday night; new bruises at the legs, hair acrid with smoke. Her dress – a gauzy shift dimming neon underwear – is dirty at the sleeves and hem. She pitches her bag hard at the floor and drops boneless to the couch, forearm covering her eyes.

'*Well, now that's done: and I'm glad it's over.*'

'What's done?'

'Julian.'

'Ah,' says Robin. For two years, he has waited for this.

'Where did you see him?'

'At the Glass Mirage opening. I hate him.'

She reaches for Robin's hand, brings it to her temple, and he reflexively massages the coiled beginnings of a migraine. 'I didn't expect to cross paths with a ghost tonight, Robin, but that's what happened. The ghost of Julian, of love, and my old life – a fucking holy trinity of a ghost. Tall, too. Drinking a beer and rather pleased with itself.'

'What happened?'

'Nothing. We just smoked and yelled in an alley. I wish he was dead.'

'No, you don't.'

'You always had a thing for Julian.' Lucy says this without venom. 'You had your chance. It only required one teeny step across the kitchen that night – any of those nights. Of course I don't wish him dead; I just wish he'd fall off the earth in a forever way. Bumping into him is too much like bumping into a nasty part of myself, serene as it does the rotten things I used to do.' She drops her arm and faces Robin. 'Do you know he let me pay for everything for three years? That he never said goodbye? Never messaged me in hospital; never messaged ever?

He just took my Silver Apples record and drove into the night.'
She is slurring, perhaps more intoxicated than Robin's ever seen
her, but has the set-jaw determination of a drunk behind the
wheel, using rumble strips to stay on the road.

'I didn't know that.'

'Well, that's because we've never talked about it.'

'No.' An unpleasant feeling wraps three fingers around
Robin's ribs, giving an experimental squeeze. 'I'll get you water.'

Lucy says she doesn't want water, but he fills a glass for her
anyway, returning by circuitous route and snapping on lamps as
he goes.

'It was a wicked thing I did to my book, Robin.' She has
forgotten she didn't want water. She has forgotten Julian for
the present. 'It was a wicked thing I did with the magazine.
I didn't think myself special, or gifted, but I was good, and
getting better. The people I most admire are not suppressing
the extreme, greedy, obsessive parts of themselves; they're
amplifying them, monetising them, making careers out of them.
That drive to be adored, to obliterate yourself in a cause, wanting
more, more, more – that's propulsion. I could have stayed
and fought. I could have lived with being rotten occasionally, if that's what it took. But I threw it away; I retreated;
I gave up.'

'Do you classify our life together as retreat?' Robin speaks
calmly, but he wishes very much that she'd stop.

'In a way. That's what monogamy is by design: a retreat from
obsession, a retreat from the chase, a retreat from your most
intense self so you're bearable to share a house with. But do you
want to live without it, that feeling with Gudrun?'

'I can live without it.'

'Oh, you *can* live without it,' she says, flint in her voice. 'Always the Stoic, Robin. Do you *want* to live without it?'

'I don't think we should talk about that now.'

She pushes up onto her elbows, ignoring him. 'Women retreat to monogamy because it's safer. They withdraw from all kinds of things – anything that makes them too conspicuous – because it's safer. Not everyone, of course. Most have tangled with worse shit than me, and the tough ones *just keep going*. But once your internal alarm starts sounding, it's very hard to shut off. The stupid thing – the stupid, very boring thing, Robin – is that even when I retreated from all sources of trouble, the alarm kept going. It's an infrasound vibration now, a fixed pulse of noiseless terror.'

Robin knows this well. Her dread of mice and rats. The way she avoids sitting unless her back is to the wall, the horror of being snuck up on. Her inherent distrust of any man older or bigger than her, manifesting in a refusal to deal with real estate agents, tradesmen; in the careful circles she draws around herself at work. Her aversion to the letterbox, the dark. A refusal to attend gigs, to write anything of length. What were quirks in Abergele have hypostatised, gaining power in proximity to their original source.

'What did Julian say, Lucy?' But Lucy, who never cries, has turned into the couch, shoulders shuddering in small advances and retreats.

Robin watches, then returns to the kitchen, patting around the benches until he finds Gudrun's whisky. He pours a tumbler, drinks it in one swallow, and resumes his position next to the couch.

'Lucy, listen. Remember what you said on the houseboat – that Julian is never wrong?'

She turns to him, face smeared. 'Yes.'

'It's not true.'

'It's undeniably true. That's one thing, after everything, that's still true.'

'It's not. How old were you when it started with him?'

'Twenty-three.'

'And Julian?'

'Thirty-one. So what?'

'When The Creep was at unhinged peak Creep, right? When the police were useless, the magazine publishers were useless, your family weren't great, and Victor was falling down stairs. I imagine it was an immense relief when Julian emerged, six-plus-feet of adult charisma and perfect taste. He had unstinting belief in his rightness, and it was in your interests to share that belief.'

She says nothing.

'Equally, your invention of The Unspoiled Monster – pure instinct, carved from marble, always just out of reach – was an invention it served Julian to assume. It was a dyad, Lucy: a two-way performance. But he's not The Unspoiled Monster; he's just Julian. And he has many obnoxious opinions you can disregard.'

'I thought there was something beneath that, though! Always looking for a tender Julian, a squishy Julian, the real Julian. Always thinking we were sympathetic travellers, game recognising game, tunnelling towards the same thing. I saw my delusion on all counts tonight, and I'm chilled to my goddamned marrow.' Lucy sits, arrow straight. 'And guess what? Julian told me from the beginning there was nothing to find; that it was a lunatic's mission and a waste of my time. But obsession means ignoring all good advice. Obsession means commitment to forgetting. "I can see – and I approve the better course, *and yet I choose the worse.*"'

Medea. There's a sway, a shudder. 'Oh god, I'm going to puke.'

He half-carries her to the bathroom. Lucy vomits, crying with the gulping fury of the very drunk. She crawls to the shower; he rinses her hair. It takes much manoeuvring to get her in the bed, but once there, she stretches to luxuriant diagonal, wet locks wefting the pillow. 'You're my moral compass, Robin.' She is smiling and sleepy. 'You'd never steal a girl's Silver Apples record and drive into the night.'

'Everyone is their own moral compass.' He sets out a bowl, two glasses of water, and a sheet of painkillers for the morning. 'You told me that – we can't use each other as human shields.'

She has stopped crying. Blue eyes flecked with grey, cheekbones violet in the dark. 'I'm done retreating.'

'Good. We'll be two burnt-out prodigies, staging a comeback.'

'I won, Robin. You were the prize, and I won.'

Over the next three years, Robin burrows further into photography, into the things people prize in his work. His perceptiveness and quiet diligence. His ability to divine what's elemental in subjects, drawing it out. His respect for the scaffolding of self-image, the construction of which performers are fiercely, oft-unwittingly protective. To disturb this visage is to inflict a grave injury, so Robin magnifies its most honest demonstrations. The keening reach in an arm's extension. The impulse of self-preservation masked in the slightest turn of a head. The exquisite control in every finger, even death-gripped around an instrument. When performed cellularly, for long enough, self-image ceases to be a performance. He knows this.

Robin finds his urges around music vivified, making and releasing three EPs: noisy, ruinous, haunted by buried melody. He collects a wild-eyed contingent who come to every gig, as small and sporadic as these gigs are. 'You're as violent onstage as you are polite off,' says Lucy, who breaks her ban on shows for Robin only. 'It makes sense now: immanence vs transcendence, the sacred vs the profane. You've harnessed your oppositional forces.'

Roland offers to help. Robin considers it, understanding his demolitions were conceived in direct defiance of Roland's lush approach; knowing that tension could be interesting, knowing he'll never say yes.

Lucy moves to an advertising agency, telling Robin she's weaponising her obsessions. He watches her do this with a mix of admiration and unease. 'See,' she says, 'that energy I used to put into manufacturing intrigue and tragedies, that toil to send the piano over a cliff – I've transposed that pointless labour into actual work now. And as well as people telling me I'm clever, they pay me proper money, and unsurprisingly that makes me happy. THE END.'

She loves the accelerated intimacy of projects, how it binds people to one another. She unearths the animating spark at the centre of things and polishes it to a silvered glare. She gets promoted. Robin perceives the raw ambition there the whole time, muffled by fear, obsession, and retreat. The money they both earn is useful. They buy rugs for the warehouse and find the winters much warmer. They put in temporary walls to create a bedroom. They take trips to Tokyo, Hamburg, Mexico City, and New York; to Lucy's brief childhood home in California, the one that means most to her after Abergele. They hire a car and tear through the desert, listening to the nine-minute version of 'Never Let Me Down Again' on repeat, Joshua trees shaking their shaggy fists, windfarms churning in the distance. The sense of continual ascent is right back at the surface. Robin avoids Spain, despite Lucy's gentle prodding. He is not ready. Instead, he buys better gear, takes better photos, gets better jobs, gets better fees, buys better gear, takes better photos.

There's the gradual turning out from their humid cinch, a gradual loosening of their monastic life. Dinner parties in the warehouse turn into party parties. Nights out to celebrate meeting implausible deadlines turn into huddled conferences in tiny bars, or laundromats and carwashes masquerading as bars, which often turn into Lucy and Robin coming home with one or two or a few people. This might amount to records and talking, or records and dancing, or what Lucy calls the late-night erotic cabaret. It's never as good as with Gudrun, but more than they could have hoped for; incompatible goods held in optimal tension.

The sight of her across the room, crooked arm thrown out, while he attends to his own erotic cabaret, will vault Robin into a heightened state for weeks, months. Maybe it feeds the recordings: the shiverbox production; the rough buzz that blooms into prismatic cascades; the hammering percussion, felted as if muffled by pillows; the spooky pockets of bale and joy; the chaos and loudness – he doesn't know. Maybe it's what keeps them in a state of suspended lubricious animation, pressed together as they walk the streets, waking each other in the night – he doesn't know either. He thinks of the Rilke letter: the merging of two individuals is impossible. That marriage shouldn't be the demolishment of all boundaries, but each person appointing the other as gatekeeper of their solitude. He shakes this out, sits with it.

'You think you're at the end of a story, then you find yourself right back in the middle,' says Lucy. She, Robin and Tabitha are having dinner in Chinatown, the lazy Susan piled with clay pots.

'I don't believe in monogamy as a principle either,' says Tabitha. 'But it's too much effort clearing the complications of an alternative.'

'*Adultery is a most conventional way to rise above the conventional.* If you can't be bothered, don't bother, Tabitha.'

'Harry is annoying sometimes, but I still prefer him to everyone else. The other night I went to a party and it was all crashing, drunk bores. Granted, I arrived late when people are well past their best, but I wasn't compelled to take anyone home.' She pushes back her plate.

'Lucy eviscerated a bore last night,' Robin says. It had been a collegial gathering of three newish friends at the warehouse, plus one messy hanger-on. The drunk had talked himself in spirals while Lucy watched him, smoking and silent. At last, he'd found himself at the dead end of his own maze. She'd stood, flint and height; he stood too, unsettled, sapped of will, and left.

'Oh god, Lucy, what did you say to him?' asked Tabitha.

'I didn't say a thing. I've learned that silence is the best strategy with bad eggs – they'll use any scrap you give them as fuel.'

It turns out that Robin and Lucy aren't predisposed to jealousy, not in this way anyway, and perhaps it's a problem, because jealousy might act as a brake on their excesses. From time to time, one or both of them will deflate. From time to time, one will suggest they slow down. 'Soon,' says Lucy, collecting bottles and ashtrays as Robin lies groaning on the couch. 'We'll have our 30th birthdays and a daisy chain of glorious fêtes. Then we'll retire to the country to live respectable lives.'

A ballroom dinner at which Lucy's team wins a big industry award. Bloated floral arrangements scraping the chandeliers. Alternating plates of tepid salmon and beef. It sets them both on edge – the terrible band, the terrible jokes, the canned music soundtracking the awkward line collecting trophies – and so they get drunk, first on glasses of acidic sparkling and then tequila shots at the bar. Lucy introduces Robin to her boss, and the three of them talk, Lucy voluble and nodding, what Robin knows is a performance of congeniality.

'He is a nasty egg,' she says into Robin's ear as the man saunters away. It's all they've talked about for weeks as successive resignations and small fires metastasised; outwardly unconnected events resolving as a disturbing pattern. She'd discovered a whole new order of bad eggness, she'd said – artful and insidious, reducing the Victors and The Creeps of the world to panto villains.

'Well, I have the award now, which means I'll get my bonus next week, and then I'm evacuating the premises, parachute inflated.'

Robin and Lucy have titanic hangovers the next day. They're walking for coffee, buttressed against each other, when Robin feels her stiffen. Striding towards them is a man in a white denim jacket.

'Hullo,' says Lucy, standing to full height. Victor, it must be Victor. 'You look like you went out for a big night in 1995 and never made it home.'

The man smiles, extending a hand toward Robin. 'Nice to see you too, Lucinda. You look like someone just knocked over your ice cream cone. Tell me, who is this?'

'Don't touch him.' Lucy steps forward and punches Victor in the face. The force doesn't surprise Robin, but her aim is a revelation. Victor staggers back, and Robin regards him, a long curiosity now satisfied. He is average in all respects except for a smear of blood at his nose. That might have been the end, except Victor returns Robin's look with a smirk, a Can You Believe This insinuation, and Robin gives him a shove – not hard, but enough to send Victor back into a hedge, a slow-motion tumble that might be funny one day.

'Do you know, Robin, that I'd have to finish his articles when he was too hungover to type?' Lucy delivers a perfunctory kick to Victor's shin, a Final Girl checking if the Big Bad is dead. 'You are old, Victor. Your obsession with the Second World War is disturbing. Your opinions on The Smiths are irrelevant.' She turns to Robin. 'And look, he has nothing to say. He never had anything of interest to say.' And they take off; half-running, half-skipping, hands braided.

Lucy's hangover has evaporated. At home, she snaps into furious action, tidying and cleaning, organising the records, pruning the plants, moving things around, hanging washing in long lines that crisscross the warehouse. Robin naps, comforted by the low hum of activity.

'I've realised something important,' she says. It's nearing sundown, and she has woken Robin with a plate of garlic bread. 'People use me as an explosive device. Victor felt impotent and bored, so he used me to blow up his life with Celeste. Julian felt like an ageing playboy, so he used me to blow up his routine and take a stab at bucolic retreat. My boss had run out of ideas and energy and let things get stale at the agency. So he used me to blow it up, to bring him new people, new clients, fresh blood. Fine – but I didn't enlist to be his silent proxy, or one of his horsemen of the apocalypse. I didn't enlist for what's happening now. People get excited by what I do for them, then get mad when I don't want to do it anymore.'

Her eyes are bright. 'Well, fuck that, I'm not doing anything for anyone ever again. Ever!' She takes a piece of bread and tears it with vigour. 'Caring and wanting and striving and feeling too much makes you vulnerable. It gets you into trouble. So from now on, I'm as closed-off as a machine. Bulletproof. Armoured. One of those beetles with their ironclad exoskeletons. You were the last high, Robin; you were the *last high*.'

There's nothing to be done with this.

Deliveries arrive all week: flowers, wine, cocaine, records, clothes, food. Linted stems of bullrushes and tight-fisted peonies. Bottles of garnet things and cloudy orange things with sediment at the bottom. Crates of heirloom vegetables still dusted with the soil they were pulled from. Envelopes of salt, expensively packaged. Boxes of American cereal: Count Chocula, Trix, Lucky Charms. Pots of eyeshadow in vermilion and topaz. Silver ankle boots with stacked heels. Flat mary-janes: one pair in black velvet and one in blue. Satin pyjamas printed with jaguars. Eighties issues of *The Face* postmarked express delivery from Ukraine. Her teenage favourites on 180-gram vinyl: *Under the Pink*, *To Bring You My Love*, *The Chronic*, *Maxinquaye*, *Loveless*. Gifts for Robin: a bottle of Acca Kappa perfume, an early edition of Mapplethorpe's *Pistils*, an effects pedal he'd been pining after.

'Are you trying to get rid of dirty money again?' he asks.

'What?' She's sorting through the magazines, stacking them by date, distracted.

'Your bonus. You're kicking it away, like you kicked Victor's money across the floor that Easter in Abergele.'

'I had entirely forgotten that incident.'

There are people over every night that week. People from Lucy's agency team, from the Costume Institute, from her old life at the magazine, people they have collected along the way. Lucy weaves through the warehouse, filling glasses. She wears a lycra catsuit one night; a tuxedo with a voluminous poet's blouse unbuttoned halfway down her chest on another. She is as incandescent as she's ever been, decisive, insufferable. Robin falls asleep to the shatter of laughter and dropped glass. On Thursday, he comes home from a show, chanting *too much as such, too much as such* under his breath as he takes the stairs. Everyone – the couches are full – looks up. Lucy is at his side instantly, stricken. He is drunk, monstrously drunk, and bleeding from the head. 'Robin! What happened?'

'I threw my microphone into the crowd, and someone threw it back.' He recalls pushing the mic to the back of his throat, a lunatic love note to Lux Interior. Jumping backwards from the stage, knocking over drinks, the mic cord a whip. She takes his arm, marching him to the bedroom. 'Does it hurt?'

'No. Likely because I'm plastered.' He sits, the flimsy walls moving.

'Then lie down.'

She removes his belt, his jeans, her hand cold around his cock, her eyes glassy. He groans. 'Shall I keep going?' And he wants to say, what's going on, you terrify me sometimes, I loathe myself tonight, but of course I want you to keep going. And what he says is please, yes, please. He thinks of the afternoon on her study couch when he had heatstroke, of being incapacitated, sick with lust, in her command. They kiss, and he navigates to her ribs, pushing through the silk of her blouse to the crimps underneath. He thinks of her and Gudrun in the bath when she described her delirium-inducing blowjobs.

'Please, Lucy, come here,' he says at length, so she peels away her clothes, lowering her full height against him. The softness has gone out of her; the hand at his nape firm, precise. It is that hand that he'll remember, a gesture of exquisite possession, of control.

They fuck in a sequence of austere movements, people who barely know each other, the sound of Lucy's guests close. She murmurs things into his mouth, into his eyelids, things he wishes he could remember later. 'I want to shipwreck myself on you,' he says. 'I want you to destroy me.' Lucy says nothing now, her face dispassionate, but there's a lucent charge down her body, her hand tighter at his neck, and she comes, her breath tearing in his ear. It's the end for him, and she twists away to stand in one neat movement.

He closes his eyes. When he opens them, she is dabbing at his forehead and covering it with plaster. 'I love you,' she says, voice low. 'You are the one uncompromised thing.'

'Luce,' he says, reaching for her hand, but she is finished, she is pulling on her clothes, she is gone.

Robin sleeps, fitful, hearing people leave, hearing Lucy prowl around the warehouse. In the morning, he finds her on the rooftop, watching *Depeche Mode 101* on her laptop.

'Have you slept?'

'Oh shit.' She pauses on Martin Gore buying cassettes to consider the sky. 'No, I haven't slept. I didn't realise it was so late. Or so early.' Her attention shifts again. 'Oh Robin, your head!'

He touches the gash, its concentrated throb joining the full-body throb of his hangover. 'Are you going to work?'

'Of course.' She stands and stretches. The stars and moons of her kimono emit wan tinselly light, the rotation of a mirror ball come sunrise. The summer had been wet, and Lucy's garden is in full fecund bloom; the last reaching gasps of magnificence before winter's inevitable die out. The cherry tomatoes branched across the wall, coaxed into late fruiting by the microclimate of close-by factories. The crimped dahlias taking their final bravura turn. A spray of cosmos, grown from seed she'd collected at Roland's. Staghorn ferns propagated from old monsters at the Abergele house and mounted like stuffed heads. The suggestive bulbs of balloon cotton bush dangling over the railing, and the gentle sway of furred salvias. The engorged tangle of succulents everywhere, the ones that so disgust Tabitha. 'Look at meeeeeee,' Tabitha had croaked in a distended voice, mocking them. 'Look at my gross flower – I made it for yooooouuuuu.' Lucy fills the watering can and starts her slow, methodical circuit.

Robin watches for a minute and then makes coffee.

'Well, I better rescue my gear,' he says, putting her cup next to the laptop. Lucy kisses him on the cheek, an absent kiss, and returns to watering.

Robin is only peripherally aware of what happens in the days that follow, due in equal part to her obfuscation and his alarmed retreat. Lucy leaving work and spending the day at the arthouse cinema, wandering between sessions and sniffling into the collar of her mother's old faux fur coat. Lucy walking through the city in the grip of a roiling panic attack, chewing Valiums until it subsides. Lucy, standing on the Bookend Bridge, watching canoeists plough through the graphite water below, tapping messages to Anika and Gudrun and Tabitha while grey-headed flying foxes glide in with the night. Lucy pitching her phone into the river and walking the eight kilometres back to Anika's; moving money around to book into a private clinic two hours out of town. Anika makes the arrangements. Anika packs a bag. It's three days until Robin may visit.

'You found me,' she says, somnolent, straightjacketed by hospital corners.

'Not easily.'

He realises that, once again, they have failed each other; not for lack of love, or want, but from sheer depletion of the self. 'I thought you were building a runway to leave me.'

'No. Jesus, Robin, no. I was trying not to go over the edge. And here I am anyway.' He turns back the covers and manoeuvres into the bed. They reorder their limbs, the relief of being bone-to-bone, atom-to-atom.

'Was it Victor?' he asks.

'If you take the long view, he definitely figures. But no, it's my fault. I got cocky, monstrous – I overreached. I knew very well what was required when I left hospital last time but did none of it. Instead, I obliterated myself in you, the most sublime extinguishing of the self. Then I obliterated myself in work, and surprise, surprise, Lupus in Fabula.'

'What's Lupus in Fabula?'

'It's the wolf in the fairytale. I left the door unlocked, and it wandered right into my kitchen. The horror show at the agency didn't help.'

'What will you do? About work, I mean.'

'I don't know. I'll have to quit and then figure it out. There must be a worthwhile outlet for my excess energy. Assuming that energy returns.'

She shifts, her hand at his hip. 'Don't look so sad, Robin. It's not all terrible. We had lots of fun.'

'We did.'

'I tried things, and I failed. I failed with the magazine, I failed with the book, and I failed with nearly everything this year. It hurts like hell, and I know it wasn't pleasant for you either, but sometimes you need that clean sting of failure to keep you alert, to propel you forward, to heighten everything else. You need it to test your limits periodically, to discern if the hard edges are where you remember them or slightly further beyond; otherwise you might stay weak and scared forever. Obviously my approach needs some refining. You have to keep some part of yourself in reserve.'

'But no more failure for now,' she adds, seeing the look on his face. 'It's time for the quiet life. Maybe not forever, but for a long time.'

'A very long time,' echoes Robin.

'I'll pull my socks up. I'll go to therapy – properly.'

'I'll go too.'

She stiffens. 'Not together!'

'Of course not – alone.'

'Good. Maybe we'll learn to differentiate our personality traits from our afflictions.' And he nods, despite how forbidding this sounds.

'Christ, I am tired, Lucy.'

'You should sleep.' And he does, falling into it with the swiftness of drowning; his head on her chest, her leg pinned between his, for the moment safe.

Later, Robin puts the house back together, tidying the tokens of the dirty money, the baroque detritus of the previous week's gatherings. He takes photos as he goes, thinking of The Associates and their 16 cashmere jumpers, the smoked salmon for the whippets; excess that serves no material purpose except to provoke extravagant action, to telegraph some extravagant need. He calls Tabitha and reports on the visit.

'The circumstances at the agency were less than ideal,' he says. 'It spiralled out from there.'

'It wasn't less than ideal, it was fucked,' says Tabitha. 'You have few choices in that situation, and they're all garbage: you stay and keep quiet, you leave and keep quiet, or you leave and set fire to it publicly. Lucy's always had her own way of doing things, though.'

Robin is heating soup, making tea. 'What do you mean?'

'She leaves and self-immolates. But prescribed burning – controlled burning.'

'Tabitha.' He sets down a spoon. 'I watched her nosedive over five weeks – nothing prescribed or controlled about it.'

'Not consciously. Not entirely unconsciously.'

This is even harder to accept. 'To what possible benefit?' The question starts as refutation; transposes to genuine inquiry. Lucy forever stalking lines of flight, weighing and reweighing her options. The possibility that by submitting so dangerously to things, so wholly to people, the only way to freedom is through violent finalities. That the bridge, kept openly in suspension, functions as emblem, as hard boundary. It's what compels her towards the most daunting alternative, whatever that alternative is at the time.

Tabitha waits for him.

'Jesus. That's pretty dark, if it's true.'

'Sure, but also kind of punk, no? Except for the expensive rest-cure bit.'

'Very punk. Very *I Abject!*, via *Notes from the Underground.*'

'I never finished *Notes from the Underground.*'

'Via the Pleasure Principle then.'

'Oh god, Freud? Really?'

'Yes. Lucy talked of it today – very rationally, given where she was.'

'Rational. There you go, Robin.'

'Fuck.'

'It's no fun for anybody involved, but it's not malicious; none of our self-preservation strategies are inherently malicious. You establish an organising framework for life, and it's difficult to diverge too far. The countless sustained exertions it takes to achieve any action of value would be too exhausting otherwise. Creating yourself through passionate action and heedless re-enactment, etc.'

'More than enough passionate action for us both.'

'I don't know, Robin. You've been on your own sprees, breaking things to make things. It's an infectious impulse, in the correct measure. How's your hedonistic calculus theory?'

'As good as your Dostoevsky.'

'Well, I've been teaching it this week. *Men calculate. Some with less exactness, indeed, some with more; but all men calculate.* And on that note, I have to get back to marking papers before I yield to my baser impulses and set the pile on fire. Let's talk tomorrow, yes?'

They say goodbye. Robin eats his soup and drinks his tea. He digs through his books, looking for one recovered on that first visit to the farm with Lucy. *Hor Mit Schmerzen / Listen with Pain* – a 17th birthday present from Roland. It's where it should be, and while the passage isn't highlighted, it leaps to him anyway. *Einstürzende Neubauten is a positive sound, possibly the most positive sound of all. Old objects, meanings, buildings and music get destroyed, all traces of the past are abandoned: only out of destruction can something really new be created.*

PASTEL DAYS AND NEON NIGHTS

Lucy checks out with a new class of anxiolytics that resemble rose-quartz molars, and a new set of rules for living. Methodically and without sentiment this time, she assesses the substance of her world, and jettisons much of what she once deemed essential. There are no fêtes for their 30th birthdays, just meals with their families and a pleasantly sedate joint dinner with Tabitha, Harry and Anika. Lucy will describe what came before – her volcanic 20s – as a distraction, an indulgence, a rejection of the larger world and her constructive place within it. A want has been cauterised, she tells Robin, the fall down the rabbit hole surely complete.

She takes a short contract at the just-elected lord mayor's office – working under the first woman to hold the post – a moratorium, Lucy calls it, while she formulates a fuller plan. Anika begins her registrarship at a rural hospital, a three-hour drive from the closest airport along red, largely unsealed roads. Tabitha and Harry take on new responsibilities at work, buy and gut an apartment, and have a baby girl, Olivia, in quick succession, and then Harry's father has a heart attack. Tabitha describes this period as The Pixilated Ghost Cycle as they're flattened by its compounding demands. Robin lets himself get overbooked, taking on an assistant to help, but makes the mistake of being too accommodating, of keeping things too close, and finds the workload quadrupled. The assistant quits, and for months Robin sleeps little, grinding through the edits, wired with anxiety, any pretence of making music dropped. He asks Lucy how the hell she manages people. She tells him she started young, that she's had lots of practice, that she enjoys it.

They're all in a stretch of tense recalibration, which at times resembles retreat from their real selves. It's only Gudrun, entrenched in London, who is still at the white-hot centre of Life; still very much Gudrun. Her emails are telegrams from an alternate lotusland, a place Lucy says she's glad is out there but in no hurry to inhabit.

So Lucy and Robin are quiet and careful, watching each other for signs of corrosion. They still go to parties but leave before the drugs arrive. They sit side-by-side at dinners, Lucy always to Robin's left. There are Christmases and weekends with Isabella and the kids, trips to Abergele to see Lucy's grandfather, trips to the mountain to see Roland and Christian. But they're happiest at home. On Saturdays, they walk to the markets and choose things for the week ahead, carting back bags of hard German bread and cherry preserves and pickled cactus on their shoulders. They spend the remaining weekends in honeyed torpor, cooking and reading, Lucy's feet in Robin's lap, rising now and then to stir a saucepan or change the record. It is contentment, a new feeling to them both, happiness so intense it can tip into melancholy.

The warehouse is the last repository of obsession. Photography gear. Music gear, dusty but still adored. The ferns under the bathtub, the jungle on the rooftop, the perpetual propagation of ivy everywhere. The piles of books that they use as side tables, as coffee tables, as tables to hold more books. The carefully labelled jars of homemade preserves and chutneys, Lucy's latest project, refracting orange prisms of morning light. The salts and spices she collects, decanted into glass and dated fastidiously. And their records, six-monthly cycles of compulsion. The J Dilla rarities, the Razormaid mixes, the Flying Nun reissues, the Dirty Sound System edits, the leaked synth-pop demos of *Pretty Hate Machine*, the Pebbles and Nuggets compilations, the Rhino Records compilations, the early minimal wave excavated from tape, the '70s psychedelia Lucy borrows from her dad in their tentative re-establishment of shared interests, the witch house and hauntological, the new stuff Lucy categorises as emotional disco, the new stuff Robin categorises as pink noise, each of their fixations a reaction to the last.

The twins, who've just finished school, come for sleepovers – always together, despite Lucy's pointed, periodic efforts to separate them. They delight in the warehouse ostranenie, its adult otherness. Robin suggests they hold their 18th birthday there.

On the afternoon of the party, Lucy's mother calls, asking where they should park.

'Curses,' says Lucy, hanging up the phone. 'I didn't realise my parents were coming. I'm afraid you've got a new job tonight, Robin: babysitting them.'

He is grateful for this role of minder, leaving Lucy to attend to the teenaged throng and their clamorous orchestra of needs. She brings them phone chargers and paracetamol and clean outfits. She hunts for their lost earrings and bags. She puts a very drunk girl to bed on the guest futon, then cleans a spray of vomit from the bath between diagnostic surveys of the room. She sets out iced water, pressing glasses on those who've overindulged. She calls taxis and guides guests down the perilous stairs, waiting with them on the street. She sits with a weeping brunette for a half-hour, a brunette who'll return with Rosemary on many subsequent nights, employing the warehouse as safehouse.

Lucy and Robin conference on the rooftop.

'I can't believe my parents are still here – Dad said they'd leave after the food. Clara and Rosemary must be livid.'

'They tried to leave ages ago, but Clara got very upset, and Rosemary got upset that Clara was upset, and there were tears. So everyone will be here 'til the end, I suspect.'

'Well, that tracks. They're a very cosy unit, those four, and it's genuinely nice to see. I'm all for secure attachment, though I still find its finer mechanics mystifying. How will the twins learn to be good without impetus to first go properly, prolifically bad?'

Robin hadn't thought about Julian in a while. They'd heard things, of course, but he has the quality of a leitmotif fading, a once-luminous quasar growing faint as the constellations of their lives pull further apart.

Then he manifests three times in three weeks. Tabitha, in flannelette pyjamas, is collecting the paper from her stoop one Saturday morning when Julian passes with a motley troupe of young goths, en route from some mischief. An anecdote passed around the Abergele crew, Julian the punchline (ejected naked from an all-night party, pausing to drink from the garden tap mid-flee, laughter alerting him to a packed house auction across the street), acquires a sinister tone when Lucy meets the ejector by chance at a dinner. The woman's telling of the story isn't funny, not one bit.

Finally, Robin sees Julian at the farewell Pink Fist concert.

They're canon now, something Lucy declared inevitable when she reviewed Pink Fist's first talisman of an EP. Twenty thousand ballot winners stream into the Paradise Quarry for a sunset performance. Roland produced their last album in his wet, resonant cathedral style, and Robin, who is shooting, asks Lucy to come, but she says absolutely not in that calm, final new way of hers, a calm finessed in therapy, a breezy calm used to soften hard limits.

'My auteur days are behind me,' she'd said. 'In music, anyway. You're Pink Fist's Diaghilev now.'

'I'm hardly a Diaghilev.'

'Robin. What do you think you've been doing this whole time? Image-making. Myth-creation. Casting spells. Anika might call you an iconoblast. I say this with ferocious love and envy – the aggregate of which is awe. Where would Pink Fist be without your photographs? Where would any of those bands be? You're so fucking good, and still annoyingly, wilfully blind to it.'

'Thank you. For saying it, for always meaning it. I'd still be hiding my pictures in shoeboxes otherwise.'

'It's my deep abiding pleasure. But I'm not going. Get back to your music – then I'll reappraise gigs.'

'Perhaps you'll reappraise your book while you're at it.'

'Very funny.'

Robin shoots the crowd as they arrive, the new class of bright young things dressed entirely in black and white. They're chopped and singing and screaming, their pills eaten early in deference to the sniffer dogs at the gates. He shoots the band backstage – Fred newly sober and sick with nerves, Inky trying on leather jackets and working the room. And then he shoots the show itself from a cage dangled above the footlights; Robin's new assistant is side-of-stage, another in the pit. A synthesis of these photos, layered and blasted in light, will form some approximation of the immaterial now.

The week threatened rain, but the day is one of those clear blazing days for the ages. The sun drops away with torturous slowness, spraying kaleidoscopic froth across the sky and the rapt faces craned towards the stage. Lucy, you silly rabbit, Robin whispers, as seven piano notes ring through the quarry in hypnotic repetition. The crowd bursts apart, unleashing their pent-up want in a roar of unhinged bacchanal. Inky, pharaonic and beautiful, leans into the mic.

They are a five-piece now; the stage spiderwebbed in cables that took Roland's crew hours to configure. The sky turns from orange to red to carbon, machines outlined in heroic glow: a Moog Voyager, a RozzBox Oddulator, an ARP Odyssey, an Oberheim Xpander, a Korg MS-20, a Metasonix D-1000, a Swarmatron. As the last particle of night falls into place, waterfalls of synth drench the quarry, cleaving to sheets of dry ice. The centrepiece is a torch song: baritone, 808 and piano;

longing, brawn and majesty. Inky sings 'The hammer, the anvil, the stirrup' over and over in corkscrewing melodic descent. His voice rolls out in a tidal wave, crashing, without pause, into one final elegy: a nine-minute version of Tuxedo Moon's 'In a Manner of Speaking', recast against coruscating death-rave percussion. A whole Russian novel's worth of plot and pathos, Robin thinks. Lucy should be here.

Backstage is a carnival. Robin is threading through the crowds to collect his equipment from the green room when his shoulder meets something hard: Julian. Julian, who'd been crewing for the support band earlier that afternoon. Julian with a lanyard at his neck and a girl at his side.

That quality of vampiric youth – of white, white teeth, of eternal leanness, of unbearably green eyes, that shocking red across his forehead – is gone. His shoulders are broader, heavier. His hair is shorter and lighter, grey where it's buzzed against his scalp, and there's a new tattoo on his forearm, something Victorian. But the rumours of him losing his looks, of going to seed, 'like meat left in the sun', said Gudrun when she saw him in London, are overstated. His spine is as straight as ever, the same power and elegance in his arms, the same persuasive tightness at his jaw. His gaze has hardened, suggesting dissatisfaction, but there's still that near-invisible shrug of his left shoulder; a distant beat that beckons to be hitched against.

'Robin!' he says, all stubbled dimples. 'How are you?' It's the first time they've crossed paths since the party in Abergele.

'Good, very good,' Robin says. The arm on his back is authoritative, beatific. 'What have you been up to, Julian?'

'Just running my game. How's Lucy?'

'Excellent. Busy.' Robin tells Julian that Lucy's hooked on politics now, a constant presence at the lord mayor's side; writing speeches, running interference, running strategies. Her lengthy walks, taken alone, are all blue-printing and world-building now. 'She's found a new kind of kick.'

The girl with Julian – very young, Clairol blue-black hair, fingers weighted with onyx – regards Robin with curiosity. Recognition tugs at him. He's sure it's Nicole, Nicole of the rust shawl next to Lucy in Abergele: identical scowl, identical dyed bob. It makes no sense – she was 16 when Robin met her at that salt-lashed cottage by the sea, and Robin can't imagine Lucy would have permitted Nicole and Julian in the same room. But given the group's centreless intrigues, played out across multiple cities and makeshift homes, it's possible.

They stand as a close trio, talking of Julian's bands, Robin's EPs (which Julian professes to have heard and loved), and Pink Fist, who Julian says peaked with their first single and are now embarrassingly bloated. The girl, radiating boredom, walks away.

'I have to ask,' Robin says, breaking into Julian's monologue about a shady promoter, 'were you ever in love with Lucy?' It has come from nowhere, this question. Or perhaps it comes from the dissonance of Julian with maybe-Nicole; the queasy knowledge of the not-funny story.

Either way, it's a blip in his passivism. Either way, it's essential he knows.

'Jesus, Robin, it was ages ago,' says Julian, pulling out cigarettes and motioning at the fire escape. 'You guys have a great thing. You were always going to have a great thing.'

Robin follows him outside, and the door slams, the sound of the crowd extinguished by the nothing-sounds of the alley.

'That's not why I'm asking. I'd like to understand. You made a dent in her life.'

'A dent! That's dramatic.' Julian flicks open a lighter, flame sending that old bright cast across his hair. 'That's not how we were, Robin; that's not how I am.' He shrugs. 'We called it Lust with Potential. It was fun. Then it wasn't. The end.'

Robin weighs this. 'She said you were the most honest person she knew. Totally selfish and frequently an asshole, but honest.'

'A very Lucy thing to say.' Julian laughs a little. 'What did she call me?'

'The Unspoiled Monster.'

'Ah yes, The Unspoiled Monster. I was never quite sure what it meant.'

'The id, I suppose. Or the defensive ego.' It's done now, so Robin keeps going. 'Apparently, she was tunnelling for the real person beneath that; some tender, other Julian.'

'My buried sweet and tender hooligan,' Julian quips. Then a strange look steals across his face, transient. He takes a drag, exhaling in a tunnel at the ground. 'Well, it might be in there, somewhere. Good of her to try.'

The girl has found them, holding three beers. Robin murmurs no thank you, and she scowls.

'We're going to the after-party,' says Julian, stubbing out his cigarette. 'Come with us.' His arm is on Robin's back again, warm and insistent, radiating the bass-note throb of his pulse. A monster, slightly spoiled now. Unknowable, invulnerable, carved from alabastrine.

'I've got to get home and work on these shots,' says Robin. And Julian, saluting cordially, walks into the night.

THE PLEASURE PRINCIPLE

Anika, on a fortnight's break from the hospital, comes to stay. Robin and Lucy have been in the warehouse for six years, their shared accumulation of objects and habits acting like covert magic to keep them there. They talk about moving overseas, to the country, back to Abergele, about a baby or a proper garden, but nothing chimes with the force of impetus, not enough to disturb the present's density.

'Six years is the longest I've lived anywhere,' says Lucy. She sets out a jug of lipstick-cherried sweet pea flowers, a block of Havarti, a loaf of bread, a bowl of lychees. 'I can't tell if I'm rusted in, wilfully anchored, or just overwhelmed by the alternatives – anxiety being the dizziness of freedom, etc. This is where bonfires were useful. You can trust the devastation of a lovely fire."

'Anxiety is mostly just the dizziness of living,' says Anika. She's wrapped in the stars and moons kimono, expertly removing the tops of her boiled eggs. 'You're hardly alone in navigating the tightrope between the finite and the infinite, Lucy; weighing contentment against possibility. Still, if you're happy with your life here, stay.' She watches Robin butcher his first egg. She takes his second, makes a neat decapitation, and passes it back. 'Of course, I enjoy having this city pied-à-terre at my disposal, so that's selfish advice. And given you've been talking about this all night, there's doubtless some buried mechanics already in motion.'

Anika is correct. Over the next day, discrete circumstances assume the stacked order of vertebrae, pulled taut and demanding action. Robin sits on the kitchen bench, making calls about moving boxes. 'My problem,' he says, 'no pleasure.' The room pulses; a new throb of urgency. He knows it's a culmination of minor and major acts performed jointly over years, but it's still disconcerting, still dizzying. He knocks over a jar of silver cachous, scattering mirrorball pearls across the floor. He sits to pick up the glass and stays sitting, chest tight.

Anika watches. 'That's *not* the way to get things done, Christopher Robin. I have beta-blockers if you need them.'

So he eats one, and has boxes delivered, and they start to pack, Anika helping between her saved-up visits to galleries and cinemas. Lucy wraps plastic around a few pot plants, making a mess of it; decides it's crazy, they can't take them, she's tired of looking at them, anyway. She dispatches a group text and for days people descend on the warehouse, plants ribboning soil down the stairs as they're carried off to new homes. In the throes of this expulsive pleasure, Lucy collects more and more things to give away. She invites Tabitha and Harry for dinner so they can join Anika in taking first pick through the spoils.

*

'Holy shit,' says Tabitha. Lucy has laid clothes on the floor along with the other cast-offs: all the preserves and spices, all the magazines except *The Face*, the records that didn't stick, the books that won't be reread. Tabitha picks up a red shift. 'Are you honestly getting rid of all your dresses? You've got a rainbow of curiosities here: circa 1955–1992.'

Lucy shrugs. She's in a white-shirts phase now: starched origami, papal extravagance, skeletal pleats, severe borderline-erotic lacing. 'They're either curiosities or an expensive form of repetition compulsion.'

'You don't have to pathologise everything, Lucy.'

'I'm not pathologising: I'm marking a life segue from obsession to fascination. Besides, they don't make sense anymore; especially not now. I've archived five – five is enough.'

'If you say so. But save a few more: if you're too serious and well-behaved, for too much of the time, all your smothered goblin impulses will erupt in a horror show midlife crisis. God knows, it happens enough at the university.'

Robin had planned on ordering pizza, but Lucy, packing the cupboards, stroking Roland's old dishes, said, fuck it, there was time for one last fête, and so the menu is Regency vs Darkwave, the table bisected. Lucy attends to Regency: prosecco jelly, candy carnations, a tray of oysters, butter pressed from a salmon-shaped mould, smoked mousses and terrines from the markets. Anika takes Darkwave: squid-ink pasta, black beer, black grapes, black olives, black roses. The moon rises through the windows, its rabbit glowing with storybook omniscience. In a mood of special occasion, they open bottle after bottle; quickly loud, quickly giddy.

'To abundance, rapture and mystical communion,' says Anika, raising a glass. 'To *jouissance*.'

'*Jouissance* is a specifically female experience, if you wish to get technical,' says Tabitha.

'Correct. But we'll let Robin and Harry stay if they continue to behave themselves.'

Robin starts playing minimal synth records (Darkwave) interspersed with parlour-room concertos (Regency), but lets it collapse, lets Harry take over. Lucy tells Harry not to touch the mixer, and Harry says he was fixing the levels, that they were all wrong. 'Wrong for you, perfect for me. Put them back, please – we've still got a week here.' Harry shifts the levers a smidgeon, a content man at his most content, and rejoins the table. Lucy sits on his lap, crushes his neck in a messy hug. He crushes her back, fills his glass to the top.

'Heya Anika,' he says. 'I saw you in *The Politics of Dancing* last week.'

Anika beams. 'Oh, did you? I watched it at the Orpheum yesterday! Weren't my tits magnificent?'

'They're eternally magnificent and you know it,' says Lucy.

'Yes, but I'm glad they were captured at that precise moment. I was a veritable *Gesamtkunstwerk* then, a total work of art. As are you, Lucy! You need to watch it.'

Lucy stands, crosses her arms. 'I don't believe I do.'

The Politics of Dancing has just come out, a documentary about the city's music scene and its long uneasy history with the city's powerbrokers. Robin hasn't seen it either, but had done promotional shots with the directors. Tabitha asks who these directors are, being her business to know such things. Robin says a Simon and a Robert; that it was a quick shoot, they didn't talk much. Lucy says they're older, Victor's ilk. Robin, sniffing danger, tells Tabitha there's a press pack on the bench somewhere, that there's a preview screener, that she should take it. Tabitha nods, and by tacit mutual agreement they end the conversation.

They drink, nobody in the mood to stop. Harry collects magazines and preserves and then unearths a Max Headroom T-shirt, wearing it midriff-short for the rest of the night. Lucy collects books for his daughter. Tabitha takes the spices and the red shift with daisies, a high-school favourite of Lucy's. 'I nearly got arrested for solicitation in that dress,' says Lucy. 'I'd always wear it with patent heeled mary-janes, an homage to Courtney Love that was clearly misinterpreted. It set the tone for all my future interactions with police.'

'Yes, but you were a blonde girl in a vintage dress, not a brown girl in bondage tape,' says Anika. 'My arrests were always nearer than yours. Like the night I set off home from our *So Young So Cold* party with the door takings in my bag: three grand worth of $5 notes. Thank fuck Gudrun was with me. Thank fuck I wasn't carrying one of your film canisters, Lucy.'

Talk drifts back to *The Politics of Dancing*: the secret files on every one of a certain age who'd ever played an instrument, attended a protest, written an article, presented as other. The clandestine distribution of liquor licences and dubious rezoning. The profiling and harassment. The illegal demolitions that flattened century-old theatres in the blackest pitch of night. The scattering of whole neighbourhoods and communities. The series of fires that broke out downtown with near-supernatural specificity, taking out particular nocturnal pleasure spots but not others. Just before midnight, Anika locates the press pack. She hands the DVD screener to Robin, head tipped in expectant request.

'I don't think –' he begins, but Lucy has seen the exchange.

'If you must,' she says. So Robin hooks the stereo to the projector, another thing that needs packing, and they make a nest on the couch.

Robin lived in a different city then, but the terrain, the emotional topography, is familiar. Misfits finding each other in derelict buildings and flooded carparks and fire escapes, the nothing-realms of no value to anyone else until it's time to raze them for apartments. The pock-marked outcasts in the euphoric thrall of blinding white noise and contained mostly pantomime violence. Brainsick mixtape loners, finding solace in the crush of strangers. The furious necking in dim corners, ballistic with lust and possibility. Everyone careless with their elastic bodies and second-hand instruments. A universe of need condensed into minor spaces, snatched in the fiscally-void hours – a necessity, but a near-mystical intensifier too. Terrible want blooms in Robin.

It boils over at an afternoon festival, horses crashing through temporary barricades, skies opening, batons thrashing. Harry was there; mohawk soaped into position because he didn't own gel, the rain melting it, the soap blinding him. Eight stitches, a broken arm, a permanent record. Lucy says she was grounded that weekend. She's sitting on the floor in her slanted, swayback way, one arm against Anika's leg, the other against Robin's. Robin kisses her head, smells rosemary shampoo. She squeezes his ankle.

They're nearing the end. Anika rises on her haunches, meerkat-alert, and shushes Harry to deliver her commentary. Late September 2001, a discothèque turned basement club, soon to be condemned. The main stairs had been boarded up; the only way in or out via a lumbering dumb waiter – a death trap, a death wish, a delicious novelty. The floor is carpeted in bubble wrap. Telephone receivers on spiralling cords garland the room, and medical gloves bloated with shaving cream dangle from the ceiling. A dayglo mural on the back wall declares 'MAGIC DOESN'T HAPPEN'. The night, a semi-regular Thursday event, is called Stock Exchange. Projections of pixilated ones and zeroes fall like hard rain.

Anika crosses the screen in her purposeful stride, a naked Voluptas trailing lime and orange builders' string. Purple strobe illuminates her powerful back, then the promised magnificence of her breasts.

'I've seen them many times,' says Tabitha, 'but the impact is never diminished.'

'Thank you,' says Anika, pleased. 'I was tied to a pylon for an hour; the night's performance slash installation art. Four girls wearing zebra masks cut me down with kindergarten scissors – they should have filmed *that*.'

Lucy says nothing. She is sitting very straight now, her face unreadable.

A band, a band that became Important, the reason the footage is here, a band no one in the warehouse particularly rates, climb onto the makeshift stage, a pool table fizzing with cables. Beneath the table sit Lucy and Julian.

Robin watches, chest tight again. He hadn't told Lucy about his encounter with Julian at Pink Fist. He'd been worried this might knock her equilibrium askew. He didn't want to know if the girl was Nicole. He wanted no more wolves or spectres in their lives. He feels almost seasick pleasure in keeping the encounter to himself.

The old Lucy wears a gold lamé jumpsuit. Her hair is bone-bleached, asymmetric; a forelock sweeping across one eye, the back razored to expose her neck. Julian wears a thin black tie, a schoolboy shirt, an aggressively tailored jacket. His eyebrows are pencilled darker. The two are cross-legged, face to face; a hard mess of knees, her left hand buried in his right. Naked adoration lights her face, painful in its intensity. Julian's face is open, unguarded, as near to ecstatic as it gets. Lucy gesticulates with her free hand as she talks, pressing her face to Julian's ear every so often for emphasis; her mode of punctuation. Julian has a cigarette in his free hand, and for each inhalation, he holds it to Lucy's mouth so she can take greedy, rapturous drags. A pas de deux, concocted in private, unwittingly performed in public.

'Goodness, lady,' says Tabitha. 'Were you together then?'

'No,' says Lucy, voice even. 'We didn't fuck for another week, if that's what you mean by together, although we made out briefly that night. We're on drugs, obviously.'

'They must have been sensational drugs.'

'A powerful candyflip,' says Anika. 'Norepinephrine, serotonin, dopamine. A dash of oxytocin and vasopressin. And immense quantities of MDMA, if I recall.'

Without taking her eyes from the screen, Lucy makes a liminal gesture, and Anika, reading it correctly, reaches into her bag and passes forward an onyx case.

Lucy steps through her ritual of snapping, flicking and inhaling, her fingers in kinaesthetic extension. Despite its lengthy hiatus, this ritual is as familiar to Robin as a hymn. She shakes her ironed bob and lets it fall back in a scrim against her face. She stretches her legs to their full length, appraising her inky tights, the hard carapace of her studded black boots. Her countenance is cool, sibylline.

'It's curious, isn't it?' she says, exhaling so a sulphurous cloud gathers around her. 'How vital something feels at the time, and how silly it all seems later.'

NOTES

WORKS CITED

Page 16: Albert Camus, *The Stranger* (Vintage Books, 1942)

Page 32: 'The time you enjoy wasting, is not wasted time': attributed to John Lennon, Bertrand Russell, others

Page 33: 'the blue-eyed Jewish-Irish Mohican scout who died in your arms at the roulette table at Monte Carlo': J. D. Salinger, *Franny and Zooey* (Little, Brown and Company, 1961)

Page 55: The (Hypothetical) Prophets, 'Person to Person' (Symetric Music, 1982)

Page 66: Richard Hell, *I Dreamed I Was a Very Clean Tramp* (HarperCollins, 2013)

Page 68: Bush Tetras, 'Too Many Creeps' (99 Records, 1980)

Page 94: Lewis Carroll, *Alice's Adventures in Wonderland* (Macmillan & Co, 1865)

Page 106: 'By far the most valuable things, which we know or can imagine, are certain states of consciousness, which may be roughly described as the pleasures of human intercourse and the enjoyment of beautiful objects.' G. E. Moore, *Principia Ethica* (Cambridge University Press, 1903)

Page 107: Cristina, 'Is That All There Is?' (ZE Records, 1980)

Page 108: Dramarama, 'Anything, Anything (I'll Give You)' (Questionmark Records, 1985)

Page 117: Anthony Haden-Guest, 'Les Enfants Terribles de Rock'n'Roll' (*New York Magazine*, 1984)

Page 120: Simone de Beauvoir, *The Ethics of Ambiguity* (The Citadel Press, 1948)

Page 132: D. H. Lawrence, *Kangaroo* (Text Classics, 2018)

Page 174: Alexis Petridis, 'If you're brave, do it like we did' (*The Guardian*, 2007)

Page 188: Voltaire, *Mérope* (Nabu Press, 2010)

Page 188: letter to Joë Bousquet, 13 April 1942; Simone Pétrement, *Simone Weil: A Life* (1976), tr. Raymond Rosenthal

Page 188: Brian Eno, *A Year with Swollen Appendices* (Faber & Faber, 1996)

Page 188: Věra Chytilová, *Daisies* (Criterion Collection, 1966)

Page 207: Coil, 'The Anal Staircase' (Force & Form, 1986)

Page 223: 'Glamour is resistance': cabaret performer Justin Bond quoted in *The Evening Standard* (2005)

Page 231: 'Well, now that's done: and I'm glad it's over': T. S. Eliot, *The Wasteland* (*The Criterion*, 1922)

Page 238: Vladimir Nabokov, *Lectures on Literature: Madame Bovary* (Houghton Mifflin Harcourt, 1980)

Page 249: Jeremy Bentham, *An Introduction to the Principles of Morals and Legislation* (Hafner Press, 1823)

Page 249: Klaus Maeck, *Einstürzende Neubauten: Hör mit Schmerzen = listen with pain* (Die Gestalten Verlag, 1997)

Page 261: Søren Kierkegaard, *The Concept of Anxiety: Simple Psychologically Orienting Deliberation on the Dogmatic Issue of Hereditary Sin* (Princeton University Press, 1844)

ACKNOWLEDGEMENTS

The music anecdotes of *Compulsion* draw on many sources. Simon Reynolds' singular *Rip It Up and Start Again: Postpunk 1978–1984* (Faber & Faber, 2005) was a much-thumbed and much-loved resource for its forensic examination of the period, specifically The Human League's accounts of making *Dare!* and *Love and Dancing*. (It was also my introduction to The Associates, for which I'll be forever grateful.) S. Alexander Reed's excellent *Assimilate: A Critical History of Industrial Music* (Oxford University Press, 2013) provided essential backgrounding; as did Benjamin Whalley's eminently rewatchable *Synth Britannia* documentary (BBC, 2009); and Daphne Carr's *33 1/3* oral history of *Pretty Hate Machine* (Bloomsbury, 2011), a sublime evocation of fandom. The 'Blue Monday' tea kettle anecdote appeared in Peter Hook's *Substance: Inside New Order* (Simon & Schuster, 2016), a delightful, if grumpy, read. Tom Pinnock's interview with Julian Cope for *Uncut* in 2018 ('I had to release *Fried* to prove I was still a functioning human being') and François Zappa's interview with Eleven Pond's Jeff Galea (*El Gara Je De Frank*, 2019) provided A++ first-person reflections; as did the *Offbeat* 1989 TV interview with The Sisters of Mercy's Andrew Eldritch (in chain-smoking, hilarious form). The observations on Gary Numan's song structures are derived from *Mad World:*

An Oral History of New Wave Artists and Songs That Defined the 1980s (Lori Majewski, Jonathan Bernstein, Nick Rhodes, Abrams, 2014).

Eternal vibes courtesy of Derek Ridgers' photographs of the Blitz Kids (collected in *The Others*, Idea, 2015); Tim Sweeney's weekly dispatches from a real and imagined 1983 via his *Beats in Space* podcast; Veronica Vasicka's lovingly exhumed masterpieces for Minimal Wave Records; and the 1989 film *Depeche Mode 101* (David Dawkins, Chris Hegedus, D. A. Pennebaker, Amsco Publications).

Sarah Bakewell's *At the Existentialist Café: Freedom, Being, and Apricot Cocktails* (Penguin, 2017) and Stephen West's *Philosophize This!* podcast both sharpened my lifelong fascination with existentialism and offered a vital contemporary lens on its principles. Simone de Beauvoir's *'the fête'* – an 'impassioned apotheosis of the present in the face of anxiety concerning the future' – is the animating force of *Compulsion*. Thanks to Emily DeWitt's *Future Sex* (Faber, 2018) for bringing this *Prime of Life* god particle to my attention.

Finally, thank you to everyone who coaxed *Compulsion*'s fever dreams into a book.

Meredith Curnow, Justin Ractliffe, Patrick Mangan and the team at Penguin, who made the editing process one of the great pleasures of my life. I'm enormously grateful for their acuity (on plot, pace, yacht rock, keyboards), their playlists, and their patience as I burrowed down rabbit holes.

Benython Oldfield at Zeitgeist Agency, for his early insights on the (very raw) text, and finding *Compulsion* a home.

Rose Mulready, for her elemental guidance, tireless feedback and prose-poem texts of encouragement.

My grandfather Alf, for his life-shaping gift of books and the utopia of Caves Beach (where the happiest parts of *Compulsion* were written).

Maura Edmond, Chloe Gordon, Emma Rodwell, Alaina Gougoulis and Adrian Potts of Book Nookie, for the decade of germinative table talk, and boundless, near-saintly support.

Siobhan Thakur, for her iconoclytes, iconoblasts and numerous other treasures. Daniel Boud, for letting me into photography's occult powers over many shoots. Patrick McIntyre, for always treating my work seriously (two beats before I took it seriously myself). And all those who contributed kissing styles, top fives, mixtapes and fêtes over the years, especially Andrew Collins, Mark Gomes, Anna McEwan, Lysandra Godley, Giordana Caputo, Thea Baumann, Louise Terry, Lorelei Vashti, John Edmond and Alison Bird.

And thank you, Jonathan, for everything. I'd cut out my organs for you; I really would.

I ABJECT!: A MIXTAPE

1000 Ohm, 'A.G.N.E.S.' (Ariola, 1982)

A Number of Names, 'Sharevari' (Capriccio Records, 1981)

Adult., 'Kick in the Shin' (Ersatz Audio, 2003)

Anna, 'Systems Breaking Down' (RCA, 1982)

The Associates, 'White Car in Germany' (Situation Two, 1981)

Black Devil Disco Club, 'The Devil in Us' (Lo Recordings, 2006)

Bolz Bolz, 'Take a Walk' (Longhaul, 2001)

Boy Harsher, 'Morphine' (DKA Recordings, 2016)

Cabaret Voltaire, 'Just Fascination' – 7" version (Virgin, 1983)

Charlie, 'Spacer Woman' (Mr. Disc Organization, 1983)

Chris + Cosey, 'October (Love Song)' (Rough Trade, 1983)

Chromatics, 'Famous Monsters' (Italians Do It Better, 2020)

Comateens, 'Ghosts' (Jupiter Records, 1981)

Cosmetics, 'Black Leather Gloves' (Captured Tracks, 2010)

Crash Course in Science, 'Cardboard Lamb' (Press Records, 1981)

The Creepers, 'Baby's on Fire' (It Tape, 1986)

Cristina, 'What's a Girl to Do' (ZE Records, 1982)

Crossover, 'Phostographt' (International DeeJay Gigolo Records, 2002)

Das Kabinette, 'The Cabinet' (Klosette Records, 1983)

David Bowie, 'I'm Deranged' (Columbia, 1995)

Depeche Mode, 'Master and Servant' – Slavery Whip Mix (Mute, 1984)

Deux, 'Game and Performance' (Andre Records, 1983)

Do Piano, 'All The Time' (EMI, 1986)

Dot Allison, 'Substance' – Felix da Housecat Remix (Mantra Recordings, 2002)

Drinking Electricity, 'Breakout' (Survival Records, 1982)

Einstürzende Neubauten, 'Fiat Lux' (Rough Trade, 1989)

Eleven Pond, 'Watching Trees' (Game Hen Records, 1986)

Ellen Allien, 'Stadtkind' (BPitch Control, 2001)

Fad Gadget, 'Collapsing New People' (Mute, 1984)

Fatima Yamaha 'What's a Girl to Do' (Dekmantel, 2015)

Figure Study, 'Wait' (Dark Entries, 2013)

FPU, 'Crockett's Theme' (Turbo, 2002)

Freddy The Flying Dutchman And The Sistina Band, 'Wojtyla 5 Disco Dance' (Polydor, 1979)

Gary Numan, 'Metal' (Beggars Banquet, 1979)

Gina X Performance, 'No G.D.M.' (Crystal, 1979)

Glass Candy, 'Digital Versicolor' (Italians Do It Better, 2007)

Goblin, 'Tenebre' (Cinevox Records, 1982)

The Golden Filter, 'Black Monday' (The Vinyl Factory, 2014)

Grauzone, 'Eisbär' (Off Course Records, 1981)

Guyer's Connection, 'Pogo of Techno' (Tonstudio Max Lussi, 1983)

The Hasbeens, 'Make the World Go Away' (Clone, 2006)

Helen, 'Witch' (ZYX Records, 1983)

The House of Fix Feat. Circa, 'Way Out' (Tresor, 2003)

The Human League 'Rock 'N' Roll / Nightclubbing' (Virgin, 1980)

The (Hypothetical) Prophets, 'Person to Person' (Symetric Music, 1983)

Japan, 'Life in Tokyo' (Hansa, 1981)

Jay Harker, 'Bela Lugosi's Dead' – The Voice Mix (Dorian Gray, 2002)

Jenny Hval, 'Female Vampire' (Sacred Bones Records, 2016)

John Foxx, 'Underpass' (Polydor, 1980)

John Maus, 'Quantum Leap' (Upset! The Rhythm, 2011)

The Juan Maclean, 'You Can't Have It Both Ways' (DFA, 2002)

Krisma, 'Black Silk Stocking' (Polydor, 1977)

Ladytron, 'The Reason Why' (Emperor Norton, 2002)

LaTour, 'People Are Still Having Sex' (Smash Records, 1991)

The League Unlimited Orchestra, 'Things That Dreams Are Made Of' (Virgin, 1982)

Linda Lamb, 'Hot Room' (International DeeJay Gigolo Records, 2002)

Linear Movement, 'The Game' (Minimal Wave, 2008; originally recorded 1983)

Liquid Sky, 'Rhythm Box' (International DeeJay Gigolo Records, 2003; originally recorded 1983)

Martin Dupont, 'Inside Out' (Facteurs d'Ambiance, 1987)

Material, 'Secret Life' (Jungle Records, 1986)

Metro Area, 'Miura' (Environ, 2001)

Ministry, 'The Angel' (Sire, 1986)

Miss Kittin & The Hacker, 'Stock Exchange' (International DeeJay Gigolo Records, 2003)

Mount Sims, 'No Yellow Lines' (International DeeJay Gigolo Records, 2004)

Night Moves, 'Transdance' – extended 1984 mix (GC Recordings, 1984)

Nine Inch Nails, 'Memorabilia' (Nothing, 1994)

Northern Lite, 'Treat Me Better' (1st Decade Records, 2001)

Oppenheimer Analysis, 'The Devil's Dancers' (Minimal Wave, 2005; self-released 1982)

Playgroup, 'Make It Happen' – Zongamin Remix (Playgroup 2003)

Propaganda, 'Dr Mabuse' (Island, 1984)

Ruth, 'Polaroid / Roman / Photo' (Paris Album, 1985)

Serge Gainsbourg, 'Love on the Beat' (Mercury, 1984)

Sexual Harassment, 'I Need a Freak' (Great, 1982)

Silver Apples, 'Oscillations' (Kapp Records, 1968)

Soft Cell, 'So' (Metropolis, 1982)

Stereo, 'Somewhere in the Night' (Carrere, 1982)

Störung, 'Europe Calls' (Minimal Wave, 2019; originally recorded 1982/1983)

Suicide, 'Diamonds, Fur Coat, Champagne' (Island Records, 1980)

Telex, 'Raised by Snakes' – Razormaid Mix (unofficial, 1984)

Throbbing Gristle, 'Hot on the Heels of Love' (Pass Records, 1981)

Toktok vs Soffy O*, 'Missy Queen's Gonna Die' (Fuel Records, 2001)

TVAM, 'Porsche Majeure' (Static Caravan, 2015)

Ultravox, 'Mr. X' (Chrysalis, 1980)

Visage, 'The Damned Don't Cry' – Razormaid Mix (Polydor, 1982)

XLover, 'So Blue' (International DeeJay Gigolo Records, 2005)

Yoko Ono, 'Walking on Thin Ice' – Felix da Housecat Tribute Mix (Twisted America Records, 2003)

Z Factor, '(I Like to Do It) in Fast Cars' (Mitchbal Records, 1983)

tinyurl.com/yk8kdkux

Kate Scott was born in Newcastle and grew up in Melbourne, California's Mojave Desert, Nimbin and Brisbane. She began her career as a music journalist at age 18, before becoming the editor of (now defunct) street press magazine *Rave* at age 22. She interviewed hundreds of national and international artists, and her pieces were syndicated nationally.

She spent 10 years with The Australian Ballet as their in-house writer, then head of marketing, and was Managing Editor of *Luminous: Celebrating 50 Years of The Australian Ballet*, a 360-page coffee table book. She now lives in Thirroul on the NSW south coast, works as a freelance strategist, and has two rabbits, Iggy Pop and Lou Reed. *Compulsion* is her debut novel.

Kate Scott acknowledges the Dharawal people, on whose lands she lives and works. Sovereignty was never ceded.